Next Time I Fall

Whisper Lake #7

BARBARA FREETHY

Fog City Publishing

PRAISE FOR BARBARA FREETHY

"I am always ready for a return trip to Whisper Lake. I love the small town and the friendly people who live there. Barbara Freethy is a master of suspense and romance. She makes her characters come to life on the page." NJ - Goodreads

"ALWAYS WITH ME is a heartwarming second chance romance, with a captivating mystery, that keeps you reading and wondering what happens next." Doni - Goodreads

"A beautiful second chance love story with a bit of drama and mystery. I loved it!" Peggy - Goodreads on ALWAYS WITH ME

"Tragedy haunts her, regrets shadow him and passion lures them into a mystery as dangerous as their feelings for each other. Freethy captivates with a sensuous game of tainted hearts and tempting romance. My Wildest Dream is a hotbed of intriguing storytelling. Brodie and Chelsea are sure to get under your skin." Isha C – Goodreads

"My Wildest Dream has just the right mix of romance and suspense to keep the reader interested from the first chapter to the final page. I loved everything about this book. Visiting Whisper Lake is like coming home and reuniting with old friends. You won't be disappointed. Norma – Bookbub

"I have just finished CAN'T FIGHT THE MOONLIGHT and WOW such an emotional story. Absolutely loved this book...and can't wait for the next one!" Booklovers Anonymous

PRAISE FOR BARBARA FREETHY

"A fabulous, page-turning combination of romance and intrigue. Fans of Nora Roberts and Elizabeth Lowell will love this book."
— *NYT Bestselling Author Kristin Hannah on Golden Lies*

"Freethy has a gift for creating complex, appealing characters and emotionally involving, often suspenseful, sometimes magical stories." — *Library Journal on Suddenly One Summer*

"Barbara Freethy is a master storyteller with a gift for spinning tales about ordinary people in extraordinary situations and drawing readers into their lives." — *Romance Reviews Today*

"Freethy is at the top of her form. Fans of Nora Roberts will find a similar tone here, framed in Freethy's own spare, elegant style." — *Contra Costa Times on Summer Secrets*

"Freethy hits the ground running as she kicks off another winning romantic suspense series...Freethy is at her prime with a superb combo of engaging characters and gripping plot." — *Publishers' Weekly on Silent Run*

"PERILOUS TRUST is a non-stop thriller that seamlessly melds jaw-dropping suspense with sizzling romance. Readers will be breathless in anticipation as this fast-paced and enthralling love story evolves and goes in unforeseeable directions." — *USA Today HEA Blog*

"I love the Callaways! Heartwarming romance, intriguing suspense and sexy alpha heroes. What more could you want?" — NYT Bestselling Author Bella Andre

NEXT TIME I FALL BLURB

After three years of being a single mom, café owner Chloe Morgan is finally ready to take another chance on love. She's found the perfect man in Joel Bradshaw. He checks all her boxes when it comes to stability, commitment, and accountability.

And then Joel's best friend, Decker Hayes, comes to town…

Decker is attractive, sexy, and great with her kid, but Decker is a self-avowed wanderer. He doesn't make plans. He doesn't think long-term. He's not someone a woman should count on. Decker is exactly the kind of man Chloe doesn't want.

And Chloe is exactly the kind of woman Decker doesn't want. Decker is not a family man. He isn't even sure what family really means. Chloe is also dating his friend, which makes her off-limits.

But as Chloe and Decker are thrown together during a house remodel and the unraveling of an old family mystery, they find themselves falling for the absolutely wrong person.

Neither one wants to risk another broken heart, but when love shows up, anything can happen…

I hope you enjoy this single mom, feel-good, small-town romance!

NEXT TIME I FALL

CHAPTER ONE

"Did you know your tenant was a hoarder?" Hannah McKenna asked.

Chloe Morgan stared in shocked silence at the living room of her family's rental house. The room was filled with so many towering piles of stuff that she could barely see the furniture. "I had no idea. Eleanor never let me in the house. On the few times I stopped by, she met me on the porch with homemade cookies. She always said everything was fine."

"Are we having cookies?" her son Leo asked, tugging on her hand.

She shook her head at the hopeful look in his four-year-old eyes. "Not now."

"Can we have cookies later?"

"We'll see how good you are," she said vaguely, as he let go of her hand to look at a train that appeared to wind its way along a track from the living room to the dining room. That made little sense. Eleanor Johnson had been in her eighties when she'd passed away two weeks ago, and she hadn't had any children living at the house. Nor had she had any family, so why did she have a train? That was only one of a thousand questions running through her head.

"Maybe you should tell your parents that this is their problem."

"It's not their problem; it's mine," she said. "My parents want to sell the house and, in return for my help, they'll split the profits with me. That's a huge chunk of money that would make a difference in my life."

"This is going to be an enormous job, Chloe. The paint is faded. That ceiling looks like there have been some leaks." Hannah waved her hand toward the spotted ceiling in the dining room. "And who knows what other horrors are under all this mess?"

"It's probably not as bad as we think," she said, trying to stay optimistic. "It can be cleaned up. Let's check out the upstairs. Come on, Leo."

"Can't I stay here and play with the train?" he asked.

She hesitated. "All right. But don't touch anything else and don't leave this room. Understand?"

He nodded and went back to pretending his stuffed turtle was taking a ride on the train. She led the way upstairs.

"I just don't understand how anyone lives like this," Hannah said, as they stepped into the master bedroom.

"It's sad," she agreed. The sight of the unmade bed and the lingering scent of perfume in the air made her feel even more depressed as she thought about how Eleanor had spent some of her last weeks on earth surrounded by this mess. "I wish I'd known. Maybe I could have helped Eleanor while she was alive."

"I'm sure she didn't want anyone to know."

"Probably not. Eleanor never complained about anything. She always sent her rent check on the first day of the month. When something broke, I'd send someone over to fix it, but I never came into the house. She always wanted to handle things on her own, and I respected her privacy."

"It makes sense."

"But now this house, my parents' investment, is in really terrible shape. My grandmother would turn over in her grave if she could see this place." The house had originally belonged to her grandmother, but after her death nineteen years ago, they'd rented it to one of her grandmother's friends, a widow named Eleanor Johnson. She'd lived here ever since. "I need to make this right," she added.

"You have a business to run and a kid to raise," Hannah pointed out. "Do you have time to make this right?"

"I have to make the time. Thankfully, I might get some help. Joel has a friend who's a contractor. Apparently, he's at loose ends after a job got postponed, so he's coming to Whisper Lake." She glanced at her watch. "He's supposed to meet me here in half an hour."

"Well, that's good. But you might need someone who lives here. This job could take some time."

"Unfortunately, everyone who lives here is booked. Now that the snow is melting, everyone is diving into their construction jobs. Joel assured me that his friend is really good and is interested in picking up some work."

"Joel seems to come up a lot in conversation," Hannah observed. "What's going on with you two? I thought you said you were just friends."

"It's moved beyond that. We're dating, but we're taking it slow."

"Why?" Hannah asked with a laugh and a sparkle in her brown eyes. "Fast can be fun, Chloe."

"I have a child to think about. I have to be careful who I bring around."

"I get it. Maybe you should bring him around your friends more, so we can tell you what we think about him."

She smiled at that. "He doesn't need to be interrogated, which you will all do if I give you the chance."

"That's what friends are for. So, tell me more about Joel. What do you like about him?"

"Well, he's a good guy, and he checks a lot of my boxes."

"Like what?" Hannah persisted.

"He wants to live in Whisper Lake. That's a big one."

"Are you sure about that? I thought he was just here while his company develops the property on the west shore. I know that's at least a two-year project, but what about after that?"

"He's staying. There is so much land available for development in this area, he could work here for years. He's been in New York City most of his life, and he finds the quiet here very appealing."

Hannah didn't look like she completely believed her, but for once, she kept that opinion to herself. "What else do you like about him?"

"He's ready for a relationship. He wants a family. He wants children, which is important." She paused. "I like that he's a normal guy. He's not addicted to danger. He doesn't need an adrenaline rush to feel alive."

Hannah gave her a pointed look. "Now, you're talking about Kevin."

"It's hard not to compare everyone I meet to my ex-husband," she admitted. "But I'm trying not to do that. Like I said, it's early days. We'll see how it goes. I'm not very good at dating. I fell for Kevin when I was sixteen. And I was married a long time."

"It's been three years since the divorce."

"And I have gone out with a few guys, but they were not anything close to right. And I need to be careful. I can't make another mistake."

Hannah frowned, concern in her gaze. "I understand. But I have to say one thing."

She steeled herself for whatever was coming. "What?"

"I don't want you to run so far away from the kind of man Kevin is that you pick someone for the wrong reasons. Just because someone isn't like Kevin doesn't make him the best match."

"I know that. But I've had a lot of time to think about what I want in a future husband and what I don't want."

"Okay, I had to say it."

"I know you're being protective, but I can take care of myself." She paused as she looked around the room. "But first I need to take care of this house."

Hannah suddenly squealed and grabbed her arm, pointing across the room. "Maybe you should take care of that first. Or we could just back away and never return, not until you get someone in here to clean up."

At first, she didn't know what Hannah was talking about. Then she blinked at the sight of an enormous spider moving across the floor. She wasn't a big fan of spiders, but clearly not as scared as Hannah was. She was already inching her way to the door. "I can't believe after all the things you see as an ER nurse that you're turning pale at the sight of a spider," she chided. "I thought you were the brave one."

"Not when it comes to creepy-crawly things. Let's get out of here."

"I'm not going to let a spider run me out of this room. I'll take care of it."

She moved across the floor, lifted her leg, and smashed her boot down on the spider. She hit the spider dead on, but she raised her foot and smashed it again, just for good measure. As she did so, she heard a loud cracking sound and suddenly the floor fell out from under her.

She flailed her arms as she fell, then grabbed on to the leg of a nearby dresser to stop her slide, but at that point, she was up to her waist, with rough edges of boards cutting into her skin between the gap of her sweater and leggings.

"Mommy?" Leo shouted. "I can see your legs."

"It's okay," she yelled. She turned to Hannah, who was staring at her in shock. "Go downstairs and get Leo out of the house. I don't want the ceiling to come down on top of him."

"What about you?"

"I'm okay. Just get Leo." As she finished speaking, the doorbell rang, followed by the sound of a man's voice.

"Hello? Anyone here?" he called out.

"My mommy is up there," she heard Leo say. "Those are her legs."

"Hannah, go," Chloe said.

"I'm on it," Hannah replied. "I'll call 911 after I get Leo."

Chloe gripped the leg tighter, feeling the pull of gravity. She really did not want to fall any farther. Through the slats in the broken floor, she could see Hannah's dark-red hair.

"Leo, come here," she heard Hannah say, following up with, "Who are you?"

"Decker Hayes," a man replied. "I'm supposed to meet Chloe Morgan. Is that you?"

"No. Chloe is upstairs."

"Chloe is my mommy," Leo interrupted. "She's stuck in the ceiling."

"I can see that," the man said with humor in his voice. "Nice legs."

She flushed at the comment, thanking God she was wearing leggings and not a dress.

"I'm calling 911," Hannah said. "Come on, Leo. We're going to wait out front."

"Hang on. I can probably get her out without calling the fire department," Decker said. "Are you hurt?" he yelled.

"I'm fine," she shouted. "I just don't want my son to get hit by falling wood."

"They're going to wait outside," he replied. "I'm coming up."

She blew out a breath, not thrilled about that, but she'd rather have him try to help her than have the Whisper Lake Fire Department rescue her. That would be juicy gossip that would go around town for weeks.

A moment later, the man entered the bedroom, walking carefully across the room. He stopped a few feet away, a smile crossing his very attractive face. He was a tall man with thick brown hair and green eyes. He wore jeans and a navy sweater that clung to a very broad chest.

"I'm Decker Hayes," he said.

"I figured. Chloe Morgan. Do you think you can get me out?"

"I'll give it my best shot." He cautiously moved forward. "Can you let go of the dresser?"

She was a little reluctant to let go of the only thing preventing her from crashing through the floor. "And do what?" she asked.

"Grab my hand."

She looked at his now outstretched arm. "I don't know if you can pull me out."

"I can do it," he said confidently. "Trust me."

"I don't even know you."

"Joel does. You trust him, right?"

She really didn't know Joel that well, either, but this guy was his friend, and he would probably do everything he could not to drop her through the ceiling. Plus, she didn't have any other choice. "Okay." She took one hand off the leg of the dresser.

Decker's fingers wrapped around hers, his grip strong and warm, and she could feel the power in his body. His eyes met hers with encouragement. "I've got you," he said.

An odd, shivery feeling ran down her body at his words. It had been a long time since she'd felt like anyone had had her back. She'd been going it alone for so long. A rush of emotion made her eyes water, which was completely stupid. She could not cry now. She had enough problems.

Blinking the tears away, she said, "Okay. I'm letting go."

As she released her grip, he grabbed her other hand and pulled her up and out of the broken floor. At the sound of more breaking wood, she scrambled to her knees, then to her feet, as he pulled her toward the doorway.

When they got into the hall, she looked back at the floor. A few more pieces of floor had fallen through the hole, making it another foot bigger. If he hadn't gotten her out of there when he had, she might have ended up in the dining room.

"Looks like this job just got more expensive," Decker said.

She turned back to him, suddenly realizing he was still holding one of her hands. She pulled it away, wishing her heart wasn't beating so hard or that her breath wasn't coming so fast. Licking her lips, she said, "Thanks for getting me out."

"No problem. There must be a lot of rot in that floor."

"And spiders," she said. "I was stomping one to death when I put my foot through the floor."

"Well, I hope the spider is dead," he said with a smile.

"I definitely got him, but at what cost?"

"Probably a high one. And Joel didn't mention that your tenant was a hoarder."

"Joel didn't know. I had no idea, either. Eleanor Johnson lived here for nineteen years before passing away two weeks ago. I haven't been inside this house in years. The home actually belongs to my parents, but they don't live in town anymore, and I'm in charge of getting this place ready to sell." She shook her head as she let out a breath. "It's mind boggling that someone could have been living here surrounded by so much junk. And I'm thrilled the floor didn't give way when my eighty-five-year-old tenant was in here."

"That would have been bad."

"I should get downstairs, make sure Leo is okay."

"I'll look around and meet you outside."

"All right." She hesitated. "I'm almost afraid to take another step."

"You'll be okay going down the stairs."

"You should be careful in here."

"I will be."

She moved down the stairs and out of the house, feeling more than a little relieved to get into the fresh air. It was a sunny day in early April, and with Easter just four days away, it was feeling like spring in Whisper Lake. While there was still snow on the surrounding mountains, it had disappeared at lake level a few weeks ago.

"Are you okay?" Hannah asked, her sharp brown eyes searching her face for the truth.

"I'm fine."

"No cuts that need tending to?"

"I'm fine, Nurse Hannah," she said with a smile. Hannah was not only her friend since childhood, she was also a nurse at the local hospital, and as a result, she'd taken care of more than a few of her cuts over the years. "See?" She lifted her sweater just to make sure she wasn't lying.

Hannah took a closer look. "Not too bad, just some scratches."

"Mommy," Leo said, interrupting their conversation. "Look what I found." He held up a long stick that he was dragging around the dirt in the neglected garden.

"Be careful with that," she said, thinking again how grateful she was that Leo hadn't been hurt by any falling floorboards.

"Where's your rescuer?" Hannah asked.

"He's looking around the house. He said the job just got more expensive."

"I can believe that. This house is a disaster." Hannah paused, giving her a mischievous smile. "But on a positive note, your contractor is pretty hot."

"I didn't notice," she lied.

"How could you not notice?" Hannah challenged.

"I was focused on not falling through the floor. And it doesn't matter how good-looking Decker is. I'm trying to hire him, not date him. He doesn't even live here. He's just staying here for a few months until his next project starts."

"All right. I get it. He's just passing through. And you don't date people who are just passing through."

"Exactly."

"Where's he staying while he's in town?"

She cleared her throat at that question. "Joel asked if Decker could stay in the apartment over the café."

Hannah laughed. "Above your café, huh? Well, that sounds perfect."

"Stop. He's just going to do some work for me. If he still wants to after he goes through the house. And if his bid isn't completely out of our budget."

"Looks like we're about to find out," Hannah said.

As Decker strode through the front door, Chloe had to admit he was a very attractive man in a rugged, doesn't-know-how-good-he-looks kind of way. His hair was a little long, a little tousled, and there was some dust now on his shirt, probably from the house, but there was power and strength and purpose in his stride, in his gaze, and her heart raced as that gaze settled on her. She tried to shrug it off. This was crazy. She was dating his friend. Her reaction was probably coming from too much adrenaline. It would pass.

"What exactly do you want done?" he asked.

"Well, before I saw the place, we thought that the two bathrooms should be remodeled, that the house should be painted, and maybe some new tile or cabinetry in the kitchen. The floors, too, probably need to be redone."

"Definitely. You made sure of that," he said with another smile.

"Do you think all the floors upstairs are that fragile? Why would it suddenly break apart?"

"I suspect you have a leak in the bathroom that rotted the floor. It will take some discovery to see how far the damage goes. It's difficult to know if there are any other structural problems in the house. It will have to be cleaned out to be sure that there are no other surprises."

"So, what do you think?" she asked him.

"I think you need me."

His gaze bored into hers, and she felt like there was a double edge to his words, one that made her go on defense. "I need the house fixed," she said, wanting to make that point clear. She didn't need him. She needed his construction skills. "I'll also need to see a price. My parents have a budget, and I can't go over that."

"I'll work up a bid. Joel said you might rent me the apartment over your café?"

"Yes. Do you want to see it now?"

"That would be great. I can get settled and then get started on your bid."

"Well, I'm going to head to work," Hannah said, interrupting their conversation, a thoughtful gleam in her brown eyes. "I'm sorry I freaked out over that gigantic spider, Chloe. I feel a little responsible for what happened."

"You were totally responsible," she said. "How are you so afraid of spiders? You look at broken bones sticking out of people's arms and legs."

"That's different," Hannah said with a helpless smile. "The bones don't crawl toward me."

"Well, I'm sure we would have discovered the problem in the floor at some point."

"By the way," Hannah said, turning to Decker. "We didn't actually meet. I'm Hannah McKenna, one of Chloe's oldest friends. I really appreciate you getting her out. You saved the day."

"Happy to help," he said.

"Well, I'm sure I'll see you around," Hannah said.

"I hope so."

As Hannah headed to her car, Chloe turned to Decker. "Shall we go?"

"I'm ready."

"Leo, come on. And you're not bringing the stick," she said, as he started toward her.

He gave her a sad look. "But it's the best one I've ever found."

She smiled at his dramatic words. "There are plenty of sticks in our backyard. This one stays here."

Leo dropped the stick and followed her to the car, climbing into his car seat. Luckily, he was easily distracted by the stuffed dog waiting next to his seat. By the time she'd started the engine, he was already playing a new game.

Sometimes, she was amazed at how adaptable her four-year-old was. His bad moods never lasted long, and while he pushed back sometimes, he rarely put up a big fight. He was eager to be good, to make her happy. And she wanted to make him happy, too. That wasn't always easy, since she had to be both mom and dad.

Her divorce had become final three years ago, although her ex-husband had been gone a lot even before that. In special forces for the military, Kevin was often deployed overseas, sometimes disappearing for months at a time. He loved being a soldier, and, ultimately, he'd chosen his job, or his calling as he liked to refer to it, over being a husband and a father. She wanted to hate him for that, but it was difficult to hate someone who was being a hero in so many other ways.

She knew she'd made the right decision for herself and even for Leo. He needed a stable home environment, and hopefully, one day, Kevin could spend more time with his son. Because in the past couple of years, he'd only seen him a couple of weekends a year. Someday Leo would have a lot of questions, but luckily, that day wasn't today.

As she drove back to the café, her mind moved to another man, her gaze drifting to the rearview mirror, to Decker Hayes. With all the contractors in town busy for the next few months, she needed him to fix up the rental house. But there was something about him that told her he was going to be trouble—trouble that would be living in the apartment above her café.

CHAPTER TWO

CHLOE MORGAN WASN'T what he'd been expecting, Decker thought, as he followed her into town. Not that he'd really thought about it that much. But Joel's girlfriends in the past had all had a similar vibe: tall, thin, sophisticated, and stylish. While Chloe Morgan was a pretty woman with light-brown hair and beautiful, hazel eyes, she was barely five-four, and her black leggings and sweater hadn't been the cutting edge of fashion. She was also a mom with a cute little kid.

Was Joel ready to take on a single mom, to be a stepdad?

Decker certainly wouldn't have thought so six months ago when Joel had been massively in lust with Sylvie, a New York fashion designer who he'd been in a relationship with for several years. But that relationship had ended shortly after Joel had moved to Whisper Lake. Apparently, Sylvie had come to Whisper Lake with Joel and had spent two weeks here, but had not liked the small-town life at all. Joel, however, had suddenly become fascinated with the idea of leaving New York and moving to the mountains, becoming a new man.

He could understand why Joel wanted a change. He'd lived in big cities for most of his life. He had stepped in to run his father's huge construction company after a decade of toiling away at every job to prove he was worthy of taking over his dad's legacy. And it hadn't been just the legacy that had hovered over Joel's head, it had been his father's enormous shadow. In New York, it was impossible to get away from all that. But in Whisper Lake, in this beautiful, mountain resort town, Joel could be completely himself.

But he couldn't quite believe that Joel would really be happy with small town life forever. Maybe Joel would prove him wrong. He'd certainly been enthusiastic about the changes he was making in his life. Joel had told him he was doing the opposite of what he used to do, and apparently dating a single mom with a kid was part of his new persona. Now that he'd met Chloe, he saw the appeal.

Chloe was beautiful in a very natural, girl-next-door kind of way. He smiled to himself at the memory of her flushed cheeks and the embarrassed expression on her face when he'd found her trapped in the floorboards. His smile faded as he remembered the feel of her hands in his, the way she'd looked at him, the breathless catch in her voice.

It had just been an adrenaline-charged moment and nothing else, but it had caught him by surprise.

Not that anything would or could happen. She was involved with Joel, and he had never gone after a friend's woman. He wouldn't start now. He also wasn't interested in dating a woman with a child. He liked his dates single, childless, and free of baggage and drama. Simple, easy, and fun were the words he lived by. It made his life so much easier.

As he followed Chloe into town, his thoughts drifted to the last time he'd been here. He'd only been six years old, and he wasn't sure he'd remember anything about the area, but there was a sense of familiarity running through him. He couldn't pinpoint one business, one sign. It was just a shadowy feeling of recognition.

When Joel had told him he'd moved to Whisper Lake, he'd been a little shocked. It was like Joel had pulled a memory out of his past and put it right in his face. Once Joel had invited him to visit, he hadn't been able to think about anything else, and he didn't know why.

He'd traveled all over the world with his father. Whisper Lake had just been one of the places they'd gone to and that had been twenty-seven years ago. *So, why was there this gnawing feeling of something he couldn't define at the back of his mind?*

Well, maybe he'd figure it out while he was here. He had two months until his next construction job started in Santa Barbara, a few hours away from his home in LA. That's where he'd spend three months before he moved on to another job, another city, another adventure.

That mantra reminded him of his dad, of every trip they'd ever taken. His father had believed in living a life of adventure, and it had been one hell of a life. It just hadn't lasted long enough.

He shook that depressing thought out of his head as he drove into a small lot behind a two-story restaurant. The Blue Sky Café was on the first floor, with an apartment on the second floor. The location in the middle of downtown was perfect. Hopefully, the apartment wasn't a disaster like the house he'd just seen.

After parking his rental car, he grabbed his overnight bag and backpack and met Chloe and Leo at the back door.

She gave him a surprised look. "Is that all your luggage? Aren't you planning to be here for a few months?"

"I travel light."

"Got it. Well, come on in."

She opened the back door and stepped into a hallway. He saw a couple of restrooms, a door marked Office, and caught a glimpse of a bustling restaurant just beyond. Chloe and Leo headed up the back stairs. She inserted a key into the door, and he followed them inside.

The apartment was one room with large windows overlooking the street. There was a queen-size bed, a small dresser, as well as an adjacent sitting area with a loveseat and a chair. A small kitchenette and a bathroom rounded out the living space.

Leo ran toward a fluffy beanbag chair in the corner of the living room and plopped down on it with a delighted giggle.

"Some of the furniture is a little old," Chloe said, turning the smile she was giving to her son onto him.

His gut clenched at that inviting smile, which seemed to instantly fade when she realized who she was looking at.

This woman had some guardrails up. He knew she was divorced, but he knew little else, and he found himself more curious than he would have thought.

"Anyway," Chloe continued, clearing her throat. "You're welcome to stay here if it works for you. I replaced the mattress last year for my previous tenant, so it should be in good shape."

"This is fine," he said. "What happened to your tenant?"

"She got a job in Denver. She moved out about a month ago. I was thinking about fixing it up before I rented it again, but then Eleanor died, and I realized the house would have to take priority. That's why I told Joel I'd be happy to rent it to you for a good price until June. That's when you have to leave, right?"

He nodded. "End of May. I have a job in California that was postponed, so I ended up with some unexpected free time."

"That must have been frustrating to think you had a job starting and then it didn't happen."

"It happens more often than I'd like, but I've learned to roll with it. Do you own this entire building?"

"My in-laws own the building, my former in-laws," she amended. "I'm buying them out gradually. They used to run the restaurant and manage this apartment, but they moved to Florida about six years ago, and I've been in charge since then.

"Sounds like you're in charge of a lot of places for a lot of people."

"You could say that. Everything was running smoothly until recently." She licked her lips. "You've come to Whisper Lake at a good time. Everything is opening up again after the winter. This weekend you'll be able to see the town in action."

"In action?" he asked curiously. "What's going to happen?"

"A massive Easter egg hunt and pancake breakfast on Saturday. And on Sunday, you'll find plenty of Easter brunches at various restaurants. Whisper Lake doesn't let any holiday go by without a celebration. After several long months of cold and snow, everyone is excited to be outside again."

"Sounds like fun. I was thinking I was coming to a sleepy small town."

"Not sleepy and not so small anymore. The last few years, we've had a lot of growth. Joel's resort development is just another sign of how the community is growing."

He gave her a thoughtful look. "That should be good for your business."

"It is. I'm not complaining. I don't mind having more people around, more businesses popping up, but there are some in town who don't feel the same."

"There always are," he said. "It sounds like things have changed a lot since I came here as a child."

Surprise ran through her eyes. "You've been here before?"

"When I was six. I don't remember much. I know we stayed at a cabin on the lake. I hadn't thought about that trip in years until Joel mentioned he'd moved here. Then a few memories came back."

"Like what?" she asked curiously.

"There was an ice cream place with waffle cones. It smelled like sugar."

Chloe smiled. "You must be talking about Sugar Dreams. It's a small shack by the public beach. It's been there for sixty years, I think. It still has the best ice cream in town."

"I'll have to check it out." He sniffed. "This place doesn't smell too bad, either."

"Gus is making chili for our special tonight."

"Living here, I have a feeling I'm going to be hungry a lot."

"I'm hungry," Leo announced, interrupting their conversation as he somersaulted his way out of the bean bag chair, ending up off-balance and with a giddy smile. Leo had some of Chloe's features, her smile, and her light-brown hair streaked with gold highlights. But Leo seemed more carefree. Maybe he got that from his father, whoever that was.

"You're always hungry," Chloe teased as Leo ran toward her, throwing his arms around her waist. She ruffled his hair. "We'll go downstairs and get you some dinner."

"Maybe I'll go with you," he said. "I haven't eaten since breakfast."

"Of course. And dinner will be on the house tonight. It's the least I can do after you saved me from falling through the floor."

"No need to thank me. I'm glad I was there."

"Me, too. I didn't want the entire Whisper Lake Fire Department coming to my rescue. It would have been the talk of the town for at least a week." She held out her hand, revealing a set of keys. "One key for the apartment, and one for the café. They will work on both the front and back doors."

"Thanks."

"Can we eat now?" Leo whined.

"Yes," she said, as she headed downstairs.

He locked the door behind them and followed her into the café, which was a warm, bright space with wood tables and chairs, along with a couple of cozy booths and a counter hosting a dozen seats. It was a little before five on a Wednesday evening, so there were only a couple of tables that were taken.

Chloe swung Leo onto a stool at the counter, and he took the seat next to the little boy while she moved behind the counter.

"What would you like to drink?" she asked. "We have sodas as well as beer and wine."

"I'll take a beer, whatever you recommend."

"Great. I'll get you a menu, so you can decide what you want to eat."

"I don't need a menu. I'll take the chili. It smells amazing."

"It tastes amazing, too."

"Mommy, I want mac and cheese," Leo said.

"I know what you want." She pulled out a tablet and entered their order. Apparently, technology was alive and well in the small town. "I'll get the drinks."

As soon as Chloe turned her back to grab drinks from a large refrigerator, Leo gave him a smile and then surprised him by climbing onto his lap. Leo put his hands on his face and giggled.

He couldn't help but smile back. "What are you doing?"

"Meow," Leo said, his tongue darting in and out.

"Ah, you're a cat."

"Meow."

"I had a cat once. His name was Freddie."

"Was he a white cat?"

"No, he was a black cat with a white stripe on his head. Some people thought he was a skunk. They'd run when they saw him coming."

Leo patted his cheeks as his little face drew closer. The kid clearly had no boundaries.

"Leo," Chloe said as she returned with their drinks. "Remember what I told you about touching other people's faces? Get back in your seat. Your mac and cheese is coming soon. You can start with some fruit and milk." She set a glass of milk on the counter and a small plate of sliced strawberries, bananas, and apples.

Leo climbed off his lap and onto the adjacent stool.

"Sorry about that," she said, putting a beer down in front of him, as well as a large bowl of salad. "The chili will be ready soon."

"Thanks, and you don't have to apologize for Leo." As Leo meowed, Decker laughed and said, "Or should I say your cat?"

"He loves to be a cat. Or a dog. He's very interested in animals. He's dying to have a pet, but I can't take on another responsibility right now."

At her words, he couldn't help but notice the tired gleam in her eyes. She seemed to have her hands full. He couldn't imagine how difficult it was to be a single mother.

"I'll check on the food."

He dug into the salad she'd brought him while she returned to the kitchen. The lettuce was crisp, and the vegetables tasted like they were right out of the garden. The salad immediately perked him up. It had been a long day of traveling, and he had eaten nothing healthy in hours.

"Hello," an older woman said, as she came around the counter with a suspicious and cool smile. She was quite tall, with dark hair and deep-set brown eyes. "I'm Marian. Are you a friend of Leo's?"

"As of a few hours ago. I'm Decker Hayes. I'm renting the apartment upstairs."

"Oh, you're the contractor. It's nice to meet you. I'm Marian Lassen, the assistant manager. I'm here most days, so I'm sure I'll be seeing a lot of you."

"Judging by how good this salad is, I'll be eating here a lot."

Marian smiled. "It's the best place in town."

Chloe returned with Leo's pasta and his chili. "I hope it's not too spicy," she said. "Sometimes Gus gets a little heavy-handed."

He scooped up a spoonful. "I like it spicy. This is perfect."

Chloe smiled. "I'm glad you like it. Gus and his sister Amy are my cooks, and they're exceptionally good. A lot of other restaurants in town have tried to lure them away, but they've been incredibly loyal."

"How long have you been running this place?"

"I've been working here since I was sixteen and running it since I was twenty-six. That's when my former in-laws moved to Florida. Before that, Joan was the manager and Jerry was the cook. But after Jerry had health issues, they retired somewhere warm and put me in charge."

"That was an enormous responsibility to take on."

"It was, but I was working here all the time, anyway. My ex-husband is a soldier, and he was deployed a lot. This place became my second home, and the employees are family to me. I couldn't run this place without them, especially Marian. She has really helped me keep this place going since Leo was born. Anyway, what do you think about the house? Are you interested in the job?"

"I am, but I need to go back in the morning and dig a little deeper. Then I can give you an estimate. Joel said he could help me find some day laborers, maybe a tile specialist to help with the bathrooms and kitchen. I can do it all, but a one-man show will take longer."

"I'd like it done as soon as possible."

"Which works for me, since I have a limited amount of time available."

"I wish I'd known that Eleanor was living like this. I could have offered to help her get organized."

"I'm surprised it didn't get around that she had a problem."

"I have to believe she never let her friends come inside. She doesn't have any relatives. I contacted her attorney after she passed away. He said she didn't leave any instructions about her personal property, and he wasn't aware of any relatives. What little money she had went to a local shelter for women and kids. But maybe there's someone he didn't know about. Someone who would want some of her things."

"If not, I'm sure there must be a junk service in town."

She frowned. "I can't just hire someone to clean it all out."

"Why not?"

"It feels too cold, like none of the things she treasured mattered at all. I need to at least look through what she left behind, see if there's anything of value."

"Her things might have mattered to her, but she's gone," he said. "That might sound cold, but it's the truth. To anyone else, her things will probably have no significance."

"If I could find a close friend, some of her personal things might be meaningful to them."

He thought she was about to do a lot of work for nothing, but that was her choice. Clearly, she had a big, kind heart. She was running a restaurant and two properties for people who were not in town, not to mention raising a child. Now, she wanted to find someone to give her tenant's things to. She was too nice, which was probably why she looked so tired. And he wanted to ease some of her burden.

"Why don't we meet at the house tomorrow after I look around?" he suggested. "We can talk about exactly what you want and look at what's there. Do you have time?"

"I could meet you after the breakfast rush tomorrow, around ten-thirty. Leo will be at preschool and daycare until three, so I have a few hours."

"That works for me."

She tucked a piece of loose hair behind her ear. "Maybe things will look better tomorrow."

"I've often found that to be true," he said. But in this case, he felt her optimism was probably misguided.

"I really hope you can take the job. Most of the contractors around here are busy for the next few months. They've all been waiting for the snow to clear."

"Joel mentioned that."

"Joel never told me how he knows you. He just said you were a friend from school."

"We met in high school in San Francisco."

She straightened at that piece of information. "San Francisco? I didn't realize Joel had lived in California."

"His father was overseeing a development there, and the family came with him for two years. The family went back to New York after Joel's graduation, and he and I headed off to college together in LA. Since then, we try to get together every couple of years, but it's not as often as we'd like."

"Did you grow up in San Francisco?"

"I grew up all over, but I lived in San Francisco for about four years."

"Why did you grow up all over?"

He shrugged. "My father's job took us around the world. He was a photojournalist and an incredible writer."

"Sounds like an amazing childhood."

"It was an adventure, that's for sure." He paused as the door to the café opened, followed by a familiar voice. He smiled as Joel entered the restaurant, wearing a navy-blue suit with a light-blue tie, which was a typical look for Joel. They both worked in construction, but Joel had always been more comfortable in the office or the job site trailer while Decker had enjoyed getting his hands dirty. But he was surprised that Joel hadn't gone more casual since moving to this small town.

"Decker," Joel said with a cheerful grin. "You made it."

He got to his feet as they exchanged a brief hug. "I'm here."

"It's great to see you." Joel stepped away from him, then walked around the counter and gave Chloe a quick kiss, which seemed to fluster her a little.

"Can I get you a drink or something?" she asked quickly, moving forward so that Joel had to step back around the counter, which seemed to make her more comfortable.

That was a little odd. But he knew little about their relationship. Maybe they were still at an awkward stage. Although, in his experience, awkward stages never really became much of anything else. If it wasn't easy from the beginning, it rarely got that much easier.

"Actually," Joel said. "I wanted to see if Decker wanted to get a drink and some dinner, but it looks like he already ate."

"I can still drink," he told Joel. "And we have a lot to catch up on."

"Hopefully, we'll have lots of time to do that," Joel said. "What did you think of the job Chloe needs done?"

"It would be a challenge, but I'm definitely interested. I need to take a better look tomorrow."

"I'm sure you can help her," Joel said confidently.

"I'm going to try." He got up and pulled out his wallet, but Chloe waved him away.

"I told you, dinner is on the house," she said. "Consider it a welcome to Whisper Lake meal."

"All right. Thank you." He turned to Leo. "See you later, buddy."

"Meow," Leo returned.

He laughed and said, "Meow" back, which made Leo laugh and Chloe smile. Then he turned to Joel, who looked at him in bemusement. He shrugged in response. "Sometimes, you just have to be a cat."

"Sure," Joel said. His gaze moved to Chloe. "I'll call you later."

"Have fun," she replied.

"We will," Joel returned. "Goodbye, Leo."

Leo said, "Meow".

Joel just ruffled Leo's head and then headed out the door. "I don't remember pretending to be an animal when I was a kid," he said, when they left the restaurant. "Chloe says it's just a phase."

"Probably. I have to say I'm surprised you're dating a woman with a child."

"A few months ago, I decided to say yes to everything I would have ordinarily said no to, and it has been an excellent strategy. I'm happier than I've been in a long time. Chloe is different from other women I've dated. She's down-to-earth and sweet—always smiling. She's easy to be around. There's no drama. No agenda. It's refreshing."

He felt an odd sense of envy at Joel's words, which made little sense, because he was living exactly the life he wanted to live. And he always picked women who were drama-free. But he couldn't quite equate the word easy with a single mom and a child. "Let's get a drink. You can tell me all about your new life."

CHAPTER THREE

THEY ENDED up at an Irish bar, and after ordering a whiskey, Decker had time to catch up with Joel. "How long has it been since we've seen each other?" he asked.

"Four years?" Joel said, a question in his eyes.

"That sounds about right."

"It's been too long, but you're not an easy man to pin down, Decker. I never know where you're going to be."

"I've been in Los Angeles for most of the past few years."

"Most?" Joel challenged. "You had a job in Hawaii, one in Park City, Utah, another in San Diego."

"That's true," he admitted. "I met some people with second homes that needed remodeling. It was nice to pick up work in other locations. I get itchy feet if I stay in one place too long."

"You sound like your dad."

"We were definitely cut from the same cloth. But let's get back to you and your new life goals. How on earth are you going to run your very large construction company from this small town?"

"I have a plan. I want to downsize the Manhattan office and set up satellite offices. Whisper Lake would be one. I'd have another in San Francisco to cover the west coast. I think we could be more efficient by operating across the country instead of in one location."

"And what does your father think about that?"

"It shouldn't matter what he thinks. He stepped down as CEO last year, and he put me in charge. It's my company now."

Despite Joel's words, he heard the tension in his voice. "It's difficult for me to believe he actually retired."

"Me, too, because he spends almost as much time at the office now as he did when he was working. He has trouble letting go, which makes things difficult, because clients and partners still trust him more than they trust me. And senior management has been giving me grief, especially my father's best friends, who don't love that I got the company instead of them. But it has always been a family business, and it was always going to be mine. I just need my father to step back and let me do what I was born to do." Joel blew out a breath and drained his whiskey, then called the server over to ask for another.

Having met Joel's father, he understood the pressure Joel was under. "I'm sure your dad will eventually back off," he said. "I know he's always been proud of you."

"I wouldn't say that," Joel muttered. "Most days he acts like I'm an idiot. It's nice to be away from him."

"Is that why you want to live here? Because I thought you loved New York. You used to say the city energized you."

"It did at one time, but now I feel claustrophobic when I'm there. Everyone wants something from me. Everything is about networking and going to the right parties and showing up at the new restaurant and living this life that seems so unreal. So, I'm walking away from it all. I'm going to be a mountain guy."

"Maybe you just need a vacation."

"That's what I thought at first, but I've been here five months now, and I can finally breathe again."

"And you're not bored?" he challenged. "I know you, Joel. You like upscale restaurants, museums, and the theater. You like expensive suits and traveling. You're not a mountain guy."

"I could be. I want to be. I've done all that other stuff. I don't care about any of that anymore."

Despite Joel's words, Decker wasn't completely sold. "And Sylvie is definitely out of the picture?"

"Sylvie didn't like it here. She said it was too small and too dull. When I told her I wanted to make Whisper Lake my home base, she thought I was out of my mind. She couldn't get on a plane fast enough. She didn't even try to like it. We're at different stages in our lives."

"I thought you were crazy about Sylvie."

"I was. But I want to settle down and make a life somewhere. She wasn't ready for that." Joel cleared his throat and grabbed his second glass of whiskey as soon as the server set it down. He took a long swig. "So, that's over. And now I've met Chloe. She's great. Don't you think she's great?"

"She seems great. But she has a lot of baggage, including a child, a very young child. You ready for that?"

"I want a family, so why should I shy away from someone who has a child? I never considered it in New York because a lot of my friends are single, and the city is full of wonderful adult activities. But here, there are so many family things. It's almost like you're the outsider if you're not in a relationship and you don't have a family."

He frowned. "That makes it sound like you're settling, Joel."

"I'm doing exactly what I want to do. And once you get to know Chloe, you'll know why I like her so much."

"Is her ex-husband around?"

"He's a soldier. He's overseas somewhere and doesn't come home much. They've been divorced for three years. She said they were high school sweethearts and simply outgrew each other. It doesn't sound too messy. Anyway, we'll see how things go. It's early days."

"If you're happy, I'm happy."

Joel grinned. "What about you? Are you happy?"

"I'm great. And I'm looking forward to exploring. I told you that my dad brought me here when I was a kid, so it will be interesting to see what I remember."

"That's right. Well, you're going to like it here. And we can go biking, hiking, sailing. It will be like the old days."

"Didn't you tell me the job was very busy right now?" he asked with a laugh.

"Yeah, it is. But hopefully, I can carve some more time out of the schedule. It's tricky because we're pitching to build another development on the north shore. If we can get that job, that will support my satellite office plan. So, tell me about Chloe's rental property. I know her parents have a tight budget. If I can help in any way, I will. I know they're hoping to get it up for sale within two months, and I guess Chloe will get a portion of that sale in return for managing everything. I think she could really use that money."

"I'm not sure of the timing yet. It depends on what Chloe wants to have done and what kind of rot we find in the house. It's apparent that at least one leak ran unchecked for a long time."

"That's too bad."

"But it's difficult to see what's there, because Chloe's tenant was a hoarder. That house is full of junk, mountainous piles of stuff. Just getting that out of the house will take some time. But I'm confident we can work something out."

"Good. I wanted to help her myself, but I've got everyone tied up on my project, and we're already a little behind. But I may be able to come up with some day workers for you. Also, tools and a truck, courtesy of the company."

"That's very generous."

"I want this to work for Chloe, and I'm happy to have you here, so a double win." He paused. "This town is going to change you, Decker. You mark my words. In a few months, you'll be a different guy. You won't want to leave."

Joel's words sent an odd shiver down his spine. He didn't want to be a different guy, and he would leave, because that's what he did. He never stayed in one place too long. He didn't even know how to do that.

An odd memory flashed through his head. His dad dragging him out to a car parked at the curb. He felt sad. He wanted to cry. His dad had pointed at the setting sun over the horizon and said, 'That's where we're going, Decker. If I could teach you anything, it would be this. Never look back. The future is always better than the past.'

He'd wanted to believe his dad, because it made him feel better, so when they'd driven down that road, he hadn't looked back. It had been the same with every goodbye after that. In fact, he rarely said goodbye. He just moved on.

"Decker?" Joel asked, bringing his attention back to the present. "You okay?"

"I need another drink," he said.

"And I need some food," Joel said, waving to the server. "We'll order and then you can tell me what you've been up to the last couple of years. You know, it is possible to post photos online, share your life."

"I prefer to live my life, not memorialize it."

"You can do both. Your father did. He took photos everywhere you went."

"Not of himself. Not of me. And aside from spectacular landscape or historical photos, I think most people's photos make them feel bad."

Joel gave him a bemused look. "That's not true. I like to look at my photos. Remember the good times."

"Sylvie photos don't make you feel bad?" he challenged.

Joel's smile faded. He took out his phone and opened up his photos. "I look at this picture now," he said.

Decker stared at Chloe's smiling face. The photo had been taken at the beach. Her hair fell loosely about her shoulders. The sun was shining on her beautiful face and her striking hazel eyes were a shimmering mix of colors: brown and gold and green. He started, realizing he was staring far too long.

Thankfully, the server came over to take their order, and Joel set down his phone, erasing Chloe's image from the screen. But Decker could still see her in his head, and that bothered him. He never poached someone else's woman, and Chloe was Joel's girlfriend. She wasn't going to be anything more to him than a landlord and maybe an employer.

And he didn't want her to be anything more. Chloe was a woman with all kinds of baggage, and while Joel might not care about all that, Decker certainly did. They'd just be friends while he was in town, and then he'd be gone.

Thursday morning, Chloe headed to the rental house, feeling a mix of emotions as she walked into the home that had once belonged to her grandmother. She'd spent many afternoons at this house, cooking with her grandmother, while her parents were working. Seeing Eleanor's mountainous piles of junk made her feel sad for the home that she remembered, and also for Eleanor, who clearly had some mental or emotional issues. But they had been masked by Eleanor's cheerful attitude and physical health. She'd come into the café now and then to have lunch, usually with a book in hand. But something had been off, probably something no one had known about. She should have checked on Eleanor, on the house, but she'd gone with the thought that no complaints meant no problems. That had been a bad assumption.

"Don't know where to start?"

She jumped at the sound of Decker's voice, whirling around to see him standing in the doorway between the kitchen and the dining room. Since meeting him yesterday, she'd tried to convince herself he wasn't that good-looking. But he was looking hot in worn jeans and a short-sleeve black T-shirt that highlighted his broad shoulders and muscular biceps. This was a man who worked with his hands, and who was tan and fit from building houses in California. He clearly hadn't spent the winter in the snow.

"Everything all right?" Decker asked, giving her a speculative look.

"Sorry, I was lost in thought." She cleared her throat. "Actually, I was lost in the past. This used to be my grandmother's house. I was thinking about how different it looked when she lived here. She used to have photos everywhere. She'd always bring out a camera when we were together. She wanted to immortalize every occasion. I think it was because she didn't have very many photos of my grandfather after he died, and she said she always regretted that."

"I'm assuming your grandmother also passed away?"

"Nineteen years ago. I was fourteen. We had baked cookies the day before. I thought she was feeling good, and maybe she was, but the next day she had a heart attack and passed away. Everyone said it was good that she didn't have to suffer, but it never felt good."

"Sorry."

"And I'm sorry for rambling on about my grandmother."

"What happened after your grandmother died? Is that when the house got rented to your hoarder?"

"Yes. And I think we should call her Eleanor. She was more than just a hoarder. She was a person, a nice woman."

"My turn to apologize," he said with a tip of his head.

"Eleanor moved in about three months after my grandmother passed away. She was a widow, and one of my grandmother's friends. I thought she was the perfect tenant. She never complained or asked for anything, and my parents were happy to have the house rented to someone they could trust."

"Where are your parents now?"

"They moved to Chicago ten years ago. My mom went back to work when I was in high school, and eventually, her ambitions took her to a much bigger city."

"What does she do?"

"She's a graphic designer for a media company. She's very talented."

"And your dad?"

"He's a lawyer. He can work anywhere, so he followed my mom. He wanted her to have her dreams. She stayed home while I was young and put her career on hold to take care of me and to support my dad. It was her turn. But I miss them being around. I wish they were closer, but they have their lives and I have mine." She blew out a breath. "Anyway, what can I do to help you here?"

"Why don't you look around down here and come up with a plan? I'd suggest calling someone to pick up everything, but if you want to go through things and separate them into donations, garbage, or recycle, that would be helpful. The sooner we can get the personal items cleared out, the faster I'll be able to get down to work on the bones of the house."

"I don't know where to start," she said with a sigh.

"Pick a pile and go. Be ruthless."

"That's not really my personality."

A smile lifted his lips. "If you want me to start the renovation quickly, then..."

"I know. I need to figure out what to do with Eleanor's belongings. They shouldn't feel that personal to me. I didn't know her that well. I should be able to be objective."

"Or you might start looking through Eleanor's things and get lost in her life," he said.

His prediction was probably a little too close to being accurate. "I know I don't have time for that. But I am curious why Eleanor came to be like this. I wonder if she was a hoarder before she moved in or if it happened after that. This isn't a town where it's easy to keep a secret obsession, but she was able to do that."

"I don't think you're going to discover her secrets by going through her trash."

"I think trash is the best place to find someone's secrets," she returned. "Like the wrapper on a bar of chocolate that you snuck away from your spouse or your kid."

"Did you do that?" he asked, his grin broadening.

"Maybe. I'm just saying that what people throw away can be very revealing."

"Well, I'm not interested in the trash, so I'll leave that to you. But I have to ask, don't you run a restaurant? Aren't you raising a child on your own? Do you have time to figure out an old woman's life, someone who isn't here anymore, who has no family to care about any of this? What does it matter?"

"You ask some good questions," she conceded. "But maybe that's the problem. Eleanor doesn't have anyone but me to sift through her things, and I feel like I should show her belongings some respect."

He gave her a doubtful look. "It's your time to waste. Speaking of your time—are you going to be involved in picking out tile, paint, cabinetry, lighting fixtures, all the things that you may want to replace?"

It felt like he was adding a million things to her *To-Do* list. "I hadn't thought about it, but I guess so," she said slowly. "But we are going to put the house up for sale, so it's not like I'll be living in it. I just want it to look clean and fresh, so maybe you could make some of those decisions, or does it cost extra?"

"I'm happy to pick up some samples and drop them off, but I prefer you make the final decisions. That way, we both know you're getting what you want. Joel mentioned that there are some bigger stores in Bixby."

She nodded. "Yes. It's about a twenty-five-minute drive. But that's where you'd probably find the most abundant selection of home repair materials. There are some smaller stores in town for basic stuff." She paused. "What about tools?"

"Joel is helping me out with that and also with a truck, which I'll pick up later today."

"It sounds like you're going to take the job."

"I still need to get you a bid, but I'm getting some details lined up, so if we decide to move forward, we can do that quickly."

"Speed is a priority," she said. "I better get started. What are you doing?"

"I'm trying to figure out where the leak is upstairs and how far the rot goes."

"It sounds like we're both looking for answers," she said lightly. "I have to say, I think there's a better chance my search will be more interesting than yours."

"I wouldn't bet on it," he said dryly, as he headed for the stairs.

She moved to the coffee table where there appeared to be a collection of salt and pepper shakers ranging from holiday themes to cats and dogs and other animals. As her gaze swept the collection, she had a feeling Decker might be right. She might be about to waste an enormous amount of time. But she couldn't just dump everything without looking at it first. And maybe, just maybe, she'd find something meaningful among the mess.

CHAPTER FOUR

AN HOUR LATER, Chloe felt more discouraged than optimistic. She had cleared off the coffee table and emptied the two side tables on either side of the couch. She'd started four piles for charity contribution, trash, recycle, and personal items that needed a longer look. So far, she had two plastic bags filled with items to donate, a box of magazines that dated back ten or more years for recycling, and a bag of trash for items that had been broken.

She'd found a couple of photo albums and some other random notes and Christmas cards that she'd put aside to look at later. She could take those items home and look through them after Leo went to bed. While she was here, she needed to focus on clearing things out and making some space.

Decker had been making considerable noise while he was upstairs. It sounded like he was pulling the house apart, and more than once, small pieces of wood had fallen through the hole in the ceiling. Now, she heard his footsteps on the stairs, and as he came into the room, she tried to ignore the little tingles that ran down her spine every time he came around.

"Well?" she asked, noting the dirt on his jeans, which

matched the smudges on his face. All of that should have made him less attractive, but it didn't.

"The problem is limited to the master bedroom and bath. The other bedroom and bath across the hall are fine."

"That's good news."

He nodded. "I'll detail what else I think needs to be done and work up a bid based on what you've told me you want, but you can add or delete once you see all the numbers."

"How long will it take to get everything done?"

"Two months, depending on the availability of labor and materials." His gaze moved past her. "It looks like you're making some progress. Find any secrets yet?"

"Unfortunately, no, but there's still a chance."

"Well, you have a lot more trash to go through. Are you in the mood to get some lunch? Or do you need to get back to work or to Leo?"

The restaurant was covered, and she didn't have to pick up Leo until three, so she could say yes. But should she? Why not? "I could eat. What did you have in mind?"

"I'll leave that to you, but I think dessert should include a trip to Sugar Dreams. I've been thinking about that ice cream since I got here."

"Then we should eat by the lake. I know just the place."

He glanced down at his clothes. "Should I change before we go?"

"You're fine. This place is very casual."

"All right. But I am going to wash my hands."

As he headed into the guest bathroom, she blew out a breath, wondering again what she was doing. She pulled out her phone and called Joel. Maybe he'd like to join them for lunch. Unfortunately, he didn't pick up. But it was fine. It wasn't a date. She needed to stop overthinking things. Decker was her tenant and, hopefully, her contractor. The least she could do was take him to lunch and show him around town.

Chloe led Decker down a long pier next to the harbor to a restaurant simply named Good Eats. "It's not fancy, but the food is great," she said. "Tammy Hall is the owner now. She took over for her dad about fifteen years ago."

"Another family-owned business," Decker murmured. "Like your café."

"Yes. There are a lot of family-owned businesses in town. You'll find very few chains or franchises."

Decker opened the door for her, and she preceded him into the wood-paneled restaurant that offered six tables inside as well as a patio with another dozen tables.

They paused at the counter to order their food, grab drinks, and then went out to the patio to find a table in the sun.

"This is an amazing view," Decker said, as he sat down across from her, his gaze sweeping the boat harbor, the lake, and the surrounding majestic mountains.

"There are magnificent views everywhere in Whisper Lake. Mountains, forests, lake, rivers...we have it all."

"You should work for the Chamber of Commerce."

"I've done a lot of work with the chamber. And I sell to tourists every day. My location on Silver Street gets a lot of visitors, and they always want to know where to go and what to do."

"You love it here, don't you?"

"For the most part. Sometimes the long winter gets tedious, especially with a four-year-old who wants to play outside. But the rest of the year..." she shrugged. "It's home. When I was a little girl, I used to think the mountains were my bodyguards. They were so tall and strong and protective. I always felt safe with them overlooking me." She smiled. "Silly."

He smiled back. "I can see why they would make you feel that way."

"Does this view feel familiar to you?"

"Yes, but I'm counting on the ice cream to bring some more detailed memories back."

"That's a lot to ask from an ice cream cone," she teased. "How long were you here before?"

"I have no idea, maybe a week."

"It sounds like you came in the summer if ice cream was the big memory."

"It was hot; I remember that. My dad took me swimming in the lake, and I got a bad sunburn." He paused. "It's funny the things that stick with you."

"Was your mom on the trip?"

"No, she died when I was three," he said shortly, as he took a sip of his soda.

As the shadows crossed his face, she felt a wave of compassion. "I'm sorry. That's very sad."

"I don't remember her. I wish I did. I barely remember my dad talking about her."

"Do you have any photos?"

"No."

"That seems odd."

"I'm sure there were some around at some point, but I didn't end up with any."

She still thought that was strange, but she let it go. "So, it was just you and your dad."

"Just us," he said, sitting back as the server dropped off their meals. "That was fast."

Too fast. She'd wanted more time to talk to him, but he was now focused on his food. Since she was hungry as well, she dug into her steak salad, thinking about the very little he'd told her so far. She shouldn't pry into his life any further, but she really wanted to. She waited until they were done with lunch before turning the conversation in a more personal direction.

As the server removed their plates, she lingered over her coffee, unwilling to call an end to lunch just yet. "Tell me a little more about yourself," she said. "If I'm going to hire you, I'd like to know more about you."

"Do you want me to give you a resume?"

"Just an idea of who you are, what you've been doing. You live in Los Angeles, right?"

"That's where I'm currently based, but my jobs take me all over the country. I don't like to stay in one place too long."

"Why the need to keep moving around?"

"It's a big world. I want to see as much of it as I can."

"Like your dad."

"Yes."

"How did you get into construction?"

"When I was sixteen, a friend of a friend's dad told me I could do some labor for him during a school break. I enjoyed working outside, and the money was decent, so I picked up a hammer. The rest is history."

"You're glossing over a lot of years," she complained.

"If you're concerned about my level of experience, I'm more than capable of doing your job. I'm sure Joel will vouch for me."

"I'm not concerned. I just like to know who I'm working with." She paused, thinking about his unusual upbringing. "Does your father still travel a lot?"

"No. He passed away when I was twenty-one," he said tersely.

Her jaw dropped. "Oh, my God! What happened? He must have been so young."

"Thirty-nine. He was on a research trip in Africa, and he got struck by lightning and died."

She stared at him in astonishment. "Are you serious?"

He nodded, a grim set to his mouth. "Yes. The odds are like a billion to one, but it's what happened. While it was a freakish way to go, in some ways, it was exactly right. My father lived on his own terms. He did what he wanted to do when he wanted to do it. Not that he was selfish; he wasn't. He was very generous and kind and interested in people. Everywhere he went, he became the center of attention because he was funny and genuine. But he couldn't live according to anyone's idea of structure or purpose. He had to be free, and he was. He was perfectly well until he wasn't. In fact, he had told me a day earlier that trip was the trip of his lifetime. He wished I'd gone with him, but I was in college then and trying to find my own life rather than follow him around in his." Decker paused. "His words were more prophetic than he knew."

"That's awful, Decker."

"I'm glad he didn't suffer. I couldn't imagine him getting sick and having to be trapped or stuck somewhere. He would have hated that."

She had a feeling he needed to think that to feel at peace with a death so sudden and so tragic. He'd been through a lot in his life. She never would have guessed, because he appeared lighthearted and carefree, but there was deep pain somewhere. "You've lost both your parents," she murmured. "That's not right."

"It is what it is," he said pragmatically. "I had a great childhood. Growing up with my dad was amazing. It was one adventure after the next. Our time together was short, but it was good. He always told me to move forward, never look back. That's how he lived his life and how I try to live mine."

His words made her realize that her first instincts were right —Decker was just passing through. He'd be gone in the blink of an eye, and she didn't need to know any more about him. Because that's all she really needed to know.

Not that she even needed to know that, because she wasn't going to date Decker; she was seeing Joel. That's who she should learn more about.

"What about you, Chloe?" Decker asked, interrupting her thoughts. "Did you grow up in a happy two-parent household?"

"I did, and I feel kind of guilty for saying that."

"Don't feel guilty. That's great. And it's rare."

"I was lucky," she admitted. "My mom stayed home with me

until I was in high school, then she went back to work. After they moved away, it felt a little different. At first, they'd come back every few months, or I'd go visit them, but once I had Leo, it was harder for me to travel, and their lives had gotten very busy. We definitely don't see each other as much as I'd like."

"Have you thought about moving to where they are now?"

"No. I have my business, my home, my friends. I need all of that to make my life work."

"Have you ever lived away from Whisper Lake?" he asked curiously.

"Yes. I went to college in Denver. After graduation, Kevin and I got married sooner than we'd planned because Kevin was in the Army and was going to be stationed at Fort Bragg. We wanted to move there as a married couple."

"You were young."

"Yes, too young, in retrospect. We lived on the base for three years. Then Kevin went into special forces, and he was called up for long deployments. I was lonely. I decided to move back to Whisper Lake and help his parents run the restaurant. I never lived on a base again, although I did sometimes spend time with him wherever he was."

"Sounds like you spent a lot of time living his life."

His words echoed the same thought that had run through her head a million times. "I spent too much time doing that," she admitted. "But I was in love. Neither of us knew how we'd be tested, how we'd change, how we'd disappoint each other. I'm sure in Kevin's mind I failed him as much as he failed me. But none of that matters now. We just need to be good co-parents for Leo."

"Joel said your ex isn't around much. How does he co-parent?"

"Kevin tries to talk to Leo once a week, but sometimes it's two or three weeks. He comes home when he can, but his life is at the whim of the Army. Last year he was gone somewhere for four months. I didn't even know where he was. But it was easier not to know because we weren't married anymore, and I was no longer depending on him for anything."

"That's rough."

"It's complicated," she said. "Kevin loves Leo, but he is obsessed with his military life, his band of brothers. His family is the men and women he serves with. That's the relationship he has always put the most effort into. And that's just him. He has best friends that seem to be able to have their family and their career, but Kevin just can't juggle that. He has to be solely focused on what he's doing." She paused. "But I don't want you to think he's a bad guy. He's smart and brave beyond belief. Anyway, I don't know why I'm telling you about him. You can't possibly be interested in my failed marriage."

He met her gaze. "I don't think ending something means you failed; you just changed. That's life. You did what was best for you and your child. Your ex probably feels the same way."

"I think he does. I wish I could give Leo the ideal family, mom and dad living in the same house, loving one another, but I can't. I just have to do the best I can. Thank you for not judging."

"I rarely judge anyone. My dad used to say unless you're walking in someone's shoes, you can't possibly know how they feel, what challenges they're dealing with. You can imagine, but you can't know, because every single person on this earth has a secret life."

She thought about his words. "I think your dad was right. Anyway, it's all good now. Or at least, as good as it can be. Leo is smiling most days, which makes me smile."

Decker grinned. "You seem like a person who smiles a lot."

"No one likes to talk to someone in a bad mood."

"So you fake it."

"Sometimes. But I think actions drive feelings, so if you act positive, then you feel better."

He nodded. "I agree. No point in wallowing in misery and self-pity. That doesn't make you any happier."

She thought he probably put on a good face a lot of the time, too. Losing both his parents so young had to have put a dark shadow over his life. But he wasn't living in that shadow. He was out in the sunshine. And he looked good in the sunlight, with the warm beams of light dancing through his dark hair. But he probably looked good in any light.

"Speaking of smiles and making people happy," Decker said. "You've definitely put a smile on Joel's face."

She started at his words, realizing she hadn't given Joel much thought since she'd sat down with Decker. "Joel seems great. We're still getting to know each other, but I like what I've learned so far."

"He's a good guy," Decker agreed.

Decker looked like he wanted to say something else, but then he just picked up his soda and took another drink. When he lifted his gaze back to hers, something passed between them. She didn't understand it. Or maybe she just didn't want to understand it.

"Well," she said, a little too loudly. "I think it's time for ice cream."

"It's always time for ice cream." He took out his wallet. "And lunch is on me."

"We can split it."

"Don't worry. You'll be paying me plenty of money in the next few months."

She sighed at that reminder. "Okay, then. Thank you for lunch. I'll get the ice cream. Is there any other place you're interested in seeing while we're out?"

He hesitated. "I was thinking about the cabin we stayed in. I feel like my dad knew the person who lived there or who let us stay there. Maybe it was even a relative, but I'm not sure."

"Do you know the address?"

"No. But the backyard was on the lake."

"A lot of houses and cabins back onto the lake."

He thought for a moment. "There was a gas station two

blocks away with bright red pumps. There was a black lab that used to lie next to the cash register."

"You're talking about Ernie's Gas," she said. "I know the station. It's been there for years. If the house is a few blocks away, we might be able to find it."

"Do you have time?"

She checked her watch. It was almost two. "I have about an hour before I pick up Leo."

"Then we better get going."

CHAPTER FIVE

DECKER HAD second thoughts about trying to find the vacation spot. He was definitely going against his father's directive to never look back, but when the gas station came into view, a surge of excitement ran through him. He recognized the red pumps immediately.

"That's it," he said, as Chloe slowed the car down. "That's where we'd go to get gas, and sometimes we'd just walk over to pick up snacks." He pointed to the street behind the station. "We would walk down that street."

"Let's check it out."

Chloe turned right at the corner, and as she drove down the street, he scanned the houses on the lakeside, looking for something familiar. He found it in a birdhouse hanging from a large tree. "Stop. That's it."

Chloe pulled over to the curb. "The one with the birdhouse?"

"The one next door," he said, his gaze moving to the one-story white house with the peeling paint. It looked weathered and sad. While it was early spring and most of the lawns hadn't yet come back from the winter, this particular yard felt abandoned.

"It doesn't look like anyone lives there," Chloe commented.

"No, it doesn't." He got out of the car, not completely sure why. He walked up to the front door and rang the bell. There was no answer.

Chloe had gotten out of the car and moved across the yard, a curious gleam in her eyes. "What are you doing, Decker?"

"Just looking around. I don't think anyone is home."

He headed through the side yard, where a gate was barely hanging on its hinges. When he reached the back of the house, he saw more neglect, but he also saw the lake, the shimmering blue water that took him way back in time. Memories suddenly washed over him.

"I want to go swimming, Daddy," Decker said, as he walked to the edge of the yard. There were a lot of weeds surrounding the path that led down to the beach, and he wanted to explore, but his dad kept arguing with the brown-haired lady, who had gone into the house to take a phone call.

"Maybe later," his dad said tensely.

"Why can't we go now?"

"Because I have to deal with…something," he said, his gaze moving toward the house.

"The lady is making you mad," he observed.

"I'm fine. Don't worry."

"I like it here. Can we stay here after the summer ends?"

"I don't know. Probably not. But there's a new adventure waiting just around the corner." His dad stiffened as the woman came out onto the back deck. "Stay here."

He watched his dad move up the steps to the deck. "What did he say?" his father asked.

"He wants to talk to you in person."

"Dammit!"

Decker jumped at the sound of his dad's loud, angry voice. "Dad?" he questioned.

"Stay here," his father ordered. Then he and the lady went into the house.

"Decker?"

Chloe's voice brought him back to the present, but his heart was still thudding against his chest.

"Where did you go?" she asked.

"Just thinking about when we stayed here."

"It didn't look like a happy memory."

"I'm not sure what it was. I was out here, and I wanted to go swimming. My dad was arguing with a woman. I don't know who she was."

"Was it a girlfriend? You came here after your mom died, right?"

"Yes. The lady in my mind seems older than him. Not a girlfriend." He frowned, then shook his head. "It doesn't matter. I don't even know why I came here."

"Something about your stay here is bothering you," she said.

"I don't know why. It was a long time ago."

"But..."

He met her gaze. "Ever since Joel told me he was working here, I started having weird dreams about our trip, bits and pieces of memories that make little sense. I don't know why there's something tugging at my brain."

"But there is something. Maybe it has to do with the argument you witnessed. You said you came here on vacation, but your dad was upset, and he was arguing with a woman. That makes it seem like he had a reason to come here besides just wanting to visit the lake."

He nodded. "It feels that way, but it doesn't matter. We should go."

"I bet we could find out who owned this house thirty years ago," Chloe said. "My friend Keira used to be a real-estate agent. She lives in Miami now and is pursuing a career as a fashion designer, but she has a manager running her real-estate business here in town. I'm sure someone in her office could track down the title."

"We probably rented this house. The title wouldn't matter."

"They might. Let's see who your dad might have rented it from."

He gave her a thoughtful look. "Don't you have enough to do, Chloe?"

"Yes, but I'm intrigued."

"Why?"

"Because I don't think you'd be so bothered by that trip if there wasn't something to figure out. And I like mysteries."

"I don't think it's a mystery."

"It's something. Can I try to find out?"

"Fine, but don't spend over five minutes on this."

"I'll just make a call." She checked her watch. "Do you want to get that ice cream before I take you back to the house?"

"Maybe we'll push that to another day. I'm full." That wasn't the only reason he didn't want to go for ice cream. His stomach was churning with what he'd remembered, and he was almost afraid to visit that ice cream shop in case it brought back more memories.

Never look back, his dad had told him repeatedly. Maybe having Chloe make that call was a mistake, but he couldn't quite bring himself to tell her to forget it.

After picking up Leo from school, Chloe spent the afternoon helping him color Easter eggs and decorate them with stickers, which involved plenty of messy fun. While she loved being with Leo, and usually he took all her focus, today her mind kept drifting back to Decker and his odd reaction at the rental house he'd stayed in as a child.

There was a story there, and she wanted to know what it was. She was intrigued not just by his odd memories, but also by him. He suffered tragedy, lived an adventurous and unusual life, and seemed happy and confident in who he was, except when he'd been at the house. And that was why she wanted to know more.

When Leo finished decorating his eggs and ran into his bedroom to play with his horse farm, she pulled out her phone and called Keira.

"Hello?" her friend said, answering somewhat breathlessly.

"Are you running?" she asked.

Keira laughed. "Only in from the car. How are you, Chloe? It's good to hear your voice."

"It's good to hear yours. How is Dante? Are you enjoying Miami?"

"Dante is amazing, and Miami is growing on me. It's very different than living in the mountains, but I've made some fantastic connections in the fashion world. And I'm making lots of trips to New York when Dante is on the road, so it's all working out."

"I'm glad you're happy. I hope you're not lonely."

"Well, I miss my girls," Keira said. "But you're all very good at keeping in touch. I'm looking forward to our girls' getaway in June. I hope that's still on."

"I'm in. I already have my parents lined up to babysit that weekend," she said. Her group of friends, most of whom were married or engaged now, had made a vow to get together at least once a year for a three-day weekend, and she couldn't wait.

"Perfect," Keira said. "What's going on in Whisper Lake? Are you still dating that guy you mentioned last time we spoke?"

"I am," she said. "It's...good," she said, wishing she sounded more convincing, because Joel was a great guy.

"You don't sound that sure."

"We're still getting to know each other."

"Well, I'm glad you're getting out there," Keira said.

"I'm definitely getting out there. We're going to karaoke tonight," she said, wanting to turn the conversation away from Joel.

"Oh, man, I miss Micky's and karaoke. Sing one for me."

"I'm hoping to do more cheering than singing."

"You have a beautiful voice, Chloe. You should stop being so shy about using it. How's Leo doing?"

"We just finished coloring Easter eggs. He's excited about the hunt on Saturday."

"I'll bet."

"So, I have another reason for calling. I need a favor."

"Sure. What is it?" Keira asked.

"I need to find out who owned a house about thirty years ago. Would you be able to find that out for me?"

"Probably. Text me the address, and I'll check it out. Can I ask why you're interested?"

"I met someone who stayed in the house a long time ago, and he has some memories he can't figure out. We went by the home, but it doesn't look like anyone is living there. It's probably a long shot that we could track down the former owners, but if it's easy enough to run a search…"

"It's easy."

"Okay, I'm texting you the address now. He said they stayed in the house twenty-seven years ago."

"Got it. I'll call you back and let you know what I find out."

"Thanks, Keira." She set down the phone and cleaned up the kitchen. Her neighbor's daughter, Jessie, was coming over to watch Leo while she went to Hannah's party, so she'd make spaghetti for both of them.

She'd barely gotten dinner started when her phone rang.

"I got the information," Keira said.

"That was fast."

"I just ran a title search on the house and the year you gave me. There have only been three owners. At the time in question, the house was owned by Eleanor Johnson."

She sucked in a shocked breath. "Are you serious? Eleanor Johnson? The woman who lived in my parents' rental house the last nineteen years?"

"I think it's the same one. She bought the house with her husband Hank Johnson when it was built fifty years ago. She sold it twenty years ago when her husband passed away. The current owner is Jeff Hodges."

"I don't know that name."

"It wasn't familiar to me, either. Do you want me to dig in further?"

"No, that's fine. I can't believe Eleanor owned that house. It seems like such an odd coincidence."

"Why is it a coincidence? Who's this friend you're getting the information for?"

"He's actually Joel's friend," she said. "I just met him. He lives in LA but came here to visit Joel. He's a contractor and had some time in his schedule, so he's going to remodel the rental house. He mentioned that he'd spent some weeks here one summer a long time ago. He wanted to see the house where he'd stayed." Her voice drifted off as she realized how crazy this story was sounding. "Anyway, he was just curious who owned the house, and I said I'd help."

"You sound pretty interested in this guy and his story."

"More so since you just told me Eleanor used to own the house. I wonder if that was where she lived or if it was a rental property."

"Hang on. I'll see if Eleanor owned any other property in Whisper Lake at that time."

Chloe waited, hearing Keira clicking away on her computer keyboard. A moment later, she came back on the phone.

"Eleanor and her husband owned a house on Middleton, so the other house was probably a rental. Looks like both properties were sold after Eleanor's husband died, but to two different parties. Do you care about that?"

"I don't think so. Thanks for doing this, Keira."

"No problem. Let me know if you need anything else."

"I'm sure I won't," she said firmly, trying to convince herself as much as Keira. "I need to worry about my own life, not someone else's very distant past."

"I was going to say that, but I didn't want to waste my

breath," Keira said with a laugh. "I know you, Chloe, and when you get curious, you can't stop yourself from asking questions."

"Well, I'm going to try. We'll talk soon." As she set down the phone, she wondered if the odd coincidence meant anything. She didn't see how it could. But she'd pass the information on to Decker and let him decide.

CHAPTER SIX

MICKY'S BAR and Grill was packed when Chloe arrived for karaoke night. Her friends had grabbed a large table by the stage, and it looked like the beers were already flowing. Hannah and Jake were sitting next to Gianna and Zach and across the table were Lizzie and Justin, Adam and Molly. There were four empty chairs, so she slid into the one at the head of the table next to Hannah.

"You're alone?" Hannah asked, disappointment in her eyes. "I thought Joel and Decker were coming."

"They should be here soon." She'd heard from Joel an hour earlier, whose dinner had apparently been moved up, so he would be able to make it, and he'd invited Decker as well. It would be nice to have them here. While she adored her friends, she was getting tired of always being the single one at the table. "No Chelsea and Brodie?" she asked.

"They were going to come, but Chelsea got nervous when Layla got a cold, so they passed. New mother jitters," Hannah said with a smile.

"I remember those. And Layla is only two months old, so I can see why they'd want to stay in." Chloe looked over at Lizzie, who was Chelsea's sister, and had recently announced that she was three months pregnant. "How are you feeling, Lizzie? Or should I ask? You're practically glowing." Lizzie always had a smile on her face. She was an innkeeper and a naturally happy and welcoming person, but she looked even more radiant today.

"I'm great," Lizzie said. "The morning sickness seems to have finally passed. I didn't have it as bad as Chelsea."

"Thank God," her husband Justin said.

Chloe smiled. "That's great. I'm glad you're feeling better."

"Just in time for Easter. You're coming to brunch at the inn, right?" Lizzie asked. "And Joel, too."

"I'm definitely coming. Joel has a friend in town, so I'm not sure if they want to hang together. You'll meet him tonight. Decker is coming with Joel."

"Well, Decker can come to brunch, too. I'm not cooking, so the more the merrier," Lizzie added with a laugh. "And you know we have plenty of space in the dining room. I have a couple of guests this weekend with kids, so we're setting up some videos for the children. The adults will play trivia after brunch. I even have prizes."

She smiled. "You're always up to something, Lizzie. It sounds great."

"I'm looking forward to getting to know Joel better. It seems like things are going well with you two."

"It's good, but you all need to relax. It's early. We'll see where it goes."

"It's just good to see you're enjoying yourself," Lizzie said.

"I am." She paused, her heart skipping a beat as Decker approached the table in dark jeans and a button-down shirt. "Hi," she said, getting to her feet. "You made it."

"I did, but..." He gave her a somewhat apologetic look. "I'm afraid it's just me for the moment. Joel got hung up at his dinner meeting. He said he'd be here as soon as he could."

Disappointment ran through her, but she pushed it away, telling herself that Joel was not like Kevin. He wasn't choosing to be gone for weeks at a time; he just had a meeting that had run late. "Well, I'm glad you came now." As they took their seats, she introduced Decker to the rest of the group.

Over pitchers of beer and a dinner featuring Micky's famous ribs and sides, the conversation flowed fast and easily. Decker got along with everyone. He had quick comebacks to Hannah's sarcastic wit, could trade adventurous outdoor experiences with Jake and Zach, and had plenty of travel experiences to talk about with Justin. Decker also found common ground with Gianna, who had lived in LA, and asked Lizzie questions about her inn, a subject Lizzie was always happy to discuss.

Chloe spent most of the time listening, happy to learn more about him through her friends. But as Decker became the life of the party, she couldn't help thinking that it hadn't been this easy when she'd introduced Joel to everyone. They'd been welcoming and Joel had had no trouble talking, either, but it hadn't felt quite so easy. Maybe that's because her friends weren't deciding if Decker was worthy of dating her. They were just being themselves, and so was he.

As their plates were being cleared, Decker turned to her. "Are you pissed off that Joel is so late?"

"It's fine. He's busy. I just want him to get to know my friends. They're very important to me."

"They're great. You're lucky."

"I am," she agreed. "They love you."

"What's not to love?" he asked with a laugh.

She couldn't help smiling. "I'm sure there's something I'll discover if you stick around for a while."

"That's my secret. I never stick around too long."

"I don't think that's a secret," she said lightly. "You mentioned you don't like to stay anywhere for too long. Is that to lower expectations? You don't want anyone to get too close?"

"I just like to put my cards on the table."

She nodded, but as their gazes clung together, she cleared her throat, thinking they were getting a little too personal. "I found out who owned the house you stayed in."

His brows shot up in surprise. "You did?"

"Yes. I called my friend Keira. She ran the title on the house, and you're going to be surprised who the owner was."

His gaze grew wary. "Who?"

"Eleanor Johnson."

At first, he looked confused, and then a sparkle of awareness entered his green eyes. "Eleanor Johnson? Isn't that the name of your tenant? The one whose stuff we're clearing out?"

She nodded. "That's the one. Eleanor and her husband owned the house when it was rented to you. They had another house somewhere else in town, so I guess that was a rental. It's a strange coincidence, isn't it?"

"Yes," he said. "Very strange."

"But what does it mean?"

"It probably means nothing."

"Except that at some point in your life, you had a connection to Eleanor."

He thought about that, then shrugged. "I guess so, but I don't know what that connection is beyond the fact that she might have rented my father her house. And since she passed away, I don't think I'm going to find out what that connection was."

"We could try."

He frowned. "I think I'd rather leave things where they are." He paused, relief running through his gaze as it moved past her. "Look who's here."

She turned as Joel came up behind her. He leaned over, giving her a quick kiss that hit the corner of her mouth because she was so surprised to see him. "Hi," he said with an apologetic smile. "Sorry to be so late."

"It's okay."

"Sit here," Decker told Joel, as he slid into the empty seat by Jake, allowing Joel to sit next to her.

"Thanks," Joel said.

As he greeted her friends, she put a smile on her face. She was annoyed that he was late, irritated that he'd interrupted her conversation with Decker, and was feeling generally out of sorts. But that was stupid. Joel had made an effort to get here. She should appreciate that.

"How was your meeting?" she asked when he turned back to her.

"It was good," he said, excitement in his gaze. "My company is bidding on another piece of land on the north shore of the lake. If we get that, we'll be able to build an amazing development near the ski area. It will be its own resort, a destination within a destination. It could be huge."

"That sounds great. Is there a lot of competition?"

"Two other companies are in the mix. The fact that we're already building on the south shore is a point in our favor. They can see our vision and that we keep our promises." He paused. "Plus, getting that land will further support my plans to make a permanent office here, which is what I want. I like this town and the people I'm getting to know," he said pointedly. "I'm sorry I missed dinner. I know you wanted me to get to know your friends better. It's a busy time, but it won't last forever."

"What are you two whispering about?" Hannah interrupted. "I hope you're figuring out what song to sing, because Chloe owes me a song."

"I don't owe you," she returned with a frown.

"I did you a favor, and you said you owe me one," Hannah reminded her. "This is my one."

"I'll do something else for you."

"This is what I want. You don't get to pick the favor you owe. You and Joel can do a duet."

"I'm not a singer," Joel said. "Sorry, Chloe. You're on your own." He paused, glancing down at his phone. "And I apologize again, but I have to take this."

Her annoyance with Joel returned as he quickly left the table.

"I'm not singing alone," she told Hannah.

"I'll sing with you," Decker said.

"Perfect," Hannah said with satisfaction.

Chloe turned to Decker as he moved back into Joel's seat. "You don't have to sing with me."

He shrugged. "Why not? It's just karaoke."

"I'm not a talented singer."

"Well, I'm great, so I can carry you."

She smiled at what was clearly mock arrogance. "Great, huh? You're not short on confidence, are you?"

"Not for singing karaoke. Are you in?"

"I'm in." Turning to Hannah, she added. "And I won't be asking you for a favor any time soon."

Hannah gave her a smug look. "I'm sure that's not true."

Hannah was probably right, but next time, she would negotiate better.

After several singers had taken the stage, she and Decker made their way to the side to pick a song. Her nerves increased after Gianna and Zach sang a duet that resulted in a standing ovation.

"I don't want to go after them," she muttered.

"We'll be good, too," Decker told her.

"I highly doubt it."

"Hannah has known you for a long time, right? If you couldn't hit a note, I don't think she'd be pushing you to take the stage."

"She thinks I have a good voice, but I haven't sung in a while. I'm rusty. And I'm nervous," she admitted. "I feel like I've been failing a lot lately, and I don't need to add one more thing."

"Then we won't fail," he said. "I've picked the perfect song."

"Hang on," she said, as he grabbed her hand and led her onto the stage.

She looked at the prompter in front of them. "What did you pick?" She'd no sooner asked when the music started, and the words came up.

"Sing," Decker said. "Don't look at the audience. Just sing."

He grabbed her hand as the music started, probably afraid

she was going to bolt from the stage. Then he sang the first line, "Don't go breaking my heart."

She looked at the prompter. "I couldn't if I tried," she sang.

Her voice was a bit wobbly, but as Decker kept going, she followed. They were singing about a love that scared the hell out of the two people who were trying to avoid it. It was probably the perfect choice for Decker, a man who wanted no entanglements. But it was also a good choice for her, a reminder that falling for yet another wrong man was not an option.

When the song ended, applause rang out, and she could hear Hannah's cheering voice above the rest. She looked at Decker, who was grinning happily.

"Told you," he said, squeezing her hand. "You were great. We were great."

"We were okay," she admitted.

He let go of her hand as they exited the stage, and she felt almost chilled by the loss of heat, but then they were back at the table, with everyone giving them another round of applause, before turning to pay attention to the next singer.

Decker lifted the pitcher of beer. "Do you need a refill?"

"A big one," she said, pushing her mug in his direction.

Chloe's face was flushed, her eyes sparkling, a gleam of satisfaction in her gaze as she sipped her beer and relaxed while other singers took the stage. She'd conquered a fear tonight, and Decker was happy he'd helped. She actually had a really wonderful voice. And once she'd gotten over her nerves, she'd sounded great.

The song he'd picked had been perfect, because he had a feeling Chloe was the kind of woman who could break his heart if he let his guard down. But he wasn't going to do that.

His smile faded as Joel came back to the table. He forced himself to move to the next chair so Joel could sit next to Chloe again, reminding him that Joel was who Chloe wanted. He'd just been a temporary stand-in.

As Joel leaned in to whisper yet another apology to Chloe, he wondered what was really going on with Joel. He'd been ridiculously late, then distracted. He claimed to want a life that wasn't all about business, but he wasn't acting that way. And he'd seen this side of Joel before, the intense, ultra-focused, ambitious side that drove him sometimes ruthlessly forward in whatever quest he was on. Was he really going to settle here in this small mountain town and let other people rush past him? It just didn't make sense.

But it wasn't his business. Joel's decision, his relationship with Chloe, wasn't for him to judge. He'd told Chloe he tried not to judge people, so he needed to stop doing that instead of making himself a liar.

His frown deepened as Joel put his arm around Chloe and kissed her on the cheek. Chloe smiled. If she'd been pissed at Joel earlier, that feeling had vanished.

Blowing out a breath, he finished the rest of his beer in one long swallow and looked for a distraction. He found it in Hannah, who had changed seats with Zach and was sliding into the chair next to his.

"Nice job up there," she said. "You have a good voice."

"Thanks. It was fun. I think Chloe enjoyed herself in the end."

"I knew she would. She used to sing all the time, but then she stopped. She stopped doing a lot of things that used to make her happy, and I didn't enjoy seeing that. We grew up together, and I remember the girl she used to be before life kicked her down a few times."

"The divorce?"

"That and all the responsibilities she had to take on. She's been picking up the slack for many people: her parents, her in-laws, and her ex-husband. Now she has to raise Leo on her own, and she's consumed with being the perfect single parent. I wanted to give her a few minutes to let loose." She paused. "I'm talking way too much. Chloe would not want me to be telling you all this, but I have to admit I'm a little drunk."

He smiled as she slurred her last few words.

"Anyway," Hannah continued. "I'm glad you got her on the stage. I don't think she would have gone up there alone." She took another sip of her beer. "What's the deal with your friend always being busy?"

He turned his head to see Joel and Chloe engaged in conversation with Lizzie and Justin. "You'd have to ask him."

"He doesn't stick around long enough to ask him anything."

"He's here now." He pushed back his chair. "I need to get going. I have to work on my estimate."

"I'm sorry. Have I made you uncomfortable? If so, I apologize."

He smiled. "I have a feeling you make many people uncomfortable, Hannah."

"I can be too honest and direct," she admitted. "But I'm also very loyal, and I always look out for my friends."

"I respect that," he said, meeting her gaze. "But if you need to warn someone that you've got Chloe's back, it should probably be Joel."

"I'll get to him if he sticks around long enough. He seems like a big city guy to me, but I guess we'll see."

"I guess we will," he muttered. He gave a general goodbye to the table of friends and then left, feeling relieved to get out in the fresh air. He needed to clear his head, and he needed to stop thinking about Chloe. She was with Joel, which meant there was really nothing to think about.

He walked to the truck Joel had given him earlier to use while he was in town, so he could turn in the rental car he'd gotten at the airport. Sliding behind the wheel, he started the engine. He headed back to the apartment, then impulsively changed directions. He drove toward the lake and past the gas station, to the house they'd gone to earlier that day.

Pulling up across the street, he cut the engine and the lights.

He didn't know why he was so drawn to this property. But there was something...

Staring at the house, he could hear voices in his head. He closed his eyes and leaned his head back, caught between wanting to remember something and wanting there to be nothing to remember.

The woman had come to the door, but his dad didn't want to let her inside.

"There's only one person I want to speak to," his father said, "and it's not you."

"I know. I'm working on setting up a meeting between you."

"He doesn't want a meeting; he wants to destroy me."

"That's not true. Just give it a little more time." She paused. "I've brought a present for Decker. Can I give it to him?"

"He needs nothing from you," his dad replied. "I provide for him. I always have."

"No one doubts that."

"Oh, yes, they do."

"Please, just give him the present," the woman begged.

"No. You know what I want, Ellie. Don't come back until you can give it to me."

His father stepped back and slammed the door in her face. When he turned around, he saw me and stopped abruptly. "Decker. You're supposed to be in bed."

"I'm thirsty. Why are you mad at the lady?"

"It doesn't matter."

"She said she had a present for me."

"You don't need any presents from her. And tomorrow we're going on a hike, so you have to go to sleep. Get back in bed, and I'll bring you some water."

"Will you read me another story?"

"We read three stories earlier," his dad said, then relented. "Maybe one more. I love you, Decker. I hope you know that. You and me—we're a team. We don't need anyone else, do we?"

"No. I love you, too, Daddy."

Decker's eyes flew open, his heart beating faster. Had the woman at the door been Eleanor Johnson? It seemed likely that Ellie was a nickname for Eleanor. Who had she been to his father? She wasn't his father's mother; her name was Catherine. Maybe his mother's mother? But her name was Debra.

But Ellie had some kind of connection to his dad, and that connection felt familial.

He wished he knew more about his family, but his father's desire to always move forward had prohibited discussions about the past. His dad had never wanted to talk about family, always saying they had each other and that was enough. He'd always felt it was enough.

But now he was wondering what drama had made it just the two of them. The woman had suggested that they'd gone to Whisper Lake to work something out. He'd thought it had just been another vacation spot, another place for his dad to write and take photographs. It had clearly been more than that, but what?

It shouldn't matter, and he would probably never know the truth. Although…

Eleanor had left her entire life in Chloe's rental house. *Was it possible there was a clue to his past in that vast pile of junk? And did he really want to look for it?*

His gut twisted in conflict. His father wouldn't want him to look. He'd tell him to leave, go home to California or anywhere else. Looking back was not where you wanted to look. It would only make you lose your balance or slow you down.

Why had his father stressed that so many times? Had his dad been afraid of what he would find if he did look back?

He started the car and drove down the street, pausing at the stop sign in complete indecision. He didn't know where he wanted to go, but he had a feeling there was probably one good choice and one bad one. *Did he want to stir up the past or leave it buried the way it had been for so many years?*

CHAPTER SEVEN

CHLOE WOKE UP FRIDAY MORNING, feeling more energized than she had in a while. The night before had been fun. She'd gotten back up on the karaoke stage, thanks to Decker, and it had gone well. She hadn't sung too badly. And having Decker as a duet partner had been amazing. He'd played to the crowd, making everyone laugh and cheer for them.

She'd also had a chance to spend time with Joel. They'd been missing each other the past few weeks, as his schedule hadn't matched up with hers. Finally, her friends had had time to talk to him. They'd seemed to like him. There wasn't much not to like. He was handsome and friendly and easy to talk to.

But it didn't feel like Joel had clicked with the group as much as Decker had. To be fair, Joel hadn't made as big of an effort as Decker to get to know her friends, and by the time he'd arrived at the bar, her friends had had several rounds of drinks and were more interested in singing and then dancing when the karaoke session ended, and a DJ took over.

She would have liked to dance with Joel, but he'd had an early meeting, and she'd had a babysitter to send home, so they'd parted company at the bar after a kiss that might have been better if it hadn't been interrupted by people coming and going in the parking lot.

Looking at herself in the mirror, she touched her fingers to her lips, trying to sink back into the feeling of his mouth on hers. But it had simply been too fleeting. Next time, she told herself, then left the bathroom.

Moving into Leo's bedroom, she found him already awake and playing with a bunch of trucks in the middle of his bed. She smiled at his sleepy eyes and messy brown hair, feeling an enormous wave of love for her little boy. Sometimes, he reminded her of Kevin, but he was a mix of both of them, and she was happy about that.

After getting him up and dressed, she fed him a quick breakfast and then they headed off to preschool. Leo was always happy to go to school, so there were no sad goodbyes, just a quick hug before he ran off to play with his friends. Sometimes, she secretly wished he was a little sorrier to see her go, but that was selfish. It was better that he was independent, because she really needed the preschool daycare to work well. It made her life a lot easier.

When she got to the café, the restaurant was packed. Friday morning had brought more tourists in for eggs and pancakes. She jumped into work, not giving the rest of her life a second thought until the rush finally slowed down around ten. She was taking her first deep breath in an hour when Decker walked in and slid onto a stool at the counter. For some inexplicable reason, her heart jumped at the sight of him. His brown hair was damp, as if he'd recently taken a shower, his face cleanly shaven, a glow to his skin.

He smiled when he saw her, and that gave her heart another jump.

"Hi," she said. "Can I get you anything?"

"No, thanks. I ate early this morning. I don't have a printer, so I wrote up the bid." He pushed a piece of paper across the table.

"Oh, great," she said, picking it up. She perused the line

items, her stomach clenching a little at the various price points. It wasn't going to be cheap to fix the house up, but as she turned the page over, she realized Decker had thrown in a discount at the end. "You're giving me fifteen percent off?"

"I always do that for friends."

"Well, I appreciate that. Even though we're not really friends. We met two days ago."

"I consider anyone I sing with to be a friend," he said lightly.

"I wanted to thank you again for that. You took off so fast last night, I didn't have a chance."

"No thanks necessary, and I wanted time to work on the bid. I know you probably need to go over this with your parents, but if you can let me know as soon as possible, that would be great."

"I'll call them today," she replied.

"I've laid out a few options if you want to go a cheaper route. You could leave the downstairs guest bathroom as is and just do some paint. The kitchen isn't in terrible shape, either, if you want to skip new cabinets and just do some refinishing. Anyway, you can think about it. In the meantime, I know I'm not on the payroll yet, but I'd like to do some cleanup at the house."

"Really?" she asked in surprise. "Why would you want to do that?"

He shrugged. "It needs to be done, and I have time."

"There are lots of other things you can do in Whisper Lake. You can hike, go for a sail, walk around town. You could take a bike ride. There's a great path that runs along the water, and it's a beautiful day."

"Joel and I are going on a bike ride later this afternoon."

"Right. He said something about that. That's good. You and Joel should spend time together."

"Well, until then, I might as well be productive. I can leave personal items for you to review at a later date."

"Sure, go for it." She tilted her head, giving him a thoughtful look. "Did you have any more thoughts about what I told you last night? That Eleanor owned the house you and your father stayed in?"

"I have thought about it," he admitted. "To be honest, I'm a little more curious to look around her house."

Now, she knew why he was so interested in sifting through Eleanor's things when yesterday he'd suggested she hire a junk company and be done with it all. "Do you think there's a clue there?"

"Probably not," he said with a wry smile. "I'm not sure I would even know if I somehow stumbled upon a clue. But I think Eleanor was the woman arguing with my dad. I remembered him calling her Ellie. Which sounds like a nickname for Eleanor."

"I would think so. There are photos of Eleanor in her house. You should be able to confirm she's the woman who was talking to your dad. You could solve at least one mystery."

"I'm not sure there is a mystery," he said slowly. "I don't even know why I'm intrigued by these particular memories. I'm not someone who thinks about things that happened a long time ago."

"It's because you're back in Whisper Lake. And I don't think it's a bad thing to look back."

"Well, whether or not I find clues, I can give you a little help—no charge."

"All right. I'll call my parents and talk to them about the job. I'll let you know what they decide."

"Then we'll talk later."

After Decker left, she looked back at the bid he'd given her, but her thoughts weren't really on the itemized list of repairs. She was still wondering about his connection to Eleanor Johnson.

"What are you thinking so hard about?" Marian asked, giving her a sharp, curious look. "It wouldn't be the very attractive man who was sitting at the counter a few minutes ago, would it?"

"More like the bid he gave me to fix my parents' rental

house," she said, holding up the paper in her hand.

"Well, that's not as much fun."

"No, it's not. And I wouldn't have been thinking about Decker. I'm going out with his friend, remember?"

"Right," Marian said.

She didn't like the gleam in Marian's eyes. "I need to call my mom." She moved down the hall and into the small office, shutting the door behind her. She sat down at the desk and took out her phone. She took a photo of the bid and texted it to her mom and then called her.

Her mother answered immediately. "Hi, Chloe."

"Hi, Mom. I just texted you the bid for the house."

"I see that," her mother murmured. She fell silent for a moment. "It's a lot of money. Does he really have to repair the flooring upstairs?"

"Yes, I stepped right through it. The wood was completely rotted from a leak in the bathroom. The house is in poor condition, Mom. Eleanor was a hoarder. I had no idea what kind of clutter and disrepair she was living in."

"Really? A hoarder?" her mother echoed. "I can't believe that. She always looked so impeccably neat when she used to visit your grandmother."

"She did dress well. I never would have imagined she was living in such a mess. No wonder she didn't complain or ask for repairs. She didn't want anyone in the house. But all that money you saved over the years is now coming due."

"Do you think we should get a second bid?"

"There are no contractors available for at least six months. If you want to wait until next year, we can get another bid. But Joel vouches for Decker, and he seems very fair in his pricing to me. He's even giving us a discount because of his friendship with Joel."

"I saw that. It's just so much money," her mother said with a sigh. "I was hoping we could make more of a profit."

"Maybe the investment will pay off when we sell."

"Let's hope so."

"Do you want to talk it over with Dad?"

"No. He told me to decide. He went on a fishing trip with friends. He won't be back until Monday."

"So, you're spending Easter alone? You could always come here, Mom."

"I won't be alone. I'm going to Aimee's house," she said, referring to one of her friends. "She's having an Easter brunch, and I can't get away right now. I have a lot of work starting on Monday."

"Well, Leo and I would like to see you sometime."

"We'll get out there soon," her mom promised. "How's Leo?"

"Getting bigger every day. He's really at a sweet age, loving and happy, easy to please."

"Enjoy that while you can."

"Hey, I was pretty easy," she protested.

"You were a very good child, thank goodness," her mom said with a laugh. "I was lucky, and you're lucky, too. Have you spoken to Kevin lately? Has he seen Leo?"

"Not since Christmas. He was supposed to come last month, but there was some kind of problem. Kevin never has any details."

"That's for sure," her mother said tartly. "I'm really disappointed in that man."

"He's doing a heroic job; I try to remember that."

"That's true, but it doesn't excuse him for letting you and Leo down."

"We're doing okay." She didn't really want to rehash the past. "I should get back to work."

"Me, too. Hire the contractor," her mother said. "I'd like to get started as soon as possible. I'll let you decide what is really necessary and what isn't."

More decisions she would have to make. "Okay. I'll figure it out. Before you go, do you know anything about Eleanor's family?"

"Like what?"

"I know her husband died. Did she have kids?"

"No, she didn't. I remember your grandmother saying that after Eleanor's husband, Hank, died that she was all alone in the world."

Which made her wonder again how Eleanor could have been connected to Decker's father.

"We'll talk soon," her mom said. "Give Leo a kiss for me."

"I will." As soon as her mom hung up, she punched in Decker's number. "Hi," she said, when he answered. "You're hired."

"That was fast," he replied.

"My mom is ready to go."

"So am I. But we need to address the junk issue as soon as possible."

"I know. I have to pick up Leo at two. I'll bring him over. He can play with the train while I go through things. Unless you don't think the house is safe."

"I've marked off any areas I believe to be unsafe. It's mainly just that one spot where you fell through the floor. What are the odds that the spider would be in exactly the wrong place?"

"Just my luck," she said dryly.

"Maybe it was lucky," he countered. "You didn't get hurt, and you revealed a problem that might have taken a long time to discover. Now, we know exactly what we're dealing with."

"That's true. You're a glass half-full kind of guy, aren't you?"

"I try to find the positive. I think you do, too."

"Some days are harder than others," she muttered. "But not today. I feel better knowing that you'll be in charge of this project."

"I won't let you down."

She slipped her phone into her pocket and headed back into the dining room, feeling like she'd finally checked one item off her To Do list. But it also meant that she was going to be seeing a lot of Decker over the next few weeks.

CHAPTER EIGHT

DECKER STARED at the array of photos on Eleanor's piano. The woman featured in many of them at various ages was the woman from his memories—Ellie. She'd been an attractive woman. When she was young, her hair had been dark brown, but in later photos, it had turned white. She was often pictured with a stern-faced man, who was probably her husband. He seemed to be annoyed that he was in the picture. Ellie didn't always look that happy, either, although she seemed to try harder to look like she was. Clearly, she had been a woman of secrets all her life.

As his gaze moved away from the photos to the rest of the living room and dining room, he wondered if there could be a clue to those secrets in the mess. It certainly seemed possible, since it didn't look like she ever threw anything away. Clue or not, he needed to clean up the house so he could do the renovation. He might as well get started.

For the next two hours, he worked in the dining room. Since it was directly under the broken flooring, he didn't want Chloe working in that area. He tried to continue the organizational system that Chloe had set up earlier. Some items were easy to decide on, like the basket containing probably a hundred spools of different colored threads, and the collection of plates depicting life in the forties or fifties. She also had three silver tea services. He had no idea why anyone would even need one. But he put them in the donation box, hoping someone would want them.

As he worked his way through the pile on the dining room table, he kept an eye out for mementos from the past. But there was nothing. The only thing that really became clear was that Eleanor had obviously had some mental health issues. No one needed to keep hundreds of ketchup packets from various takeout restaurants or menus from every restaurant in Whisper Lake. No one needed to keep junk mail catalogs from twenty years ago, which he quickly tossed in the recycle pile.

But what really concerned him were the toys piled up under the dining room table. The train actually ran through the stacks of unopened toys and stuffed animals, many of which seemed to date back twenty years. Eleanor practically had a toy store in her dining room. Shaking his head in bemusement, he started moving the toys toward the front door. They would eventually be donated, but if Leo was coming over, he could play with some of them in the meantime.

He also took a ridiculous amount of time to reroute the train, so that it didn't go into the perilous area of the dining room. If Leo wanted to play with it, it could safely run around the coffee table and couch.

When he finished with the train, he grabbed the last remaining box under the dining room table, finding more mail. This one seemed to contain more in the way of bills and letters. He tossed most of the mail into the recycle bag, wondering again why she would have kept a yellowed gas bill from fifteen years ago.

He'd almost emptied the box when he stumbled upon a dozen letters held together by a rubber band. His jaw dropped open in shock as he read the name of the addressee—it was him. Eleanor had written to him, addressing the letter to Decker Hayes. He ripped off the band, realizing none of the envelopes had been opened. They'd all been sent back saying address unknown.

The address on the first two envelopes was in Arizona. They had lived in Arizona for a year or two, but he couldn't remember the street name. The next letters had been sent to an address in San Diego, another city they'd spent a short time in, but he didn't know if the dates matched up. Clearly, they hadn't, since all the letters had been sent back. Or maybe his father had just returned them because he didn't want any contact with Ellie.

He ripped open the first envelope, his hand shaking a little as he unfolded a piece of note paper.

Dear Decker,

I loved meeting you last summer. I wish we could have spent more time together, but I'm praying you'll come back soon, and we can ride the train again. Your smile was so bright that day at the park. I don't think I'll ever forget it. I just wanted you to know that I love you and I'm sorry we didn't get to say goodbye. But one day we'll see each other again. In the meantime, here are some stickers that reminded me of you. I hope they'll remind you of Colorado.

Love Always, Ellie

His heart raced as he stared at the stickers, reminded of how much he'd loved stickers when he was a kid. He'd plastered them all over his backpack and everywhere else. It had driven his dad crazy.

But why was he thinking about stickers when he should be wondering why Ellie had written to him, telling him she loved him? *Why would she love him? Was he related to her?*

And why wouldn't she have written to his father? He wouldn't have been able to read her letters at age six.

He opened the next letter, which had arrived a month later, according to the postmark.

. . .

Dear Decker,

Merry Christmas! I sent you some toys. I hope you get them. I think you'll like what I picked out. Remember the puppies you loved meeting at my friend Clara's house? Well, I sent you some puppies to play with.

Love to you and your dad!

Ellie

Decker shook his head in confusion as her note referenced something else they'd done together. He didn't remember riding a train with her or going to see puppies. *Or did he?*

His lips tightened as he heard the horn on a train ring out. He remembered the wind in his face, the lake in the distance. Someone had been sitting next to him. He didn't think it was his dad. He smelled perfume.

As he struggled to remember the past, the doorbell suddenly rang, and he jumped, his pulse racing even more.

The door opened before he could answer it, and Chloe popped her head in, a smile on her face.

"Hi," she said, as she pushed the door open, and Leo darted past her, running straight for the train. "Sorry about the bell. Leo loves to ring doorbells. How's it going?"

"Uh...fine," he said, trying to get his head back in the present.

She gave him a quizzical look. "Is everything okay?"

"Not really."

"Why? What's wrong?" Her gaze narrowed in concern. "Did you find more rot? Will the job be more expensive?"

"No, it's not anything to do with the house. I found some letters from Eleanor to..." He still couldn't believe the connection between himself and Eleanor Johnson.

"To who?" Chloe asked impatiently.

He walked over to the table and brought back the letters and envelopes. He handed them to her. "See for yourself."

"Decker Hayes?" she said in shock, lifting her gaze back to his. "Eleanor wrote to you?"

"I read the first two. They would have been sent the first year or two after we were here. But the letters never got to me. She had the wrong address." He paused. "Actually, I don't know if she had the wrong address, if we'd already moved, or if my father just sent them back unopened."

"What did she say?"

"You can read them," he said tightly.

She perused the two notes he'd already read, then glanced back at him. "She loved you. But why? I don't understand the relationship."

"Neither do I. I have no idea why this woman would write to me, tell me she loved me, or try to send me presents."

"She must be related to you. Maybe she was your grandmother."

"I know the names of my grandmothers. Neither one was Eleanor or Ellie."

"Are they still alive?"

"Yes. But I've never met my maternal grandmother or grandfather. My mother's parents disowned her when she got pregnant at seventeen."

"They didn't come to her funeral?"

"I don't think so. I met my dad's mother once or twice, but my father didn't have a good relationship with her, so she wasn't in my life. My paternal grandfather took off when my dad was a toddler, so I know nothing about him." He tried to pace, because he needed to move, but there was nowhere to go in this small, crowded house, and he felt like he was going to suffocate. "I need air." He pushed open the door and stepped out onto the porch, drawing in several deep breaths of air.

Chloe stepped out on the porch, keeping the door to the

house open. She had the two remaining letters in her hand. "You should read these. Maybe there are more clues."

He hesitated, then took the first envelope out of her hand and opened it.

Dear Decker,

I got an ice cream today at Sugar Dreams and couldn't stop thinking about how much you loved that ice cream. You ate it so fast that the chocolate smeared across your face. You were so cute. I hope you're eating ice cream wherever you are. I was shopping today, and I found a miniature ice cream shop. I think you'd love to play with it. I have it at my house. It will be waiting when your dad brings you back for a visit. I hope that will be soon. Miss you, Decker. Tell your dad that we miss him, too.

He handed the letter to Chloe to read and then tore open the last one.

Dear Decker,

I guess you're not getting my letters. I thought I would try one more time in case you're back from one of your adventures. It's been almost two years since I saw you. You must be so big by now. I think you're probably in the third grade. Time goes by so fast. I'm still picking up presents for you that I hope you'll be able to open one day. Tell your dad I know he's a great father, and I hope he brings you back soon. There are people here who love you. Someday, I hope I can tell you that in person.

He shook his head as he gave the letter to Chloe to read. "It's more of the same and it doesn't make sense why this woman was writing to me."

"She keeps wanting you to tell your dad things, that he's a good father, that she wants him to bring you back, but why didn't she write to him?"

He shrugged. "Who knows?"

"Maybe she wrote to him, and you haven't found those yet."

"That's certainly possible. I'm not sure I want to find anything else."

"What are you worried about?"

"Lies," he said shortly. "Lies that might have been told to me by the one person in my life I trusted more than anyone else. My father was so big on honesty. I don't want to believe he had a big secret he didn't share with me."

"Maybe it's not about lies. Ellie might not have been a blood relative. She could have been a friend of the family. It sounds like there was a lot of estrangement. Maybe she was one of your grandparents' friends or a neighbor or a former nanny. She could be anyone."

"That's true. She doesn't say she's my grandmother or an aunt or anything."

"Did she ever appear in your life again?"

"I don't think so. I know we never came back to Whisper Lake. I don't believe that I ever saw her anywhere else. It's puzzling."

"It sure is, but I wouldn't jump to any conclusions until you have more information."

"I rarely do that, but this town, this house, is throwing me off-balance." He drew in another breath. "I made some progress in the dining room, so that's something."

"That's good." She paused. "I hate to throw some bad news at you, but Joel called me and said to tell you he can't do the bike ride this afternoon."

"That's fine. It's not a big deal."

"He was disappointed. He wanted to show you more of the lake and the downtown park."

He started at her words. "Is there a train in the park by the lake? Something that people ride?"

"Yes. And Ellie mentioned in her letter that you rode the train with her."

"I don't remember that, but it sounds like it happened. I need to check it out."

"Well, that park is near the bike path. Why don't you go for a ride with Leo and me? We won't be able to go as far as you could go with Joel, but it could still be fun. Only if you want to," she added quickly.

"Did Joel ask you to sub in for him?" he asked curiously.

"I volunteered. I owe you for helping me out last night on the karaoke stage, and to be completely honest, I'd love a bike ride. It's such a beautiful day. I have bikes at my house and a carrier that Leo can sit in. The start of the trail is only about a mile from there."

The idea of getting out of this house and by the water was more than a little appealing. "You're on," he said. "Can we go now?"

She laughed. "You sound like Leo. I can't tell him in advance that we're going to do anything, because he wants to do it right that second."

"Is that a yes?" he asked with a smile.

"Yes. Do you want to follow me to my house?"

"Perfect."

They went back into the house. As she told Leo it was time to go for a bike ride, he put the letters on the coffee table. Whatever Eleanor's secrets were, they were in this house, and, for the moment, that's where he wanted them to stay.

CHAPTER NINE

CHLOE'S ONE-STORY, three-bedroom house felt like her: warm and welcoming, with charming décor. It was also a little messy, with toys and picture books strewn around the living room. He was quite sure that Chloe was always cleaning up, but it was difficult to keep up with Hurricane Leo.

"Come to my room," Leo said, grabbing his hand and dragging him toward the hallway.

Chloe laughed. "I'm going to grab a sweater while you get the tour."

He smiled, allowing Leo to take him into a small bedroom at the end of the hall. This room was even more chaotic, with toys all over the floor, and a pile of clothes on the unmade bed that looked like they'd come out of the laundry but hadn't been folded yet.

"This is my horse farm," Leo said, as he knelt down in front of a fenced-in area with several miniature horses and people inside.

He squatted down and picked up a chestnut horse. "Who's this?"

"Cinnamon." Leo pointed to the other three horses. "And that's Burt, Whisper, and Midnight."

"Burt?" he questioned, picking up the white horse. "How did you pick that name?"

"He has white hair like Burt at the market."

"Got it."

"Midnight is black, like night."

"And Whisper?"

Leo shrugged, then jumped up and ran to the closet, bringing back a bucket of toy soldiers. "Do you want to play with my soldiers?"

"I don't think we have time. We're going on a bike ride, buddy."

Despite his words, Leo dumped the bucket of fighting men into the middle of the horse farm. "My dad is a soldier," he said, looking back at Decker. "He's at war."

"I heard that."

"Mommy says he's a hero. He protects people. I want to be a soldier when I grow up," Leo declared. "Then I can fight with my dad."

His heart squeezed at the words that seemed to imply more than just a childhood dream occupation, but a desire to spend more time with his father. He'd felt that way about his missing mom. He'd adored his father, but he'd missed having a mother. He had a feeling that Leo might have some of the same emotions in reverse.

"What does your dad do?" Leo asked. "Is he a soldier, too?"

"No. He traveled all over the world taking pictures and writing books."

"I like to take pictures with Mommy's phone," Leo said.

"Actually, he's not supposed to use my phone to take pictures," Chloe interrupted, giving her son a pointed look as she entered the room.

Leo just laughed, which made Chloe smile.

As she turned to him, he felt the warmth of her smile wash over him. It felt good—too good. He got to his feet. "We should get going."

"Yes," she agreed. She grabbed a sweatshirt off the bed for Leo. "You need to put this on."

"I'm hot," Leo protested.

"You won't be hot when we're outside." She got Leo into his sweatshirt and then they headed out to the garage to get the bikes.

She had a small trailer for Leo to sit in that attached to the back of a bike.

"That's cool," he said. "I was thinking you just had an extra seat."

"This works better. Leo is more comfortable, and I'm more stable."

"I can pull the trailer."

She hesitated. "If you wouldn't mind. It is a little heavy."

"I'm happy to get extra exercise. I'll be careful," he added, wanting to drive the tiny worry lines off her face.

"I'm sure you will be. There's not much traffic between here and the bike path. Just a couple of stop signs, and then we'll be off the street."

Despite Leo being in the carrier, she put a helmet on his head and on herself. She handed him an extra. "This is Kevin's. You probably don't want to wear it, but Leo will ask you a million questions about why you're not wearing it."

"I'm fine to wear it," he said, although it felt a little weird to put it on. Not because he had anything against wearing a helmet, but because it belonged to her ex-husband. He felt like he was stepping into the guy's life. That was stupid. Kevin probably hadn't worn the helmet in years. If he was encroaching on anyone, it was probably Joel, something he needed to remember. But Joel had set this ride up, so he was just going to enjoy it and stop thinking about it.

Chloe took a deeper breath, feeling better when they reached the bike path. While the streets had been fairly quiet, she could never really relax until they were on the designated trail. She flung a quick look over her shoulder. Decker gave her a smile and a nod. So, she turned her attention to the path that led through thick tall trees and wound around the lakeshore.

It was a gorgeous afternoon, the temperature in the low seventies, which was warm for early April. The sky was a brilliant blue. The snow-topped mountains adding to the picture-perfect view. She'd ridden this path a million times, and yet there were still days like today when it amazed her. She hoped it was amazing for Decker as well, although she could hear Leo babbling away and Decker occasionally answering back. She hoped Leo wasn't being too annoying. Her son had an incredible imagination, and he loved to share any idea that came through his head. Decker seemed to take it all in stride. He had an easy way with kids, something Joel hadn't really shown.

Joel was sweet to Leo, but they didn't engage very much. They didn't play together. Joel never really got down on Leo's level like Decker had done in his bedroom. But it wasn't fair to compare. She had deliberately kept Joel a little away from Leo, wanting to make sure their relationship was going to be something before her little boy got too caught up in it.

But she didn't want to think about the future right now. She just wanted to enjoy the day.

They rode for another fifteen minutes, until the path ended at a beach in a pretty cove called Waller's Bay after Edith Waller, who was once the mayor of Whisper Lake and whose house still stood on the nearby hills above the bay. She came to a stop and hopped off her bike.

"End of the road," she said as Decker put his feet on the ground.

"I want to go to the beach, Mommy," Leo said.

"I'm not sure we have time." She looked at Decker. "I know

you wanted to look at the train. We can get to it through one of the paths we passed about a mile back."

"There's plenty of time for that. I'm happy to take a break on the beach. Can I let Leo out?"

She nodded, removing her helmet as Decker did the same, then freed Leo from the carrier. They moved their bikes off to the side and walked down to the water. There was a couple with two kids having an afternoon picnic, and another woman stretched out on the sand reading a book. Otherwise, the beach was deserted.

"Not too close to the water," she told Leo, who was already looking for rocks, one of his favorite things to do at the beach.

"Okay," Leo replied, barely glancing in her direction.

Decker sat down, stretching out his legs before him, and after a moment's hesitation, she also sank to the sand.

"This is something," he said, his gaze sweeping the scene in front of them.

"One of the prettiest spots on the lake and never too crowded, because you can't park nearby. You have to bike or walk to get here."

"It's worth the effort." His gaze swung back to her. "Thanks for bringing me."

"No problem." She paused. "I guess I'm not the only one Joel stands up for work."

"Joel can get tunnel vision when he's in the middle of a project. I'm sure he'll make it up to you."

"I don't need him to make it up to me. I just need to know that..." Her voice drifted away as she realized how needy she was about to sound.

"What do you need?" Decker asked curiously.

"Nothing. Forget it."

"I'm not going to forget it. Just tell me. I won't say anything to Joel."

"I'm a little gun-shy when it comes to men who lose track of the rest of the world when they're in the middle of a project."

"We're talking about your ex-husband."

"Kevin could be a great husband and father when he wanted to be, when he gave us his focus, but most of the time, his concentration was elsewhere. I couldn't complain because then I'd be a distraction. He couldn't afford to be distracted when he was in dangerous parts of the world. I couldn't whine about not having enough attention. I had to swallow my feelings and be the cheerful, supportive wife. He was doing his duty, and I had to do mine. And I did it, for a long time."

"What changed?" he asked curiously.

"Leo," she said simply. "Kevin missed Leo's birth. I was all alone when I went into labor. It wasn't Kevin's fault. He'd been captured on a mission. I didn't know that at the time; I just knew he was missing. When I found out he was alive, I was the happiest I'd ever been. He came home injured but able to recover and for six months, I thought we were going to enter a new chapter in our lives. He was going to get out of the service, and we'd be a family."

"I guess that didn't happen."

"No. He tried, but he was bored and restless, even with a newborn in the house." She paused, thinking back to those tough days. "Kevin didn't know how to be anything but a soldier. He had to go back. And I had to let him."

"I'm sorry, Chloe," Decker said, a compassionate gleam in his gaze.

"It was a hard time, but that's life, right? You get knocked down. You get back up."

He nodded. "That's true."

"I had a lot of support, so over time, things got better." She scooped up a pile of sand in her hand, letting it slip through her fingers. "Our love didn't last, but it brought me Leo, so how could I ever regret it?"

"Regrets are a waste of time. They change nothing. They don't make you feel better."

"I agree, but it's still difficult to let them go. Have you ever wished you'd made a different choice?"

"God, yes," he said so vehemently, she laughed. "But I don't dwell on it. I move on, try to do better in the future."

"That's what I do, too, although I probably dwell on the problem a lot longer than you do. I've always been a little too eager to please, to do the right thing. My friends say I'm too nice. Maybe I am."

"If that's your worst trait, I think you're good," he said with a warm smile.

Her heart fluttered as the breeze lifted his hair, the sun putting a glow on his handsome features, his full lips, and firm jaw. His gaze shifted, as she couldn't quite break the connection between them.

Fortunately, Leo came running over, breaking the sudden tension and interrupting her wandering thoughts.

"Do you want to build a sandcastle, Decker?" Leo asked.

"Absolutely," Decker said, not a trace of hesitation in his voice. "And I'm a great sandcastle builder."

"You are?" Leo asked, his eyes widening in admiration.

"Yes. But I need a good helper."

"I can help you," Leo quickly offered.

"First thing we need to do is find some rocks and sticks. Since we don't have any shovels, we'll have to use what we have to dig."

"Looks like I'm going to get a first-hand look at your construction skills," she teased.

"Oh, no. You're not spectating, Chloe. You're helping," Decker said.

"But I am not the world's greatest sandcastle builder," she said.

He gave her a charming grin. "You will be after today. First things first. Take off your shoes."

"What do my shoes have to do with anything?"

"It's easier to move in the sand." He kicked off his shoes as

Leo did the same. Her little boy loved nothing better than to be barefoot.

She took off her shoes and socks, feeling the cool sand slide between her toes. She'd always been a beach girl, even when it wasn't summer, and sandcastle building was actually one of her strengths, but she was curious to see how Decker would do, so she let him take the lead.

It soon became clear that the rocks, shells, and sticks would not just be used for scooping sand, but also as material for walls. Decker hadn't been lying when he said he was good; he was actually amazing.

For the next hour, they worked on the castle, using her water bottle to get water from the lake to make the sand moist enough to pack down. She made a lot of the back-and-forth trips to the lake. After an hour, she was getting tired and chilly, but she couldn't find the will to end the activity. Leo was having the time of his life.

She played with Leo every day, but it was fun to have an adult partner, and Decker was great with Leo. He encouraged creativity and let Leo talk about whatever he wanted to talk about. He treated her son with kindness and respect, which only made her like him more.

"Hey, hey," Decker told her, waving an urgent hand in her direction. "Your wall is collapsing, Chloe. You need moister sand."

"Sorry, I wasn't paying attention."

"This is serious business," he said with mock outrage.

"Serious, Mommy," Leo repeated.

"Okay. I'll get more wet sand." She moved down to the lake once more, scooped some water into her bottle and then brought it back to make her sand wall more stable. "It's good now."

"It looks good," Decker confirmed. "I think we're done." He sat back on his heels, his jeans covered in sand.

"It's great," Leo said, amazement in his voice. "The best sandcastle ever."

Chloe laughed. "High praise, Decker."

"It was a group effort."

"With you in charge. You lived up to your own hype." She paused. "If you want to check out the train, we should go."

"Are we going to ride the train?" Leo asked with excitement.

"I don't know if it's running. We'll have to see," she told him. "But let's get our bikes and check it out."

"What should we do about the castle?" Leo asked.

"We can leave it," she said.

Leo frowned. "Maybe I should knock it down."

"It was a lot of work, honey. Do you really want to knock it down?" she asked.

Indecision played through his gaze. Leo turned to Decker. "What do you think?"

"You should do whatever would be the most fun thing for you to do," Decker replied.

A smile spread across her son's face and then he lifted his leg and brought his foot down on the nearest part of the castle. To her surprise, Decker immediately joined in. Within seconds, their massive castle was nothing but a pile of sand. It bothered her a little to see it destroyed, but the males did not share her sentiment. They were laughing and smiling, having as much fun tearing it down as they had had building it up.

She put her shoes back on and got to her feet. Then they headed off to the next adventure.

CHAPTER TEN

DECKER WAS sorry to leave the beach. Building a sandcastle with Chloe and Leo had been ridiculously enjoyable. Seeing Chloe barefoot, her hair blowing in the breeze, her cheeks flushed, eyes sparkling, had made him want to do anything he could to keep her in that happy moment. For a brief time, she'd been able to set down all the weight she carried and just relax and be silly. Being with them had reminded him what it felt like to be with his dad when there were no rules, no real problems, just enjoying the moment.

But that moment was over, and the sound of a train horn took his thoughts in a different direction. The sound pierced his memory, a troubling reminder of a past he didn't really want to remember but couldn't quite forget.

The train horn blasted again, louder this time, and as the path came out of the trees, he saw the open-air train chugging along the nearby track. Chloe came to a stop, and he pulled up next to her as the train passed by. There were four cars on the train with about a dozen people aboard.

"Can we ride the train, Mommy?" Leo pleaded from inside his carrier.

Chloe glanced over at him. "What do you think, Decker? Want to take a ride?"

He wasn't sure he did, but he thought he'd have one unhappy boy if he said no. "All right."

They rode across the park to the entrance and locked their bikes along the fence before heading to a small booth where an older woman was selling tickets. She greeted Chloe and Leo with a big smile. "It's nice to see you out of the restaurant," the woman said.

"It's nice to be out, Nancy," Chloe said. "We need two adult tickets and one child."

"Of course. And who is this?" Nancy asked with interest.

"This is Decker Hayes," Chloe replied. "He's going to be remodeling my parents' rental house."

"Oh, I heard about poor Ellie," Nancy said, her mouth turning downward. "So sad. I didn't know she was sick until it was too late."

"Did you know Eleanor well?" Chloe asked.

"I wouldn't say well. But she used to play bridge at the rec center with a bunch of us. She was a private person, never talked much about her personal life. I know she was a widow and didn't have any kids or relatives nearby, but she always had a smile on her face." Nancy paused. "It will be seven dollars for the three of you to ride the train."

"I've got it," Decker said, handing her a ten. "Keep the change."

"Well, thank you," Nancy said. "Enjoy the ride."

They stepped to the side as a mom and three kids came up behind them to buy tickets.

"That's the first person I've heard call Eleanor, Ellie," he murmured.

"She introduced herself to me as Eleanor. My grandmother might have called her Ellie now that I think about it." Chloe gave him a thoughtful look. "You seem a little tense, Decker."

He drew in a breath and let it out. "I don't know why I am, but...yeah."

A moment later, the train pulled up in front of them, and they got into the first row of the third car, with Leo sitting in between them. It only took a few moments for the train to fill up, and then they were off.

As the train moved through the park, past a pond, the children's playground, and through a canopy of thick trees, Decker felt the years in between trips slip away. And when the train horn blared as they came to the crossing by the bike path, his heart jumped, then beat faster as the train moved faster down a small incline.

"Faster," he said, clapping his hands with excitement.

"You love trains, don't you?" the woman named Ellie asked. "Maybe one day I'll get you a train to play with."

"A big train? With lots of cars?"

"Definitely," she said with a smile.

He looked away from her as the train moved around the pond. "Ducks," he said with glee, pointing to the ducks playing in the water.

"They love to cool off in the pond," Ellie said.

"My dad says he can swim like a duck."

"I bet he can," she said. "Your mom and dad loved this park, the ducks, this train. They once rode it six times in a row."

"They did?" he asked in wonder.

"Yes.

"My mom is in heaven. Do you think she can see the train and the ducks from there?"

Ellie didn't answer. When he looked over at her, she was wiping her eyes.

"Are you crying?" he asked.

"I got something in my eye."

As they went over the bridge, he saw his dad walking across the grass. "Daddy's here," he said, pointing to his father. "I thought you said he couldn't come."

"I guess he changed his mind," she said tersely.

When the train stopped, he jumped off and ran toward his dad. "Do you want to ride the train with me, Daddy?" His dad grabbed his hand so tight, he squealed. "You're hurting me."

His father didn't even look at him, his gaze on Ellie. "I told you no train."

"Decker loved it. I knew he would. He is your son, after all."

"This isn't working."

"It was just a train ride. That's all," Ellie said.

"Why are you mad, Daddy?" he asked.

"I'm not mad," his dad bit out. "Come on, we have to go."

"We're still on for tomorrow night, right?" Ellie asked his father.

"We'll see," his dad replied.

"Goodbye, Decker," Ellie said, looking a little sad. "I had fun. Love you."

He looked over his shoulder as his dad dragged him toward the parking lot. Ellie wiped her eyes again, and this time he was pretty sure she was crying.

"Decker?"

He looked at Chloe in confusion.

"Do you want to take another ride?" she asked.

He realized then that the train had stopped.

"I do," Leo said before he could reply.

"No, I don't think so," he said. "You two can go around again. I need to get off."

"We'll all get off," Chloe said.

"Can we go to the playground?" Leo said.

"Uh," Chloe hesitated, giving him a questioning look.

He had no words, so he just shrugged.

"For a few minutes," she told Leo. "We can walk our bikes to the playground."

"Sounds good," he said.

When they reached the playground, Leo ran off to play with another little boy he apparently knew from daycare.

Chloe gave him a searching look. "What happened on the train, Decker? You just went away."

"I rode that train when I was a kid. I was with Ellie. My father came running over at the end, and he was so angry. He told her she had no right to take me on the train and that something wasn't working. She reminded him about some meeting and then she told me she loved me. When I looked back at her, she was crying."

"I don't know if I ever saw her again after that." He paused. "Maybe I did. I'm not sure if my memories are coming in order."

"Did you remember anything else that she said to you?"

"She said my mom and dad liked to ride the train, that they'd done it like six times in a row. And she mentioned the ducks."

"If your mom rode the train, then she and your dad had been to Whisper Lake before."

"That's true," he said, realizing he hadn't completely comprehended that fact. "My mom and dad came to Whisper Lake—maybe before I was born. Or I could have been a baby, I guess."

"What do you know about your mother? What was her name?"

"Kelly. She and my dad met in Phoenix at a Christmas party their senior year in high school. They didn't go to the same school, but they started dating and having sex, and she found out she was pregnant right before they graduated. Her parents were furious and wanted her to give up the baby. My dad's mother was also very upset. Neither family wanted to support them, so they graduated from high school, got jobs, and found a studio apartment to live in. Oh, and they got married at the courthouse. After I was born, my mom stayed home with me, and my dad worked at a photography studio and waited tables. He said they had no money, but they were happy. Four years later, she was killed in a car crash. I had just had my third birthday. She was twenty-one years old."

"That's tragic, Decker. Your dad became a single father so young. I was twenty-nine when I got divorced. I had money and a house, and it was and still is difficult. I can't imagine what your father went through."

"My father said I kept him going. He had to make something of his life so he could take care of me." Decker ran a hand through his hair. "None of that information ties to Ellie or Whisper Lake. I have no idea why my parents came here together or why my dad brought me back. But clearly there's some connection between Ellie and my family."

"There will probably be more clues in Ellie's house."

"That's the only place they could be." His lips tightened. "I keep thinking about the train in the living room."

A gleam entered her eyes. "She bought it for you," Chloe said.

"She saw me years before she moved into your rental house."

"She still could have brought the train with her, or she bought it after she moved in because it reminded her of you or your father." She paused. "Maybe all the toys in the house were for you."

"Some of the packaging looked old and a few of the toys were popular decades ago." A chill ran through him as he thought of Ellie buying toys for a kid she would never see again. "This was a mistake," he said. "I never should have started down this path into my past. I'm not going to get answers, and even if I do, I doubt I'll like them, and they won't change anything."

"You're not going to be able to stop thinking about your past while you're here, Decker."

"I'm not going to be here that long. I think I can ignore the memories."

"Well, you can try. Or you could leave, but I hope you won't do that."

He was tempted to go, but while he didn't make commitments easily, when he did, he followed through, and he'd told her he'd do the job. So he'd do it. "I'm going to take care of the house for you, as we agreed."

Relief ran through her gaze. "Thank you." She paused. "There's just one thing I want to say."

"What?" he asked warily.

"I know your memories are spooking you because you don't

understand them, but there's love in your past. You don't know who Ellie was to you, but she said she loved you, and I think she loved your dad."

"My dad kept us away from her. He didn't want me to know her, and I don't know why. But I probably never will know. So, I have to make peace with that."

"Sometimes, that's all you can do," she said. "Accepting that sometimes there just isn't a good reason or a good answer is the sucky part of being an adult."

He smiled. "Truly sucky," he said. "I had fun today. Thanks for taking over for Joel."

"I had fun, too. So did Leo. You're great with kids."

"He's easy to like. He takes joy in simple things. You do, too, don't you?"

"Sometimes I forget to do that, but days like today, I remember how nice it is to just be in the moment. But I need to get back. Let me give Leo a two-minute warning. It's easier to avoid tears and complaining if he gets a heads-up."

As she walked over to talk to Leo, he dug his hands into his pockets and turned his head toward the train. The rides for the day had apparently ended. He was happy about that. He didn't want to hear that damn horn again. He just wished he couldn't still hear Ellie's voice in his ear.

CHAPTER ELEVEN

"SORRY ABOUT YESTERDAY," Joel told Decker Saturday morning as they met up in the parking lot next to the Lion's Club, where a pancake breakfast was being held. "It sounds like you had a good ride. Chloe said you went down to the beach and built a sandcastle. I bet Leo liked that."

"Leo loved the beach," Decker replied. "He's an easy kid to please."

"He seems to be," Joel said, as they walked toward the hall. "Wow, look at this line. I didn't think we were going to have to wait for pancakes."

"That must mean they're good," he said, noting that the line coming out of the hall had at least twenty people in it and the nearby picnic tables were full.

"I'd bail, but Chloe is flipping pancakes, so that's not going to work. And it's apparently for a good cause. I'm just not a big fan of pancakes. I'll be asleep in an hour."

"I love a good pancake with plenty of maple syrup."

Joel laughed. "You used to drown your pancakes in syrup, especially on Sunday mornings after a night of drinking."

"Best hangover cure," he said with a grin. "And you were right there with me."

"Not on the syrup, but definitely on the drinking. We had some wild times back then."

"It was college," he said with a shrug. "Everyone was wild. But it was a long time ago. I don't miss those days."

"You never miss anything. What is it you always say? Never look back?"

"That's right," he muttered as they joined the group at the back of the line. "But it's not always as easy as I'd like."

Joel gave him a questioning look. "Why is that?"

"Chloe didn't tell you?"

"Tell me what?"

"You know I came here when I was a kid."

"Yes. So?"

"Well, since I got here, I've been having weird memories about that trip, about my father arguing with an older woman."

Joel gave him a surprised look. "That's strange. Your dad was so easygoing. He never seemed to get angry about anything. The two of you were always chill."

"I think that's why the memory sticks out to me. It turns out that the woman is the same woman who was renting Chloe's house, the one who passed away a couple of weeks ago."

Joel's eyes widened. "No way. That's a strange coincidence."

"Exactly what I thought, but I don't know what it means, or if it means anything. It's just odd." He shoved his hands into the pockets of his jeans as he rocked back on his heels, still feeling more rattled than he should. He'd told Chloe that it didn't matter, but here he was, talking about it again. "Anyway, forget it. Tell me what's going on with your project."

"Hold on. Who do you think this woman was to your dad?"

"I don't know, maybe a relative of some sort. She seemed to be very interested in spending time with me. She told me she loved me in a letter."

Joel's gaze grew more curious. "Was she tied to your mom?"

"I think it was my dad, but I don't know, and I don't think I'll be able to find out. As you know, my dad was estranged from his parents and his in-laws. I don't see them answering my questions. I just need to stop thinking about it."

"Or figure out what it all means."

"Let's talk about you," he said, forcing a change in subject. "What's keeping you so busy?"

"The potential development on the north shore and major pushback from some senior execs about my plan to downsize New York and create satellite offices."

"That can't have surprised you. Most of those employees are New Yorkers, and they've been with your dad for years."

"Yes, and some of them should retire like he did. I'd like to fire a couple of them, but I can't do that," he said in frustration. "I know what I'm doing, Decker. They need to trust me."

"Trust takes time. Be patient."

"That's not my nature, not when it comes to business, not when I know I'm right."

"I get it, but you're going to need to get the staff on your side. Maybe you're trying to do too much too fast."

"I've run the numbers. My satellite office plan will save us money. It's a good idea."

"What about the people who don't want to move out of New York, some of whom have been there for a very long time?"

"I'm not giving up the office there, just downsizing. I'm sure we have some employees who would love the option to move out of New York City and get a bigger space for a cheaper cost somewhere else. It's just my father and his cronies who are hanging on to the way it's always been."

"It's difficult to get people to change." He paused. "I have to say, Joel, I'm still surprised that this small-town life is what you want."

"I needed to shake things up. I can't be my father's clone, Decker. I have to find my own way. Here, I can be myself. I don't have a past or a reputation to live up to. I don't have a network of people to impress. That feels good."

He nodded. "Well, I hope it works out the way you want it to."

"It will. I just need people to do what I want them to do."

"Good luck with that," he said, as the line finally moved into the hall. After paying for their pancakes, they stepped up to a long buffet. Chloe was standing behind a large flat top griddle, her hair up in a ponytail, her cheeks a rosy pink, her eyes sparkling as she flipped pancakes and slid them onto a plate. Leo was playing at a table behind her with another child, who appeared to be about eight or nine.

"There's my girl," Joel said, waving to Chloe.

Chloe looked at them and smiled.

As the warmth of her smile washed over him, Joel moved in front of him, putting him in the cold shadows. And he didn't like it. Nor did he like being reminded that Chloe was Joel's girl.

Maybe that's exactly why he needed the reminder.

When they got to Chloe's position on the line, Joel said, "Hey, babe. How's it going?"

Chloe seemed to flush even more at his words. "Fine, busy. I'm glad you guys came."

"Wouldn't miss it," Joel said. "I'll take three."

"You got it. How about you, Decker?"

"Six," he said. "I went for a run this morning."

"Just make sure his comes with plenty of maple syrup," Joel drawled.

"The syrup bottles are on the tables. You can go crazy," Chloe returned.

"Hi, Decker," Leo said, coming up behind Chloe. "Are you having pancakes? Can I eat with you?"

"Sure," he said.

"I told you I'd eat with you in a few minutes," Chloe told Leo. "I'm almost done here."

"But I'm hungry, and Decker said I can eat with him."

"You said you didn't want anything two minutes ago," Chloe reminded her son.

"I wasn't hungry then," Leo said.

"It's fine," he told her. "Leo can join us, right, Joel?"

"Of course," Joel said.

"I'm almost done," Chloe said, as Leo ran around the serving buffet. "My replacement should be here in five minutes."

"We'll be fine," he told her, taking two plates from her hand, one for himself with a large stack of pancakes and one for Leo with just one.

They made their way over to a table inside the hall where Leo slid into a chair next to him, putting him in the middle between Joel and Leo. "Maybe you want to sit next to Leo," he said to Joel.

"It doesn't matter," Joel said, grabbing the syrup bottle. He put a small amount on his pancakes and then handed it to Decker.

He doused his stack in syrup and then poured a small amount on Leo's pancake.

As Leo grabbed it with his hands, he said, "Hold on a sec." He cut up the pancake and handed Leo the fork. "Better use this or your hands will get sticky."

"I'm going to hunt for Easter eggs after this," Leo told him, as he ate. "Can you help me, Decker?"

"I have a feeling the hunt is only for kids."

"But what if I don't find any eggs?" Leo asked, worry in his gaze.

"You will. You found lots of rocks yesterday at the beach. You're an excellent hunter."

Leo's face brightened. "You're right. I bet I'll find a lot of eggs."

"I'm sure." He glanced over at Joel, who had pulled out his phone and was reading an email. Frowning, he wanted to suggest Joel be more present with the child of the woman he was in a relationship with, but it wasn't his business.

He finished his pancakes while Leo told him all about his friend's turtle who got lost in a pond. The kid was quite a storyteller. As he wiped his mouth, he glanced at Joel, who was sending a text.

"Everything okay?" he asked.

"More questions and concerns," Joel said with annoyance.

"Can they wait until Monday? Work-life balance, remember?"

"That's what I told them," Joel replied. "But my father wants to chat later, which never seems like a good idea."

While he knew Joel's father could be a headache, he also envied Joel for still having his dad. He would have loved to run a few problems past his own father. He would have liked to have had a relationship with his dad as two adults, but they'd never had that chance.

"How were the pancakes?" Chloe interrupted, as she sat down on the other side of Leo and immediately reached for a napkin to wipe his sticky face. "Are you ready to look for Easter eggs?"

Leo nodded and immediately climbed off his chair, throwing himself into Chloe's arms. "Decker said I'm a good hunter."

"He's right. And I can't wait to see what you find." She paused, turning to him and Joel. "Do you guys want to come to the hunt?"

"Sure," he said.

"Uh, yeah," Joel said, still distracted by his phone. "Let's do that."

"Okay." Chloe pushed Leo off her lap and stood up.

As Chloe grabbed her bag off the table, Leo slid his hand into Decker's.

Decker felt a little awkward, thinking that Leo should hold Joel's hand, but making a big deal of it would probably make it an even bigger deal than it was. Then Joel moved around Decker and grabbed Chloe's hand.

Decker found himself following them out the door, holding the still sticky hand of a little boy.

CHAPTER TWELVE

CHLOE FELT a little awkward holding Joel's hand as they headed to the starting line of the Easter egg hunt. She didn't know why it felt awkward, because it should feel good. She'd been going to so many things alone the last few years. It was nice to be a part of a couple.

But it was the couple behind them that made her feel strange. Leo was getting attached to Decker when he should be getting attached to Joel. And having Decker watch her stroll hand-in-hand with Joel... That didn't feel good, either. She told herself to just relax and enjoy the morning. Joel was finally free of meetings, and it was a beautiful day. All was right in her world. She didn't need to make up problems.

They were almost at the starting line when they ran into Gianna and Zach, who were with their eleven-year-old stepdaughter, Hailey.

"Hi," Gianna said, giving her a quick hug. "Happy almost Easter."

"You, too," she replied. "Hi Zach, Hailey."

"Is Leo doing the little kid hunt?" Hailey asked.

"He is," she said.

"I'm volunteering to help with the younger kids," Hailey said. "Is it okay if I take him to the starting line?"

"Sure." She turned to Leo. "Do you want to go with Hailey?" She'd barely gotten out the words when Leo let go of Decker's hand and grabbed Hailey's.

Hailey laughed. "Your hand is sticky. You must have had pancakes."

"With a lot of syrup," Leo said.

She gave Decker a pointed look.

"It was just a little," he said with a laugh. "I swear. He just picked up his pancake with his hand."

"It's fine," Hailey said. "Come on, Leo."

As the kids ran off, she smiled at Gianna and Zach. "I can't believe how big Hailey is. When she first came to Whisper Lake, she was such a little thing."

"They grow up fast," Zach said. "Which is why…" He paused, smiling at Gianna. "I know you said brunch tomorrow, but…"

"It's fine," Gianna said with a laugh. "I'll tell her."

"Tell me what?" she asked, pretty sure she knew, but she needed to hear it.

"I'm pregnant," Gianna said.

"That's wonderful. Congratulations." She gave Gianna another hug. "How far along are you?"

"Three months."

"You and Lizzie are going to have babies at the same time. Why didn't you say anything?"

"I just wanted to wait a little. And we're having a boy. We were going to tell everyone at brunch."

"I wanted to tell you all for the last two months," Zach said.

"But I wanted to wait until I was past the first trimester," Gianna said. "We haven't told Hailey yet, but we're going to do that tonight."

"I won't say a word to anyone until you announce it."

"Congratulations," Joel said.

"Great news," Decker added.

"I think the hunt is starting," Zach said. "Why don't we get closer?"

As the five of them moved to the edge of the park where the kids would be hunting, Joel's phone rang.

He pulled it out of his pocket and winced. "Sorry, I have to take this call, Chloe. I'll be right back."

"Is everything all right?"

"It's just business."

She frowned as he moved away from them, catching an odd gleam in Decker's gaze. She ignored that, turning toward the park where Leo had taken off on a sprint to get a bright orange egg. Thankfully, the hunt for the little kids had plenty of eggs that were in plain sight and when the whistle sounded, Leo came back with four plastic eggs in his basket, each one holding candies inside.

"I got a lot of eggs," Leo said proudly.

She smiled at his excitement. "You did a great job."

"Hailey helped me."

"Can Leo go to the park with me?" Hailey asked. "I'll watch him really closely."

"Uh," she hesitated. There were a lot of people around, and Hailey was only eleven.

"I'll keep an eye on them," Zach said. "Why don't you join me, Decker? I'd like to hear more about your construction business."

She felt immediate relief as Zach and Decker walked toward the playground, not just because Leo had two more adults looking out for him, but because Decker was also gone.

Turning to Gianna, she said, "So you're going to have a baby. How do you feel?"

"Thrilled. Zach and I have been trying for a while. I was getting nervous. That's why I didn't want to tell anyone until I was really sure."

"That's understandable. Any morning sickness?"

"A few queasy stomach mornings, but nothing beyond that."

"I'm so happy for you. Hailey will make a great big sister. She'll be very helpful to you."

"She loves little kids." Gianna paused, giving her an odd look. "I love being a stepmother. You know that, right?"

"Of course."

"But I am excited to have a child of my own."

"That's completely understandable."

"It will be Zach's first biological child, too," Gianna continued. "He's concerned that Hailey will feel like an outsider, because she doesn't have our blood ties the way this baby will."

She immediately shook her head. "That won't happen. Zach and Hailey adore each other, and the three of you are a family. Even Hailey's grandparents accept that," she added, knowing that Hailey's grandparents had fought Zach for a while about giving him custody after their daughter had died. "A new baby will just mean more love for everyone."

Gianna smiled. "Thanks for the reassurance."

"It's going to be great, Gianna. And I'm excited to have more moms to hang out with," she added.

"You do such a good job with Leo. I can't imagine how difficult it is to do it by yourself."

"I have a lot of help."

"Not that much," Gianna said with a knowing gleam in her eyes. "You always downplay how much you have to do, but we can all see it, and we admire you immensely."

"Thanks."

"Hopefully, now you'll have more help."

"Now?" she asked in confusion.

"Joel," Gianna said. "The guy you were just holding hands with. Where did he go, anyway?"

"He had to take a phone call," she said, her gaze moving toward the edge of the trees where Joel was still conversing on the phone. "He has a lot of business going on right now."

"But things are still good between you?"

"Um, yes."

Gianna arched an eyebrow. "That didn't sound very convincing."

"We've been a little out of sync lately," she admitted. "Like I said, Joel has been busy."

"I hope that doesn't last too long. You deserve someone who's willing to give you his undivided attention."

"I'm not sure there's a man alive who would do that," she said, feeling cynical about love.

"There definitely is," Gianna argued. "Zach is busy, but when he's with me, with Hailey, he is committed to the moment."

"You're lucky. Kevin could never do that. Even when he was with me and Leo, he was never all the way there, at least not the last couple of years." She cleared her throat. "Anyway, I'm so happy for you and Zach."

"Thanks. I want you to be happy, too."

"I am happy." She held up the Easter egg basket. "My son found four eggs. It's a good day."

Gianna gave her a sly look. "Does having Decker around also make it a good day? He's a very attractive man."

"Decker is only here for a few months. Plus, he's Joel's friend. And he's going to work for me. So, whatever ideas people have, they need to get rid of them."

"Got it," Gianna said.

Joel came back, apology in his eyes. "I'm so sorry, Chloe. I didn't realize that would take as long as it did. It looks like Leo found some eggs."

"Yes," she said. "He's at the park with Gianna's daughter Hailey."

"Having fun, I'm sure," Joel said with a smile. "Leo is one of the happiest kids I've ever met. That's a credit to you, Chloe."

"I try."

"I'm going to go check on everyone," Gianna said, as she excused herself.

"So, what's going on with all the phone calls?" she asked Joel when they were alone.

"Company politics and bidding problems on the north shore proposal. That was my father on the phone. He gave me the reins to his company, but he keeps trying to take them back. He wants me to be him, but I'm not him."

Hearing the frustration in his voice, she felt sympathy. "I understand. That's a little how it was with my café, although on a completely smaller scale. But Kevin's parents ran the restaurant for twenty years, and when I started taking over, they couldn't help themselves when it came to giving me advice. Eventually, they found other things to focus on, and realized I was doing a good job. Finally, they could step back and trust that their legacy would live on. Your dad just needs to get to that point, too."

"I don't know if he can. I keep waiting, but he gets worse, not better. My father has never had a lot of respect for me. Whatever I do, it's not good enough. Sometimes, I wonder if I wouldn't have been better off doing my own thing."

"What stopped you?"

"I've worked for the family firm off and on since I was a teenager. I was groomed to take over. And I wanted to be part of something that had been running successfully for three generations. I wanted to carry on the legacy of my father and grandfather. I just hadn't realized how big their shadows were."

As Joel continued talking about his company and his father's vision for his legacy, she couldn't help wondering how he could make Whisper Lake work as a home base. And even if that was his base, it sounded like he would still put in long hours and be in a constant state of company drama. She could only imagine how exhausting that would be. Did she want to be in the middle of that?

"Anyway," Joel said, bringing her attention back to him. "I didn't mean to dump all that on you. What's next?"

"I need to take Leo home for a nap. He's going to be exhausted after this morning."

"What about later? How about dinner tonight? Can you get a sitter?"

"Probably." She wished he'd suggested the date earlier, but she wanted to spend time with him when they weren't in a group or distracted by a four-year-old. "Let me text a few people and see. What time?"

"Any time that works for you."

"I'll see what I can come up with."

"Great. I'm going to take off now and tie up some loose ends before tonight. Does that sound good?"

"Yes," she said, as he gave her a warm kiss and then headed toward the parking lot.

As she turned toward the playground, she saw Decker carrying Leo.

"Someone got too tired to walk," Decker said dryly.

"It's nap time," she said, smiling at Leo's sleepy eyes. "I can take him."

"I'll carry him to your car. Where did Joel go?" Decker asked, as they walked toward the parking lot.

"He had some business to tie up."

"He's putting in a lot of hours."

"Yes, but we're going to have dinner tonight—if I can find a sitter. I'll have to see who's available since it's a holiday weekend. But it would be nice to spend some time with Joel."

"You should do that," Decker said evenly.

"What are your plans for this evening?"

"Probably go explore. Check out some of the other restaurants in town."

"Are there any places you remember going to with your dad?"

"No," he said shortly. "I have no memories of restaurants beyond the ice cream shack."

"Then you won't have to worry about being triggered."

He frowned. "We don't need to talk about that."

"Okay. You should try Atticus—it's a Greek restaurant on Third Avenue. It's very good. I also like Paolo's Trattoria if you like Italian."

"Thanks," he said. "I'll look at both."

When they got to her car, he put Leo into his car seat. Her little boy could barely keep his eyes open.

"Will you be able to get him in the house?" Decker asked. "I could follow you home and help."

"I do it on my own all the time. But thanks for offering." She couldn't help thinking that Joel hadn't offered to help her get Leo to the car or into the house or anything. But maybe that was a little on her. She'd wanted to be careful about Leo getting too close to anyone she was dating in case it didn't work out, which it usually didn't, so she hadn't made a big deal about Joel and Leo getting to know each other. She closed the car door and gave Decker a smile. "I hope I'll see you tomorrow for brunch at the inn."

"It's very nice of you and your friends to include me."

"The more the merrier. And you're Joel's friend. So, of course, we'd include you. Have a good night."

"You, too," he said, as he walked away.

She let out a breath as he left, her gaze lingering on him for far too long. She forced herself to turn away and get into her car, reminding herself that she had another attractive male who wanted to take her out tonight. That would be an excellent opportunity for her to get Decker out of her head.

CHAPTER THIRTEEN

IT WAS fun to put on a sexy dress and go out to dinner with Joel. While they'd been dating for about six weeks, they hadn't spent that much time together. She'd wanted to take it slow in the beginning. She was wary of relationships after her divorce, and she had a child to consider. Joel had been okay with that. He'd gotten out of a relationship a few months earlier and didn't need to move fast. They'd started out on the same page, but lately it felt like Joel had turned a couple of pages ahead of her.

"More wine?" Joel asked as they finished their meal at the Harbor View Restaurant. There wasn't much to see at night, but it was still pretty inside, with glass windows and white lights strung around the dining room, adding a warm ambiance to the room.

"No thanks," she said.

"What about dessert?"

"I could not eat another bite," she said with a laugh. "Plus, I already snuck a couple of Leo's chocolate Easter eggs when he wasn't looking."

He smiled as he topped off his wine glass. "I've never been a big fan of chocolate."

"Seriously? It's so delicious."

"I'm not really into sweets." He sipped his wine. "This is a good bottle of merlot. I've never heard of this winery."

"It's local. There are several wineries in Edmonds Valley, about a half hour from here."

"We'll have to go wine-tasting one day. I love discovering new wines."

"That would be fun, but I think you'll have to get a little less busy for that to happen."

"It has been a week," he said with a sigh.

"Do you think it will work—moving your operations here? I know that's your plan, but it seems like you're running into obstacles."

"More than I expected," he admitted. "I thought I was getting away from the intensity of the city and corporate politics, but they followed me here. I'll figure it out. I want to stay here, to have my own life. When I'm in Manhattan, I'm living everyone else's life. I'm moving at such a fast pace that I can barely breathe. I want to slow down."

He'd made similar comments before, and she'd liked hearing that he wanted to slow down, balance out his life, take a breath, but his words didn't ring as true now as they had the first time she'd heard them, because his actions didn't align with his words. "It feels like you've been going at a fast pace the past few weeks, even though you're far away from New York."

"It's just the transition. It will settle down." He smiled. "I am sorry that I've had to bail on you a few times. I hope you understand it's a temporary situation."

"I know that's what you want it to be, but..." She licked her lips, not sure how much she wanted to get into his business.

"But what?" he asked.

"You seem really charged up and excited when you're working hard, when you're competing, when you're trying to close a deal. I just wonder if a slower pace will really be what you want when you finally get it."

"It will be," he said confidently. "Some of the happiest years of my life were my high school years in San Francisco. I loved being out of New York, away from my prep schools, the competition for attention, the constant comparisons between whose family had the most money or the best vacation house. I could just be myself. College was the same. I had real friends like Decker and others who didn't care who I was or what I owned. But once I graduated, once I got sucked back into my father's world in New York, it all changed again. Then I came here, and the good feelings returned, especially when I met you. I know this is where I need to be."

She was touched by his words. "I'm glad you've been happy here."

"I care about you, Chloe. I think we could have a future."

"Why do you think that?" she asked curiously. "What makes us good together?"

Surprise ran through his gaze at her question. "Well, you're a beautiful, kind, and smart woman. You care about your friends. And you're a great mom. We'd make a good team."

His words were very flattering, but they also didn't feel that personal to her. It was like he was checking items off a list. Which reminded her of the way she often thought about him: attractive, smart, successful, fun, and wants to live in Whisper Lake.

Were they right for each other or did they just both look good on paper?

As that question rumbled around in her head, her phone buzzed. "Sorry, I need to make sure this isn't about Leo." She pulled out her phone, frowning when she saw her babysitter's phone number. "Hello? Tracy? Is everything all right?"

"Leo is fine," Tracy said quickly. "I put him to bed a half hour ago. But I just got a call from my dad. My mom fell getting out of the shower, and I need to go home as soon as possible. I'm really sorry, Chloe."

"Don't worry about it for a second, Tracy. I'm sorry about

your mom. I'll be home in ten minutes." She set down the phone. "My babysitter's mother fell, and she needs to leave."

He waved to the server. "I'll get the check."

They got back to her house fifteen minutes later. After Tracy rushed out the door, Chloe went to check on Leo. He'd kicked off his covers, so she gently covered him back up, then tiptoed out of the room.

"He's asleep," she told Joel, who was standing in the living room, looking at his phone.

"That's good," he said, putting away his phone.

"Do you want to hang out? It's not too late."

Before Joel could answer, she heard Leo's door open, and her little boy came down the hall, rubbing his eyes.

"Mommy?"

"I'm here, sweetie," she said, as he ran into her arms. "I thought you were asleep."

"There's a monster under my bed," he told her.

"There are no monsters," she said.

"I heard him growl," Leo said, his eyes worried.

"You were dreaming. But we'll check under your bed."

"Can you read me a story?"

"It's late. You need to go to sleep."

"Please? Just a short one?"

She looked at Joel, debating her options. Arguing with Leo and trying to put him down without a story would probably take longer than just reading him one. "I'll only be like fifteen minutes."

"It's fine. I'm going to go, Chloe. I have a couple of emails to answer. I'll see you tomorrow for brunch."

"Okay," she said, disappointed that he was leaving. He'd just told her how much he liked her, how great they could be together, but his actions didn't live up to his words.

Why didn't he want to wait so they could spend more time together?

Joel gave her a quick kiss, patted Leo on the back, and said,

"I'll see you tomorrow, after you've slayed some monsters."

As he walked out the door, she wished he'd offered to slay a few of those monsters for her, but apparently, he had his own problems to deal with. So she'd do it herself, which was fine. She didn't need Joel to take care of an imaginary monster, but at some point, they needed to spend more time together, because what looked good on paper might not actually work in real life, and dealing with a four-year-old was as real as it got.

"What's going on?" Decker asked in surprise as Joel walked into his apartment on Sunday morning. "I thought I was meeting you at the inn at noon."

"I have a problem, more than one," Joel said tensely. "My senior staff is about to stage a mutiny. My father is in the middle of the uprising. I need to go to New York today."

"I'm sorry to hear that."

Joel ran a hand through his hair, his gaze agitated. "I don't know if I'm going to be able to make this work, Decker. I keep telling myself I can, but maybe I can't."

"Go home and talk to your dad. Maybe he just needs to be reassured. Or perhaps you can come up with a compromise. He is your father. He wants you to be happy."

"I'm not sure that's what he wants," Joel said darkly. "It has always been about his company. That's his real child."

"No, it's not. You're his kid and he might not show it, but he loves you, and he's proud of you."

"I don't feel his pride. When I'm in New York, when I'm in his house, in the building he built, I feel about two feet tall. He looms over me."

"You're not two feet tall. You're not a kid anymore. You're a smart, capable businessman. Don't forget that. And you do a damn good job running his company."

Joel's tension eased at his words. "Thanks for saying that."

As Joel paced around the room, Decker gave him a thoughtful glance. "Is there something else?"

"I heard from Sylvie last night," Joel said. "She wants to talk. I told her we have nothing to talk about, but I know she's going to find out that I'm back in town."

"You don't have to see Sylvie."

"You're right. I don't need to deal with her. I have Chloe." He blew out a breath. "Chloe will be pissed when I miss the brunch."

"Then go to New York tomorrow."

"I can't. They're going to vote on some shit tomorrow. I need to be there for that. Chloe will forgive me, right?"

He shrugged. "I would assume so. She seems pretty understanding."

"I hope so. And I won't be gone that long, two-three days, at the most. It will be fine."

Selfishly, Decker hoped it wouldn't be fine, but that was stupid. Even if Joel and Chloe broke up, it didn't mean he would step in. He was leaving in two months. They might be in the same place now, but Chloe needed someone who would always be in that place, and that wouldn't be him. He just wasn't sure it would be Joel, either.

CHAPTER FOURTEEN

"I'M sorry Joel couldn't make it," Decker told Chloe as he met up with her on the patio at the Firefly Inn, where Lizzie and Justin were serving up mimosas. Chloe had arrived a few minutes earlier with Leo, who had gone off to play with a couple of other kids.

"Me, too," Chloe said shortly, tension in her eyes. "I guess he has a crisis on his hands."

He couldn't tell how angry she was, but there was something simmering behind her calm demeanor, a decided edge to her voice. "I know it was the last thing he wanted to do. He was upset about it."

"I'm sure he was."

He changed the subject. "This inn is nice. How long has Lizzie owned it?"

"Six years now, I think. She's a fantastic innkeeper. She treats her guests like family. You'll see that today. She invited all the guests for brunch, a movie for the kids, and a trivia game for the adults. She loves to throw a party."

"I'm impressed so far. These mimosas have a kick to them."

Chloe smiled. "Personally, I'd rather just have a glass of champagne."

He smiled back at her. "I'd rather just have a beer. But these are good, too." He tapped his glass to hers. "I tried out that Greek restaurant you told me about last night—Atticus. It was good. Not as good as your café, but good."

"Since I don't make Greek food, I'm not in competition with Atticus. It's a completely different dining experience. I also love the owner. Theo is a friend of mine. I'm happy to send him business."

"I met him." He gave me a complimentary dessert when I told him you recommended the restaurant.

"Good. I'm glad he took care of you."

He sipped his mimosa as he looked around the growing crowd. "So, did you grow up with Lizzie, too?"

"No. Lizzie, Chelsea, and Adam came into my life when Lizzie bought the inn and convinced two of her siblings to move here. Gianna, Hannah, and I grew up together. My other good friend, Keira, is in Florida at the moment, but I'm hoping she moves back at some point. Oh, and I knew Jake in high school. He and Hannah were high school sweethearts."

"Like you and Kevin."

"Not exactly like us. Kevin and I went strong from high school until four years ago. Jake and Hannah broke up at the end of high school and hated each other with a white-hot passion until about a year ago, when they reconnected. They say love and hate are two sides of the same coin. That was true for them. I'm so happy they got back together, because they really complement each other."

"Zach told me he first met Gianna at summer camp when they were teenagers."

"Yeah, they also had a big misunderstanding that didn't get cleared up for a long time."

"Zach wants me to look at some plans he has for a new house build for some wealthy celebrity who wants a state-of-the-art vacation home."

"We're getting more celebrities since Whisper Lake has grown into a thriving resort community, which is great for me." She paused. "Does Zach want you to bid on his plans?"

"I think he just wants my opinion."

"Because you're leaving."

"Yes," he said, wondering if there was more behind her question.

"Right. That's what I thought. Well, it should be interesting. I wonder if it's going to be one of those super deluxe mansions with spectacular views."

"I'm guessing yes." He paused as Hannah joined them.

"Lizzie said the buffet is open, and everyone should eat." Hannah said. "Is Joel here yet?"

"He's not coming," Chloe said shortly. "He had to go back to New York, some sort of business crisis."

"That's too bad," Hannah said, her sharp gaze assessing Chloe's mood. Then she turned to him. "I'm glad you made it, Decker."

"Happy to be invited."

"You're part of the group now. Jake wants to talk to you about hiking Stone Mountain with him one day. Just to warn you, it's a very aggressive, steep hike. He seems to think you'd be into it."

"I'd love to do that," he said, feeling excited to get into the mountains.

"Well, I'm sure he'll talk to you about it. Go get some food. And we're playing trivia after brunch. Since Joel isn't here, Decker can be your partner," Hannah said.

"Only if you want to be," Chloe said quickly. "I don't even have to play."

"You're the best player, Chloe. You have to play." Hannah gave him a questioning look.

"Well, if Chloe is the best player, I definitely want her on my team."

"Great," Hannah said, as she moved on to nudge other people toward the buffet.

"What about you?" Chloe challenged. "Are you good at trivia, Decker?"

"I'm great."

She laughed. "Sandcastles and trivia. You have an eclectic skill set."

"I am good at a lot of random things," he said with a smile. "Shall we eat? I'm starving."

"Let's do it."

As they walked into the dining room, they ran into more of Chloe's friends, and were caught up in multiple conversations as they made their way through the buffet and sat down at the round tables in the dining room. Chloe checked on Leo, who was happily ensconced at a kids' table with Hailey and some other children. Then she returned and sat down next to him.

Over brunch, Chloe's friends were all friendly and talkative. He liked the way they riffed off each other with teasing and jokes, but also an underlying love. He also liked how Chloe held her own in the group of couples. She should have had Joel by her side, not him. But Joel had left town. Joel was jeopardizing a relationship he seemed to want, and while Chloe was trying to be understanding and supportive, with her history, he couldn't imagine she was happy about Joel's abrupt departure. It had to remind her of Kevin, of all the times he'd been called away, disappearing on her with little notice.

He rarely judged other people's relationships, but he thought Joel would have to step it up if he really wanted Chloe. Because she deserved better. She deserved someone who wanted to put her first. Maybe that was Joel, but right now, the only thing he was putting first was himself.

When lunch was over, they moved into the library, where Justin and Lizzie organized the couple's trivia game. With Chloe sitting next to him on a loveseat, he was really feeling like an imposter. While Chloe's friends knew she was with Joel, the other guests at the inn were treating them like a couple. Even worse, he was wishing he was more than just a stand-in. Not that he was any more right for Chloe than Joel. At least Joel was trying to stay in Whisper Lake. That wasn't in his plans at all. And Chloe was a relationship kind of woman, the kind of woman he usually stayed away from. He was half-tempted to leave now, because he was sweating more than he should be, but he couldn't be another guy who bailed on her, not even if it was just for trivia.

"Everything okay?" Chloe asked, giving him a speculative look.

"I'm just sorry Joel had to miss this," he said.

Her smile dimmed. "It's too bad, but I appreciate you playing. It's nice not to play alone or be added on to someone else's team like a third wheel. I've been odd man out a lot the last few years."

"Well, not today," he said. "Let's kick their asses."

"Let's do that," she agreed, the smile returning to her face.

A few rounds into the game, he was thinking he might have oversold his trivia talents, but then he and Chloe went on a run together. He was surprised at how much she knew about old movies, historical events, and also sports, especially football. He could hold his own in sports, but was really good at music, geography, and current events. In the end, it was geography that made them the ultimate winners, which resulted in a grand prize of two large chocolate Easter bunnies.

"Nice," he said, as the group dispersed, and Chloe handed him his bunny trophy. "I'll save this for later."

"Really? I thought you might give it to the kids."

"They've had enough chocolate. Are you donating yours?"

"Not a chance. I'll need this soon, probably on one of the days I'm cleaning out Eleanor's stuff."

"Probably," he agreed, not wanting to think about Eleanor. "How do you know so much about football? Especially quarterbacks who played before you were born?"

"My dad was a football player. He played in college and then was drafted by the Denver Broncos. My parents lived in Denver for three years while he struggled to get playing time. He had one decent year. Then he hurt his knee and had to get surgery. He wasn't able to make it back."

"That's too bad."

"He said it probably only shortened his career by a year. He'd been hurt a few times before that, and he didn't see his future being in football. While he was recovering, he went to law school. After he graduated, he worked for his former sports agent, handling athletic contracts, which he was very familiar with."

"Interesting career path."

"It worked out well. But he still loved the game and football season was sacred in our house. Every fall weekend, a big group would gather for food and football. I guess I absorbed more information than I realized."

"You got us this bunny," he said, holding up his prize.

She shook her head. "That was you. How on earth did you know where Rodrigues Island was?"

"Because my dad took me to the island in Mauritius."

"Another place I've never heard of."

"It's a subtropical island in the Indian Ocean, east of Madagascar. There are about 38,000 people on Rodrigues Island. So it's not as small as you might think. My dad set one of his novels there, or at least a good portion of the action. We spent a few weeks there doing research. Well, my dad did research. I went snorkeling and fishing and surfing with the local kids."

She stared at him in bemusement. "What an adventurous life you've led."

"It was an amazing way to grow up. My dad would take me somewhere every summer. We'd be on the road for three months at least. Sometimes, he'd take me out of school, and I'd do my assignments on my own and mail them in. He believed I was getting the best education just by traveling the world, seeing how other people lived. It was an eye-opener. In some places, the poverty is overwhelming and yet there is love and joy, too. I'd tell anyone that if you ever want to change your perspective, get on a plane and go somewhere you've never been before, somewhere completely out of your comfort zone."

"There are a lot of places outside of my comfort zone," she murmured. "Is there anywhere you still want to go?"

He thought about that. "I've never been to the Seychelles, and I'd like to go back to Africa. There's so much of that continent I have yet to see."

"What's stopping you from going?"

"Nothing, except that I need to work to live, to eat, to have the basics. But I'll get back out there."

"Having such incredible summer adventures must have made the rest of the year seem boring," she said.

"I have to admit, I didn't love school that much. But I did like being with my friends. That was the one downside of being away for so long at a time, especially when I became a teenager. I wanted to stay home, go to parties and football games. But we didn't travel as much when I got older. My dad would take months to write a book, and he generally liked to be at home for that."

She gave him a thoughtful look. "It's interesting that someone like you, who grew up wandering the world, would choose to build houses for a living. You're creating places for people to live permanently. I wonder if there's some kind of irony in that."

"Maybe. It would probably take a psychiatrist's couch to figure that out."

"Or an astute woman," she said with a laugh. "I think you want to have it all, a beautiful place to come home to, but also a wide world to explore."

"What's wrong with that?"

"Nothing. But does anyone really get it all? There's always some compromise somewhere, especially when you love someone, when you share your life with another person. It's easier to take risks when you only have yourself to think about."

"That's true. It's why I've found it easier to be on my own."

"But being on your own isn't really having it all. It's leaving out a hugely important part of the human experience—a relationship."

"Not every relationship has to be forever. In fact, most aren't. But I'm not worried about that experience. I don't know what the future will bring, and I never say never about anything."

"I say never a lot. And I'm using the word no a lot, too." She let out a little sigh. "Sometimes, I do feel a little stuck."

"Where would you go if you could go anywhere?"

"There are so many places I've never been. You could literally pick just about any country in the world, and I would not have seen it."

"Pick one place."

She thought for a moment. "I'd like to go to an island in the Caribbean where the water is that turquoise blue and the sand is white and fluffy, and it's super warm. I think that would be lovely. But maybe too relaxing. I've also always wanted to go to Rome, see the Coliseum. That would be cool. And Africa...wow, I can't even imagine what it would be like to go on a safari. See, I told you I couldn't pick one."

"Well, you should do at least one of those things."

"Maybe when Leo is a little older." She let out a breath. "I should check on Leo. I'm glad you came today. And thanks for being my partner."

"I was just standing in for Joel," he said, then hated himself for putting the shadows back in her gaze.

"Well, I appreciate that," she said. "Tomorrow, I'll come by the house and start cleaning things out."

"I'll see you there. I'm going to take-off after I say goodbye to everyone." As soon as Chloe left, Hannah came over, and there was a purposeful look in her brown eyes.

"What the hell is wrong with your friend?" she asked. "He keeps bailing on Chloe."

"Chloe told you he had a business emergency."

"A business crisis on Easter. Please. He couldn't have postponed it a day?"

"I don't know. But I'm not the person you should be annoyed with."

"I know," she said. "I just hate to see Chloe disappointed. Is he going to be back by Tuesday? Because that's Chloe's birthday. Joel told me he was planning something for her, but now I'm worried he's not going to do it. And I've told her none of us can get together until Wednesday because I didn't want to blow his surprise."

"Do you have his number? You should call and confirm that he'll be back."

"I will, but if you talk to him, can you remind him and let him know that missing her birthday would be a big problem? I don't want her to end up alone on her birthday, but I don't want to blow his surprise, either."

"I will let him know."

"Thanks. Because if he messes up her birthday, he's going to have more than one angry woman to deal with."

"I will pass that on."

CHAPTER FIFTEEN

CHLOE WANTED to get to the rental house on Monday, but a broken burner on the stove and a sick waitress tied her up at the restaurant. She apologized to Decker, knowing that he wanted to get the junk cleared as soon as possible, but he wasn't too concerned. He was planning to pull permits and drive to the next town to get tile and floor samples for her to look at.

When Tuesday rolled around, she got a flat tire on the way to work and had to deal with that as well as more problems to solve at the restaurant. While she might have been able to find an hour in the afternoon to do some cleaning at the house, she was feeling out of sorts after getting a text from Joel that he'd been delayed in New York City.

She shouldn't have been surprised, but she was. It was her birthday, and she'd thought Joel was planning to surprise her, that he'd set something up with Hannah and her friends, because none of them were available for dinner on her birthday. That had made her instantly suspicious.

But now her suspicions were turning into a pity party. Her friends were busy. Her boyfriend was going to miss her birthday, and she didn't feel like putting on a cheerful face about it.

After picking Leo up from school, she headed home, texting Decker that she would come by on Wednesday.

She wasn't holding up her end of the bargain to deal with Eleanor's junk, but she would get to it. And Decker seemed to be busy with other things. He wasn't just waiting around for her to show up. He could clear some stuff out himself, but she had a feeling he was afraid to find any more worrisome clues about his past.

As she puttered around the house on Tuesday, she still kept thinking that someone was going to show up with a surprise, but aside from getting birthday text greetings from her friends, and a hand-drawn card that Leo had made at school, there was nothing else going on.

She shouldn't care, but she did.

When her phone rang at five, she jumped to answer it, seeing Joel's number flash across the screen.

"Chloe," he said in a rush. "God, I'm sorry. I just remembered it's your birthday. I was going to surprise you with dinner. This trip just threw everything off. I feel terrible."

"It's fine. It's not a big deal," she said.

"I told your friends I wanted to do something for you. Hannah is going to kill me."

Hannah probably would want to kill him when she found out, but she didn't want Joel getting into a war with her friends. "I'll talk to her. How are your meetings going? Are you coming back soon?"

"I'll be honest; they're not going great, but I think I can win my dad over, eventually. He's the one influencing all the other staffers. I need to get him on my side."

"I don't understand why he isn't on your side. You're his son."

"I think that's the problem. He judges me more harshly than everyone else because I'm a reflection on him. I don't want to bore you. I hope you can still go out with your friends."

"Sure," she lied. "Just come back soon, okay?"

"I'm trying, Chloe. I really am."

She could hear the sincerity in his voice. But she'd also heard that same sincerity in Kevin's voice when he'd told her he really wanted to stay, wanted to be a good husband and father, that he was trying... But Kevin hadn't succeeded, and she wasn't sure Joel would, either.

It wasn't just that he was missing her birthday; it was that his reason was the same one he'd been giving her the past three weeks every time he had to miss something. It was always about work. Maybe this was just an unusually busy time. Or maybe she was kidding herself that he was ready to balance life and work. There was certainly no evidence that he was doing that.

But maybe she was being petty, too needy. She had a job and a kid; she knew what it was like to be busy and sometimes she had to bail on people. Maybe she just needed to relax and let things be what they were going to be.

As she set down the phone, she thought about calling her friends, but then she'd have to get a sitter at the last minute, and they already had plans in a few days. She'd just celebrate then. It certainly wasn't the first time she was alone on her birthday.

Actually, she wasn't alone, she thought, as Leo came running in to ask her to play a game with him. She had the best guy in the world right here.

After a long afternoon and evening of imaginary games, she put Leo to bed, and then settled down on the sofa in front of the television. She searched for a movie to fit her mood. She'd been smiling and putting on a cheerful face for Leo for the past several hours, and she didn't want to do that anymore. She needed something dark and scary, something completely different that would take her mind off things. She wasn't usually a fan of dark and scary, but what the heck...

She found the first in a series of five horror movies and turned it on.

Within minutes, her pulse was racing too fast, and she was feeling a little horrified.

Then the doorbell rang, and she almost jumped out of her

skin. It seemed eerily reminiscent of the scene she just watched when the girl had answered the door when she shouldn't have.

Telling herself to get a grip, she went to the door and looked through the peephole, relieved to see Decker on the porch. She flung open the door, more than a little happy to see his smiling face.

"Hey, what are you doing here?" she asked.

He pulled his hand from around his back, holding up a cupcake with a lit candle.

Her jaw dropped in surprised.

"Happy Birthday, Chloe."

"I can't believe you did this. How did you even know? Did Joel tell you? Did he send you over here?"

Decker hesitated. "No. But I heard he got hung up in New York, so someone else might have mentioned you like lemon cake with white frosting. It actually took me two bakeries to find it, and then some woman named Valerie said it must be for you."

"I really am predictable," she said. "It was very nice of you to do this. Since you know my favorite cake, then I'm guessing you talked to Hannah."

He shrugged. "My source is confidential. Are you going to blow out the candle?"

He'd no sooner said the words when the candle flickered out in the breeze.

"Damn," he muttered. "That wasn't supposed to happen."

"It's kind of the way my day has been going. Please come in."

"I'll relight it," he said, as he followed her into the house and over to the dining room table.

"You don't have to do that."

"You need to make a wish."

"I really don't."

He gave her a sharp, doubtful look. "I don't believe that you are a woman who doesn't make wishes."

"Well, most wishes don't come true, so maybe I should stop."

"Or maybe your wish comes true in a way you didn't expect."

Now, she was the one to give him a doubtful look. "Is that like saying everything has a reason, and you just have to find it, because I don't know that I believe in that, either."

"Okay, you're a little more jaded than I thought. Or is that just on your birthday?"

She made a little face at him. "Fine, light the candle, and I'll make a wish."

"Make it a good one. Nothing small or boring. No wishing for Leo to pick up his dirty laundry or sleep in for five more minutes."

She smiled. "Those are actually really good wishes."

He shook his head. "I want you to think bigger."

He lit the candle, and as she stared at the flickering flame, a really ridiculous wish came into her head—that this moment might last forever. But that wouldn't happen. The flame would burn down in a few seconds. And Decker would be gone not too long after that.

"Come on, Chloe, you don't have much time left," Decker said. "Don't overthink it. Just wish."

Love, she thought. Unconditional, heart-stopping, fiery, passionate, ridiculously big, always-there kind of love. It was an impossible wish, but she stopped thinking and blew out the candle.

"Good job," Decker said approvingly.

She smiled at him. "It won't come true."

"You never know."

"Do you want to split this with me?" she asked.

"I won't have to fight Leo for that honor?"

"He's asleep."

"Well, I'll let you enjoy it. So, what are you doing?"

"Watching a movie."

His gaze moved to the television, which was frozen in a terrifying frame of a knife attack. "What the hell are you watching?"

"Something very scary."

"You watch horror movies?" he asked, his gaze filling with surprise.

"I was looking for something to take my mind off my birthday."

"And prevent you from sleeping all night?"

"Probably," she said with a dry smile. "I jumped when you rang the bell. It was just like a scene in the movie."

"Okay, this isn't going to work. Do you have any playing cards?"

"Yes, but I don't need a babysitter, Decker. I'll just turn something else on."

"Or you can show me how good you are at cards. I have to warn you I'm very good."

She laughed. "Why doesn't that surprise me? Is there anything you don't think you're good at?"

He gave her an arrogant but sexy smile. "I'll have to think about that. Cards?"

"Fine." She went into the kitchen to retrieve a deck of cards while Decker turned off the movie. They sat down at the dining room table. "What do you want to play?"

"What do you know?"

"Well, it's been a while since I played anything but Go Fish or Old Maid, but I think I can remember how to play Gin Rummy."

"Let's start with that. Then I'll teach you how to play golf."

"We're playing golf indoors?" she asked with a grin.

"It's a fun card game."

"And something you're very good at."

"You said it; I didn't." He grinned back at her with a cockiness she found incredibly sexy and appealing. "Why don't you shuffle and deal the cards?"

As she shuffled, she said, "Did you play a lot of games with your dad when you were growing up?"

"We played a lot of card games on our travels. It was the easiest game to take along. We'd play on long flights, waiting at airports, sitting in rooms in hostels or on beaches in remote areas with no Wi-Fi or other electronics. We had to go back to the basics."

"That's so interesting. To be exposed to the world through action, not just playing a video game or looking online. You were there. You were living your life."

"To be honest, I think sometimes I would have preferred to play a video game, but it wasn't an option most of the time, and I got used to low-tech entertainment."

"I want Leo to have a lot of low-tech entertainment, too. I really encourage him to make up his own games. I want him to think, to use his imagination, not to just be a spectator."

"Well, that kid has a huge imagination, so I think you'll be successful."

"I had a big imagination, too, and growing up here we made up a lot of games, especially Hannah, Gianna, Keira, and myself. A lot of those games reflected what we'd later do in life. Keira was always wanting to make costumes, and she's now a fashion designer. Hannah liked to be the doctor or the nurse, and she works in the ER at the hospital. Gianna and I were not quite so focused. She liked to draw and make things, which carried into her art, but she also liked to play sports and climb trees."

"What about you?" he asked, as she dealt the cards.

"I liked to be the mom or the teacher, something involving kids. I sometimes played restaurant, but that was a later interest."

"What about sports?"

"I was good at softball. Soccer was a little too much running for me," she said with a smile. "I liked books, too. I was a voracious reader. Going to the library was one of my favorite outings. I think that's why I'm so fascinated by your life, because I had to travel through books."

"One day, you'll change that."

"Maybe. It's easy to think about making changes and never doing them."

"That's true. We can get stuck in ruts, even if we don't know we're in them."

"There's comfort in predictability," she agreed. "Anyway, let's play."

"You're on."

For the next two hours, they played game after game. She won a little less than half of them, because Decker was very good, especially when they moved from gin to golf and then to blackjack. They talked about anything and everything while they played. It was fun and easy and just what she needed to take her mind off her birthday.

Around eleven, they called it quits. She got up and walked Decker to the door, a little sorry to see him go, but knowing her early morning would be there before she knew it.

"Thanks again for my cupcake," she said, as he put on his jacket. "And the card games. They were fun. Much better than the horror movies."

"I'll say. And everyone deserves a cake on their birthday. My new favorite flavor is now lemon with vanilla frosting."

"It's the best." As she looked into his warm, green eyes, she felt heat wash over her, and the pull of an attraction she couldn't seem to fight. "Thank you for making my night a lot better than it started out to be."

"You're more than welcome."

He looked like he wanted to say more, and her pulse raced at the look in his eyes.

"I should go," he finally muttered.

"That wasn't what you were going to say, was it?" she asked, their gazes clinging together, the attraction between them suddenly sizzling.

"No. I was going to say there's something else besides cake that everyone should have on their birthday."

"What's that?" she asked, feeling breathless from his provocative look.

"This," he said. He cupped the back of her head with his hand and kissed her.

Her heart jumped against her chest as his mouth covered hers, sending her blood racing through her veins. An intense wave of desire ran through her as she leaned in, and he took the kiss deeper.

When Decker lifted his head, she pulled him back. "One more," she whispered.

Decker obliged, and as she moved against his hard body, she had a feeling that one more wasn't going to be nearly enough. But she had to stop. *Didn't she?*

Decker answered her silent question by pulling away, his breath as ragged as hers.

He gave her a long look, filled with a mix of emotions. "I shouldn't have done that," he said. "You're with Joel."

The same guilt she now saw in his eyes washed over her. "It was just a birthday kiss. That's all it was."

"And all it will be," he said firmly. "I'll see you later."

She nodded, giving him a tense smile as he walked out the door. She closed it behind him and leaned against it, still feeling a little dizzy from their impulsive kisses.

She wanted to regret kissing him, because she was seeing someone else, but she just couldn't get there. She would get there, though. She'd have to, because there was no future with Decker. With him, it would just be fun and games.

She really wanted the fun and games, but she also didn't want to make a terrible decision. She'd already done that once. The next time she fell in love, it had to be with the right person. Decker wasn't that person. And it didn't look like Joel was, either. She had never felt like this after kissing Joel. *Why did Decker have to be the one to turn on the light inside of her?* It was just her luck to want another man who was going to leave.

CHAPTER SIXTEEN

CHLOE MADE a point of staying away from Decker and the rental house on Wednesday, needing a little more time before she saw him again, but when Thursday morning came around, she knew her reprieve was over. With Leo at school and the breakfast rush done, she really had no reason not to go to the house.

She needed to deal with Eleanor's things, and she couldn't keep avoiding Decker. Not seeing him wasn't making things better. She was just missing him, building him up in her head. She needed to deal with reality. There was no point, no future possibility of a relationship with Decker, and she didn't want to waste time or risk her heart on someone else who would eventually leave.

Although, it might be really fun for a while. And she hadn't had that kind of fun in a long time.

"What are you thinking about so hard?" Marian asked, as she passed by on her way to the register. "You've been somewhere else all morning."

"Nothing," she said. "Just distracted by a lot of things I need to do."

"Are you sure you're not distracted thinking about your man?" Marian asked with a smile.

"Joel?"

"Who else would I be talking about?"

"Uh, no one."

"What's going on, Chloe?"

"I told you I'm just going over my long *to-do* list. I need to get Eleanor's things cleared out of the house so Decker can start working."

"Then what are you doing here? I've got things covered here."

She put down the towel she'd been using to wipe the counter. "All right. Thanks."

"And don't worry about coming back today. My nephew, Ross, is on spring break and was asking me if he could help. If it's okay with you, I'll bring him on for the week."

"That sounds good. We could use the extra hands. And thanks, Marian. I don't know what I'd do without you."

"Well, you won't have to find out, because I love my job and I love you." Marian smiled. "Maybe you can also take a little time to figure out what's going on with the man that you're not thinking about."

She rolled her eyes. "Joel had to go out of town. There's nothing to figure out until he gets back. Who knows when that will be?"

As she left the restaurant, she hoped Joel would return soon, because she needed to see him, to verify her feelings. If they didn't have a strong enough attraction or weren't on the same page, then they shouldn't waste time trying to make something right that wasn't. She hadn't felt that easy connection with Joel in weeks, and she had a feeling she was hanging onto something that was already gone. Maybe because she didn't want to reach for something or someone else who definitely did not check off any of her boxes. Well, maybe one. One big one, she thought, her body tingling every time she thought about kissing Decker. But passion wasn't enough. There had to be more. She didn't have just herself to think about; she also had a child.

With that reminder firmly in mind, she grabbed some empty boxes and garbage bags from the back room and headed to the rental house.

When she arrived, she found Decker under the sink in the kitchen.

"Hello?" she called, trying not to stare at the hard washboard abs revealed by the t-shirt that was hiked up under the cabinet.

"Hang on," he said, banging on something under the sink.

She dragged her gaze away from Decker, perusing the kitchen. It looked like he'd emptied most of the cabinets. Every inch of the counters was covered with dishes, glassware, and food items. Maybe she'd start cleaning here. Any unexpired food could be donated to the food bank and the kitchen supplies could also be given to a local charity.

Decker climbed out from under the sink, his brown hair tousled, his cheeks flushed with exertion, his green eyes sparkling, and her stomach did a little flip-flop. As she swiped her suddenly dry lips with her tongue, she was reminded of the feel of his mouth on hers.

Decker gave her a questioning look, and she realized she was just staring at him like an idiot. "What are you doing?" she asked, hating that she sounded a little breathless. She needed to get a grip. They'd had a couple of passionate kisses. That was it. She really shouldn't even be thinking about that anymore.

"The garbage disposal is broken. You're going to need a new one."

His prosaic words brought her back to reality. She might be living in a fever dream, but Decker was obviously not thinking about their kiss. "Okay," she said. "I had a feeling there would be additional expenses once you started taking things apart. And you've definitely been doing that in here."

"The kitchen seemed like a good place to start." Pausing, he added, "I wasn't sure you'd be coming by. I didn't see you yesterday."

"I was tied up all day. I couldn't get away."

"Was that the only reason?" he challenged, a question in his gaze. "You weren't avoiding me because I kissed you? I know I was out of line, and I'm sorry."

She drew in a quick breath. "It was just a birthday kiss, and I'm not avoiding you. I'm here now."

"It won't happen again."

"I know," she said, because she couldn't let it happen again. It would only complicate her life.

"Have you talked to Joel?" Decker asked.

"He texted me yesterday. He's going to be in New York for a few more days. And, no, I didn't tell him you kissed me."

"You should do what you feel you need to do," Decker said.

"What I need to do is start working. Where do you want me to begin?"

"Why don't you keep going in here? I was just about to head upstairs. I don't want you in the master bedroom or the dining room area. The floor and ceiling are too fragile. I'll pull everything out of the master and into the hall. You can go through it there."

"Okay." She paused. "How are you feeling about being here, Decker? Have you looked through any more of Eleanor's personal things?"

"No. I thought I'd leave that to you. How long are you going to be here?"

"I don't have to pick up Leo until three today."

"Okay. If you want to fill up the back of my truck with garbage or anything you want to donate, feel free. I can make a run at the end of the day."

"That would be great. I hate to just throw things away."

"Me, too. I try to recycle and donate whenever I can. Someone will be happy to get this stuff." He paused. "My father loved a good flea market. I think he furnished our entire kitchen with things he bought for a dollar or two. He found a chipped plate far more interesting than something brand new. He used to say every piece had a story to tell."

"Your dishes talked?" she teased, feeling better now that the awkwardness between them was easing.

He grinned. "No. My dad came up with the stories, which were easy for him. He was a born storyteller."

"I'd love to read one of his books."

"You can probably find them online or at the library."

"I'll have to look."

"But not right now. You need to get to work," he said with a smile.

"Hey, I'm the boss."

"Then tell yourself to get to work. We have a lot to do."

"I'm on it." She waved him out of the kitchen. She'd be able to get a lot more done if he wasn't in the room.

For the next three hours, she cleaned out the kitchen, taking boxes of items to donate out to the truck and putting trash bags by the side of the house. When the kitchen counters were emptied, she went upstairs. The hallway was so packed with stuff that Decker had pulled out of the master bedroom she could barely walk through it.

Her initial head of steam quickly diminished. This would be another enormous job, and it would take more time to go through the file boxes and drawers that had come from Eleanor's dresser and desk. The kitchen had felt impersonal. It had been easy to divorce herself from the woman who had lived here for almost twenty years, but these items needed more review, more care, and she had little time left.

After debating her options, she started taking boxes and drawers down the stairs and out to the trunk of her car. She could go through things at home when she had more time.

As she was making her third trip to the car, Decker came out of the house. "Why are you loading up your car?" he asked. "I told you I'd take everything out for you."

"I don't have time to go through it all here, so I'm taking some of the personal items to my house."

"Seems like you'll just have to move everything twice."

"You're right, but I'm tired, and I have to pick up Leo soon."

"You don't have to go through everything, Chloe. I don't need any more clues."

She wondered if that was true. "Well, like I said at the beginning, I want to do it for Eleanor. Someone should look at the things she thought were important to keep."

He frowned. "I believe you feel that way, but I think you still want to find the connection between Ellie and me."

"If I find another link, do you want to know?"

He thought about her question for a long minute. "I'm not sure."

"Well, you can think about it. It might not even be an issue. I'll see you tomorrow."

Decker spent the rest of Thursday and most of Friday thinking about the boxes that Chloe had taken to her house. He'd hoped to get an answer on Friday afternoon when she came to work at the house, but a work conflict kept her away, and he was left to wonder if she had found anything. He'd told her he didn't need any more clues about his connection to Ellie, but the longer he was working in her house, the more he realized he wanted more information.

That his father had kept the relationship a secret from him bothered him, because he hadn't thought they had any secrets. He'd believed they were as close as a father and son could be. But there were things his father had never shared with him. Maybe he would have eventually, but his father hadn't gotten the chance.

He might have that chance now.

When he finished up in the late afternoon, he got into his

truck and made a quick decision that might be bad on a lot of levels, but he was going with it. He picked up his phone and called Chloe.

"Hi, Decker. Is everything okay?" she asked. "Sorry I couldn't get over there today."

"It's fine. I have some samples of tile and flooring that I wanted to show you. Can I bring them by the house?"

"Sure. That sounds fine."

"You're not going out."

"Nope, just hanging with Leo."

"Want to share some pizza while you look at the samples? You can call it a working dinner." He didn't know why he felt he needed to give her an excuse to have dinner with him, but it probably had something to do with the kisses they weren't talking about, the kisses he couldn't quite forget.

"Leo and I both love pizza," she said.

"Then I'll get enough for all of us."

"Great. But I have to ask..."

He steeled himself for whatever was coming.

"Do you just want to have dinner together and look at samples, or are you also curious about the boxes I brought home yesterday?"

He was relieved that her question was about the boxes and not about the attraction sizzling between them.

"Maybe both," he admitted. "Did you find something?"

"I haven't looked. I was going to do it tonight after Leo goes to bed. You could look with me."

"Well, let's start with pizza," he said, unwilling to commit to more. "Any requests?"

"Plain cheese for Leo, get a kid's size or a small one. I love everything: meat, veggies, whatever you like."

"Then I'll surprise you. I'll get salad, too."

"Perfect. I'll see you soon."

He smiled to himself, happy that things were back to a good place with Chloe. He would not do something stupid like kiss her again. He needed to keep things on a friendship level, a working-together level. That was the best scenario. Chloe was still with Joel, as far as he knew, although he didn't know how Joel's extended absence would affect their relationship. But he didn't want to be the one to ruin their relationship, not when he'd be gone before summer.

CHAPTER SEVENTEEN

DECKER GOT to Chloe's house a little before six. When he stepped into the living room, he felt immediately warmed and welcome. Leo had headphones on and was watching a video on a tablet while a fire in the gas fireplace blazed brightly behind him.

"I know it's not that cold, but both Leo and I love a fire," Chloe said.

"Me, too," he replied, as he carried the pizzas over to the dining room table.

"I have some wine," Chloe said. "Would you like some?"

"Sure."

"It's nothing fancy, just a cabernet that was on sale at the grocery store."

He smiled. "Sounds like my kind of wine."

"Mine, too. I wouldn't dare offer it to Joel. He's clearly a wine connoisseur."

"Joel knows his wine," he agreed. "His father has the most incredible wine cellar you've ever seen. He has wines from every important wine-making region in the world."

"So, you've been to Joel's parents' home?" she asked curiously.

"The Christmas after my father died, Joel invited me to spend the holidays in New York with his family. They were very good to me."

"They're nice people then? Because when Joel talks about his father, I can't quite figure out if he loves his dad or hates him," she said as she filled two wineglasses.

"It's a little of both, I think. His father is a hard man to please. He's smart, sharp-edged, and can be ruthless in business, although he can also be charming to family and friends. But even through the charm, you can see his hard edges. He put a lot of pressure on Joel to carry on his legacy, and he made him work his way up through the company, doing all the low-level jobs so he'd know exactly how the company was run from the ground up. Now that Joel is trying to do the job he earned, his father is complaining about everything."

"Joel told me that his dad has been stirring up trouble with some of the older employees, and Joel is losing support at the company for some of his ideas. I think one of those ideas is about him making Whisper Lake an office location for Joel and possibly others."

"He mentioned that to me. Joel's father still wields tremendous influence at the company. Joel has his work cut out for him, which is probably why he's not back yet."

"He keeps saying soon, but I think it's already too late to be soon. It has been almost a week since he left." She handed him his wine. "But I wish him well. I hope he can get what he wants. It sounds like he has earned the right to run the company the way he wants."

"I think so, but I suspect his father has a different opinion."

Chloe sipped her wine, her gaze thoughtful. "What's Joel's mother like?"

"Sweet woman, seems intelligent, but is not particularly forthright when her husband is in the room. When I was around, she let him do the talking. I know Joel gets a little frustrated that she doesn't always speak up for herself."

"He said he has a younger sister, too, but she's not in the business."

"I think she's an artist or something. She's eight or nine years younger than Joel, so I don't know much about her. When I visited that Christmas, she was probably about twelve."

"Hi, Decker," Leo said, interrupting their conversation as he came running over to the table with a miniature horse in each hand. "Do you want to play horses with me?"

"I think we're ready to eat," he said. "How about after dinner?"

"Okay." Leo said, climbing onto his chair where a bright purple plastic plate was already waiting with an array of strawberries, sliced bananas, and carrots. Leo immediately dug in, picking up a bright red berry and popping it into his mouth.

"I'll get you a piece of pizza, too," Chloe said, opening the smaller box to slip a slice onto Leo's plate. "It's hot, so let it cool for a few minutes."

He sat down across from Leo while Chloe grabbed plates and silverware for them. As she dished out salad for both of them, he opened the other pizza box and offered her two slices of the meat and veggie lovers' pizza, which she was happy to get. Then he filled his own plate.

"Thanks for picking this up," she said. "I love this pizza. I meant to tell you the best place in town, but you figured it out."

"I'm glad I picked the right place." As she finished speaking, Leo knocked over his glass of milk with one of his horses, and the milk quickly spread across the table.

"Sorry, Mommy," Leo said immediately, worry entering his eyes.

"It's okay," she said, mopping up the milk with napkins. "It was an accident. But that's why we don't play at the table. Put the horses down until you're finished eating." She got up to refill his milk and to grab a towel to wipe down the table. Then she gave him a helpless smile. "The perils of eating with a four-year-old."

"He didn't dump it on me, so I'm good," he said with a grin. "And I have eaten with four-year-old children. One of my friends in LA has twin four-year-old girls and a one-year-old. Dinner at his house is more chaotic than this."

"I'll bet. Three kids under the age of four?" She shuddered. "I can't even imagine."

"I witnessed it and still don't know how he handles it all."

"Do you see yourself with kids one day?" She paused. "Or is that too personal of a question?"

He shrugged. "I don't really think about it, to be honest. I like kids, so sure, one day..."

"You're lucky you're a man. Women in their thirties have to think about whether or not they want kids. The clock is not our friend."

"I have always been happy to be a man," he said. "Do you want more children?"

"I wouldn't mind if Leo had a sibling. I think it would be good for him, but I wouldn't do it alone. Not because it's too hard," she added hastily. "But because I would want my child to have two parents. It's difficult for one person to be everything."

"It is. But I'd rather have one fantastic parent than two mediocre ones. I also wouldn't want to split time between two parents. I grew up with a couple of kids with divorced parents, and I didn't envy the way they had to go back and forth. I was fine with just having my dad. But then, he was also a really good father."

"What was he like? I know he was an adventurer and a writer, but what was his personality? Was he quiet and introspective or outgoing and the life of the party?"

"He was a mix of both. He could be quiet and serious when he was working, but he was also very talkative and friendly. He could go into any situation and come out with a new best friend. He was very interested in the life of whoever he met. He asked a lot of questions and rarely talked about himself. He used to tell me I'd learn a lot more by listening than by talking."

"You do seem to observe a lot," she commented. "You talk easily but you also listen, like really listen. Not everyone does that. They're more likely to be thinking about what they want to say next than what the other person is trying to get across."

"I've run into people like that," he agreed. "It's like they're looking for a punchline, or a chance to be smart or witty, instead of just being engaged."

"Exactly."

Chloe sat back, sipping her wine. "I know you were happy with your dad, but you must have missed having a mother."

"I did, but at the same time, I didn't know exactly what to miss, because I didn't remember her ever being in my life. It's hard to miss something you never had. Of course, as I got older and I saw other kids with their two parents, it became obvious that I was missing something. But I had a great childhood, so I can't complain." He paused. "Leo isn't going to complain, either. He's also having a great childhood, because of you. You're putting in the time. That's what kids remember."

"I hope so," she said. "But I can't help thinking that as he grows older, I'm going to run into things I'm just not very good at, that his father would be better at doing. Like mathematical word problems, or playing hockey, or camping. I don't know how to put up a tent. And I'm an average skier. I've never mastered snowboarding. Fishing is another thing I'm not good at."

He smiled at her growing list and the serious concern in her gaze. "No one is good at everything."

"But I bet you're good at all of that."

"Well, I am good at a lot," he teased, nudging a smile out of her. "But I have never played hockey."

"Still, when your dad raised you—it was two males. What about all the man stuff I'm going to have to help him go through?"

"You'll figure it out. And you'll be able to give him the female perspective. Seriously, Chloe, you can't be everything, so don't try. Just be yourself. You have plenty of friends to help you with the rest."

"It's definitely going to take a village," she said. "I know most of it will work out, but I don't want it just to be okay; I want it to be great."

"You're going to drive yourself crazy aiming for perfection. You know that, right?"

"I am good at driving myself crazy," she admitted. "I have a small issue with control sometimes."

"You think?" he joked.

"But I can give up control if someone else wants to take it. I just haven't had anyone who wanted to do that."

The more Chloe talked, the more he wondered why she and Joel thought they were good together. They were both great people, but he didn't think they matched up that well. But that wasn't his business.

After they finished eating, Leo asked him to play, and he agreed, happy to postpone looking at the stack of boxes in the corner of Chloe's living room.

"You don't have to play," Chloe told him. "You can look through the boxes. I can play with Leo."

"I want Decker to play, too," Leo interrupted, his usually smiling gaze filling with concern.

"I'm going to play," he said quickly. "As long as I can play with the gray horse, because I used to ride a gray horse named Thunder."

"You did?" Leo asked in awe. "Was he fast?"

"Really fast," he replied.

"Where did you ride?" Chloe asked curiously.

"It was outside of London, the summer I was twelve. Have you ever gone riding?"

"Not in a very long time. But I want to take Leo when he's older. There are a bunch of good stables around town." She paused, turning back to Leo. "Why don't you put your jammies on? Then you can play before story time."

"Okay." Leo took his plate to the sink and then dashed down the hall.

"Wow, he's already taking his plate into the kitchen," he said, impressed. "You are doing a good job, Chloe."

Her eyes got teary at his words. "Thanks for saying that."

"It's true. Don't doubt that."

"I'll try not to. It is nice to talk to someone who grew up with a single parent. It makes me feel a little better. I know there will still be some difficult moments ahead for Leo, and I wish I could protect him from those times, but I know I can't. I just have to surround him with as much love as I can and hope it's enough."

"It will be enough. How does Leo like Joel?" he asked curiously.

An odd gleam flickered through her eyes. "Leo doesn't know Joel very well. I haven't wanted to make a big deal about our relationship before I was sure it was serious."

He shouldn't like that there was uncertainty in her voice, but he did. "That makes sense."

"Does it? Maybe I should have gotten them together sooner. Sometimes, it doesn't feel like they connect at all. Joel is always nice to Leo, but Leo doesn't really engage with him. And Leo and I are a package deal. Whoever comes into our lives gets both of us."

"There's time for them to connect. You don't have to rush anything."

"That's what I've been telling myself, but as Joel's trip goes on and on, I wonder about a lot of things."

"Have you spoken to him recently?"

"Not since Wednesday. He apologized again for missing my birthday, but nothing since then. What about you?"

He shook his head. "Nothing."

"Well, he's busy, and the sooner he takes care of his problems, the sooner he'll return," she said, pushing back her chair. "I'm going to put the pizza away."

He got to his feet to help, but then Leo came sprinting into the room and immediately grabbed his hand and pulled him down the hall.

"What are we going to play?" he asked, sitting down on the floor by the horse farm.

"Some of the horses are sick, so we have to take them to the doctor in the trailer," Leo said, pointing to the trailer.

"Got it." He grabbed the trailer and pulled it around. "Load 'em up." He glanced up as Chloe came into the room. "Why don't you take a break?" he suggested. "I've got this."

She hesitated. "Are you sure, Decker?"

"Positive. You're a great mom and you work too hard. Promise me you'll just relax and not start working on something else."

"I promise. Call me if you need me. Story time is in half an hour."

"We'll see you then."

Chloe felt more turned on than she had in years, and it wasn't just because Decker was charming her with his sexy smile or hot body, but also because he'd told her she was a wonderful mom, and she deserved a break. She could have kissed him for that.

Luckily, Leo had been right there, or she might have given into the temptation once more. But their chaperone had stopped her from making another impulsive mistake. She couldn't keep kissing Decker and pretending nothing was going on.

Sitting down on the couch, she realized that she also couldn't deny something was going on just because they weren't kissing each other. She just didn't know what to do about it. Decker was a good guy, but he wasn't her guy.

As if on cue, her phone rang, and Joel's name flashed across the screen. Guilt ran through her. They'd never talked about being exclusive, but Decker was Joel's friend, and she knew they'd crossed a line they shouldn't have crossed.

"Hello?" she said.

"Chloe, how are you?" he asked, his voice weary.

"I'm good. How are you? When are you coming back?"

"I wish I could say tomorrow, but it's probably going to be Sunday or Monday."

"That's too bad. What's happening?"

"A lot of business stuff. I don't need to bore you with all that. I just wanted you to know I was thinking about you."

Now, she felt even more guilty. She hadn't been thinking about him at all. "I appreciate that. How's New York?"

"It's...the same," he said, an odd note in his voice.

"What does that mean?" she asked curiously.

"I don't know. I'm tired. I've been in meetings all day. It's good to hear your voice. You remind me of Whisper Lake, where everything is so calm and peaceful."

She frowned, not thinking that was the best compliment she'd ever heard. But then the background noise on the phone got louder. "Where are you now? It sounds like you're in the street?"

"I'm outside a club. I'm going to meet an old friend for a drink."

"Well, I'm glad your trip isn't all business."

"I wasn't going to meet up, but I could use a drink."

"You sound...different," she said, not able to read all the emotions in his voice.

"What?" he asked. "I didn't hear you."

"You don't sound like yourself," she said, trying again.

"Sorry. I missed that."

As a siren blared, she said, "Don't worry about it. We'll talk later. Have fun with your friend."

Joel's answer was garbled, and then the connection broke. As she put down the phone, she felt unsettled, which was odd because Joel had called to tell her he missed her. And that should have made her happy. But it hadn't. And it occurred to her that she was falling into an old bad habit, telling herself a story that didn't match reality.

How many months, make that years, had she made excuses for why she and Kevin were out of sync? Too many. She wasn't going to do that again. She wasn't going to pretend things were good when they weren't. Maybe it would get better when Joel came back to town, or maybe it would be like it had been the past few weeks, work distractions, dates now and then, professions of mutual liking, but not a lot of heat, not a driving, urgent passion to be together.

She'd told herself that she wasn't looking for all that. She was more interested in a man who could be her partner, be steady, hold the course. Joel had appeared to be all that when she first met him, but that had changed, or maybe she'd just realized that what she really wanted was a man who made her heart skip a beat, who turned her palms sweaty, who made her tingle with just a smile.

She wanted a man who could be a father to Leo. And Joel had barely shown any interest in her son. That had been fine at first. She'd wanted to take it slow. But watching Decker interact with Leo was so much different than watching Joel, who never really knew what to say or how to act around her kid. He wasn't mean; he just wasn't present.

With a sigh, she knew she'd already decided. Now, she just had to act. But she couldn't do that while Joel was out of town. She needed to talk to him in person.

Her thoughts were distracted by the sound of Leo giggling uncontrollably, and a smile lifted her lips. She got up and went into the bedroom, seeing Decker tickling Leo, who was rolling around on the floor in absolute delight.

"What is going on in here?" she asked.

"Someone wanted to be tickled," Decker said.

"More," Leo squealed, squirming under Decker's teasing fingers.

She watched them for a few minutes, enjoying the fun they

were having together, then she realized how late it was getting. "It's time to get ready for bed," she said, instantly killing the mood.

Leo's face clouded over, but before he could burst into tears, Decker swept him up in his arms and got to his feet. "You're not a boy, you're an airplane. Let's fly into your bed," he said, taking Leo on a soaring run around the room before dumping him into the middle of his bed. "The plane has landed," he told Chloe while Leo giggled again.

"I'm not a plane," Leo said.

"Oh, my mistake."

"Can you read me a story, Decker?" Leo asked.

"I'm going to read to you," she answered before Decker could get hit up for another favor.

"Sleep good, Leo," Decker said.

"Will I see you tomorrow?" Leo asked eagerly.

"I hope so," Decker replied.

As Leo smiled happily, her gut clenched. Leo was falling for Decker, and she was terribly afraid she was, too. They might both be headed for a fall. But for now, she was just going to read a story and send Leo off into a sweet, happy dreamland.

CHAPTER EIGHTEEN

While Chloe read to Leo, Decker went out to his truck and retrieved the samples of tile and flooring he'd brought for Chloe to look at. He set everything down on the dining room table and then moved into the living room, his gaze moving to the stack of boxes and desk drawers that he'd taken from Eleanor's bedroom. The last thing he wanted to do was go through Ellie's things. But trying not to think about their connection wasn't working. He was going to be in her house for another six weeks. If there was something to discover, he might as well find it now and get it over with. And maybe there wouldn't be anything which would be even better.

He moved a couple of drawers around, not interested in the office supplies and stacks of Christmas and birthday cards, none of which had been used. But the bottom drawer held personal papers and what appeared to be several journals. He took the drawer to the coffee table and sat down on the couch. He picked up the first journal.

When he opened it and saw the handwriting, a chill ran through him. His gaze blurred as he read the first few paragraphs of what appeared to be a story—a story his father had written.

But why would Eleanor have a journal that his father had written in?

Shaking his head in confusion, he read the first page, then the second. The writing was rough. It felt like a draft. As the story took shape, he realized he was reading his father's very first book, a novel set in France during the second world war. Flipping through the journal, the writing tapered off in the middle of the fourth chapter. The rest of the pages were blank.

He closed the book and stared down at the blank cover, as his brain went back in time.

His father was sitting on the back porch as the sun went down, and he was writing in a book.

"What are you doing, Daddy?" he asked.

"Working on my story."

"Can you read it to me?"

"When you're older." His dad pulled him onto his lap. "It's a grown-up story, and one day I'm going to publish it. It will be in libraries and bookstores. I can see it now."

"What's it about?"

"It's about war, fighting for what you believe in, struggling to survive, taking chances, being brave even when you're afraid," his dad replied.

"I'm brave," he said. "I didn't cry when I fell down the steps this morning."

"No, you didn't. You were a brave boy. But you need to stop running down the stairs."

"I will. You said we could get an ice cream because I didn't cry. Can we go now?"

"I need to write a little more before dinner. We'll go later."

"Maybe Ellie could take me now."

His dad suddenly looked mad. "No. Ellie is not taking you."

"Why not?"

"Because I said so. Go play," he said, urging Decker off his lap. "If you're good, we'll go in an hour."

Decker's heart raced with the brief memory. His dad had

been writing in this book on their trip to Whisper Lake. They'd never been back, so he must have left the journal behind. That seemed strange. *Why would his father have left his journal in the rental house?* It was his work, his words.

But somehow Ellie had ended up with the book.

His father must have had to rewrite the story from scratch after they left Whisper Lake. He could have just asked Ellie to send him the journal. Maybe he had. Maybe Ellie had refused.

Decker's brain whirled with questions. He dug deeper into the drawer, looking for more information and finding it in the unopened letter addressed to his father at their address in Phoenix. Like the other letters he'd found, this one had been sent back with the words *wrong address* scrawled across the front.

He opened the envelope and pulled out a sheet of paper.

Dear Ryan,

By now, you've realized that you left your journal behind. The journal with your wonderful writing in it. Well, I have it. No. I didn't find it. To be perfectly honest, I took it that last day. I thought if you couldn't find it, you might not leave. Or if you left, you'd realize where it was, and you'd come back to get it. But a month has passed, and I haven't heard from you.

I'm sorry for doing something so petty. I just want you to come back or to at least talk to me. I know the visit didn't go the way you wanted, or the way I wanted. Repairs take time. That's not fair to you, I know. But love and pain often go hand in hand, and this is a situation where both are equally difficult.

Please call me or write to me. I'll send you back the book. I feel so guilty for my part in everything—things that happened long before you even knew us. But I can't change all that now. I just want us to find a way to reconnect in the future.

By the way, I think you're a wonderful writer. You have an amazing gift. I hope you finish the story you left behind, that I haven't prevented you from achieving that.

Regretfully, Ellie

Now he had even more questions. *Why hadn't his father gone back for his journal, for his book?* He must have known he'd left it behind. *And what the hell had Ellie done to feel guilty about? More importantly, what was his father's tie to her?*

Frustration ran through him. Ellie never said enough in her letters. It was all just teasing words. He dug through the rest of the drawer but found nothing else that was personal, just bills and letters from friends, none of whom had names he recognized.

He looked up as Chloe returned to the living room.

"Leo is asleep," she said. "You tired him out. He usually wants more stories, but he was asleep before I finished the second one." She paused. "Did you find something, Decker?"

"The beginning of my father's first book. It was in a journal he wrote in when we came here. Ellie stole it, thinking he'd come back to get it or would have to talk to her in order to retrieve it."

Confusion ran through her eyes. "I don't understand. How do you know that?"

"There's a letter from Ellie to my father that she sent after we went home. It wasn't opened." When Chloe sat down on the couch next to him, he handed her the letter. "You can read it."

As she read the letter, he got to his feet and paced around the living room, pausing by the mantel to look at the family pictures Chloe had on display. There had never been any family photos in any house he'd lived in. When he was older, he'd occasionally frame something of his dad and him and give it to his father as a birthday present, but that was it. The extended family had never been a part of his life. He'd thought it was normal, but it wasn't.

Chloe's mantel display was what you would normally find in a family home: photos of Leo with his father, his mother, and his grandparents on both sides, as well as Chloe's friends and other people he didn't recognize. Leo's world was full of people. His life had been so much smaller.

"This letter talks about apologies and repairs, love and pain," Chloe said, drawing his attention back to her. "Ellie had to be related to your father."

"It feels that way, but I already told you what I know about my father and his side of the family, which is next to nothing."

"She wasn't a grandmother, maybe an aunt." Chloe paused. "Ellie was married. Maybe her husband was the link. His name was Hank."

"Which doesn't ring a bell. I never heard about anyone named Ellie or Hank."

"Do you remember Hank from your visit here?"

He thought about that. "I think there was an older man that we went to see." He struggled to remember more, but the memory wasn't there. He shook his head in bemusement and a little anger, but he didn't know exactly who to be pissed at. "I feel like I've opened Pandora's box. I want to put the lid back on, but I can't."

"What do you want to do?"

"I have to keep looking for answers. I won't be able to stop thinking about this weird connection."

"I wouldn't be able to stop thinking about it, either. Should we keep looking?"

"Maybe tomorrow. I need to process this revelation before I hit another one."

"Do you want me to look without you?"

"You can, but don't feel like you have to. I'm sure you're tired, and this isn't your problem."

"I want to help you, Decker," she said, getting to her feet. "It's only fair after you helped entertain my kid all night."

"That was fun."

"Really?"

"Yes," he said, seeing the doubt in her eyes. "Why would you think it wasn't?"

"Most people get bored playing little kid imaginary games."

"Well, I'm not most people."

"No, you're not," she breathed.

He sucked in a breath as her gaze shifted. He saw the need in her eyes at the same time he felt the yearning in his gut. Chloe was so damn beautiful. "I wish..." He stopped himself just in time. "Never mind."

"What were you going to say?" she challenged.

"That I should go home," he said. "I put the samples on your table. Take a look and let me know if I'm close to what you want."

Her gaze moved to the dining room. "Okay, I'll do that soon." She paused, looking back at him. "But I don't think that's what you were going to say."

"Well, it's what needed to be said," he said tensely. "Will I see you tomorrow at the house?"

"Leo has a playdate in the afternoon, so I can come by for a while."

"I'll see you then."

He dug his hands into his pockets, so he wouldn't reach for her, wouldn't kiss her again. The pull was still so strong, he had to force himself to leave. He jogged out to his truck and slammed the door, releasing a small amount of frustration with that forceful move.

He'd come close to screwing things up again. He'd almost told Chloe he wished she wasn't taken, but she was taken, and Joel was his friend.

He needed to remember that.

Decker had just finished loading up his truck Saturday afternoon for another run to the dump when he got a call from Joel.

"Hey, what's up?" he asked. "Are you back?"

"No. It will probably be Monday."

"I thought this was supposed to be a quick trip. What's going on?"

"Too much to get into, but it doesn't look like I'll be able to base myself in Whisper Lake, not if I want to keep my position as head of the company. I've tried to make it work, but my father's influence is too strong. We're a New York-based company, and he wants me in Manhattan. I don't have a choice."

"You have a choice. You could leave the company and work for someone else or start your own business. You're smart, capable, and you have your own financial resources, don't you?"

"Not at a level where I could compete with the company I'm running now."

"That company may not be able to compete without you running it."

"That's true." Joel paused. "There's something else. I saw Sylvie again."

"And..."

"She'd like me to move back to the city. She thinks I'm trying to define myself outside the circle of my father's influence, but Whisper Lake is too remote, too far outside the circle."

He thought Sylvie might be right. "What about Chloe?" he asked. "What about your plans to live in a small town and balance life and work?"

"I care about Chloe. She's a great person. But my career is very important to me. I've been working to get this job for ten years. I know Chloe will never leave Whisper Lake, and I wouldn't ask her to. But how can I give up the business? This is my family legacy."

He leaned against his truck, unsure how to answer that question. He didn't think Joel could give up the business. He didn't believe Whisper Lake could work as a home base. But he also knew that any answer he gave Joel would be influenced by his feelings for Chloe. That wasn't right. Joel was his friend.

"Nothing to say?" Joel asked in surprise. "You usually have an opinion. I want to know what you think, Decker."

"There's a reason you wanted to leave New York City and start over here. If you go back to the city, won't you have the same desire again? What's changed?"

"My father claims I'll get more latitude as long as I'm working out of New York."

"What does that mean?"

"He'll stay out of the business if he feels more confident that I'm carrying on his legacy the way he envisioned."

"It's your life, Joel. Your father did exactly what he wanted to do. You should do the same."

"I want to do the same, but realistically, I need my father's support."

"Then you have to pay the cost for that support. But you should be honest with Chloe. You should tell her what you're thinking, how you're feeling."

"I don't want to talk to her until I know what I'm going to do."

"Why not include her in the conversation? If you want a future with her, then she should be part of this, don't you think?"

"This is a decision I have to make for myself. Don't say anything to her about the possibility that I won't be able to work there full time."

"I don't want to be in the middle."

"How are you in the middle?"

"I'm working for Chloe. I see her all the time."

"How's the house coming along?"

"Slowly. There's so much junk to clear out, I'm spending most of my time doing that. Chloe is helping, because she feels some moral obligation to her tenant to not just dump her stuff without looking through it."

"Chloe has a kind heart," Joel said. "She really is great, isn't she?"

"Yes, she is. You should get back here soon, talk things over with her."

"As soon as I can."

Decker regretted his promise to stay silent as soon as the call ended. Joel might say things weren't decided, but they were. Joel would choose to run his family business over anything and anyone else. He was an ambitious man, and Decker could never see Joel being satisfied in Whisper Lake, not for the long term.

Short term, yes. He was defining himself outside of his father and his family's presence in New York. But that's where the business was, and ultimately that's where Joel would be.

He also didn't like that Joel had seen Sylvie again. But he wasn't surprised about that, either. Sylvie was the kind of woman Joel usually dated. Tall, thin, sophisticated, someone who knew all the right people and could network and charm her way into wherever she needed to go. Sylvie was frenetic energy and drama. She was a party girl, and until recently Joel had liked to party.

Sylvie had broken up with Joel because he'd taken a huge detour from his life. Now he was talking to her and thinking about going back to the city.

Chloe was going to get hurt by another man who was putting his career first.

Maybe that wasn't fair. Joel had tried to make things work in Whisper Lake. If he couldn't do it, he couldn't do it. But Joel needed to tell Chloe that. He needed to free her up.

And then what...

He tensed at the question running around inside his head. If Joel and Chloe weren't together, then there was nothing standing in his way. He could ask her out. He could kiss her again. He could stop trying to pretend there was nothing between them but friendship and a work relationship.

And then what...

He wasn't staying here. He had a life and a business elsewhere. He also wasn't a long-term kind of man. And Chloe needed a forever guy. That wasn't him. He'd been raised to keep moving forward: new people, new experiences, new, new, new.

It had been a good philosophy for a long time.

Now he wondered if there was a reason his father didn't look back...a reason that had to do with Ellie.

He started as Chloe's car turned into the driveway, his heart flipping over as she stepped out of the car, wearing black denim and a brightly colored cardigan over a white t-shirt, her hair pulled up in a ponytail.

"Hi," she said, a smile on her face as she approached. "I meant to come by earlier, but I had to wait for a delivery at the restaurant."

Where's Leo?"

"He has a playdate. The boys are having so much fun that their mom invited him to stay for dinner, so I have a few hours free." Her gaze moved to his truck. "It looks like you've been doing my job for me."

He shrugged. "I was here, and it had to get done. There's nothing personal in this load."

"So you looked?" she asked, a quizzical gleam in her eyes.

"I looked," he admitted. "But I didn't find anything."

"I haven't had a chance to go through the rest of the stuff in my house. I looked at the samples you left, but I haven't made any decisions. I'll do that tonight or tomorrow."

"You have a little time, but not a lot."

"I know."

He stiffened as a gray sedan turned into the driveway. "Who's this?" he asked, as an older woman climbed out of the car. She had white hair and wore tan slacks and a thick sweater.

"It's Janet Richey," Chloe replied. "One of Eleanor's friends."

"Chloe, is that you?" Janet asked.

"It's me, Janet. How are you? I haven't seen you in a while."

"I was visiting my sister for a few months," Janet replied. "I just got back to town, and I'm so sad about Ellie's passing."

"It's very sad," Chloe agreed.

"I heard you were fixing up the house, and I don't know what happened with Eleanor's things, but I gave her two quilts I had made to use when she was feeling ill. They're not worth a lot of money, but they're sentimental to me, and I was wondering if I could get them back."

"Of course, but I'm not sure where they are, or if we've

already donated them. Eleanor left quite a few personal items behind."

"I know," Janet said. "I'm aware of Eleanor's desire to never throw anything away. She had the quilts downstairs in the living room last time I was there." Janet's gaze moved past Chloe to him, and her jaw dropped. "Oh, my God!"

"What's wrong?" he asked, as her gaze searched his face.

"You look just like him," she said in amazement. "Well, not just like him, but a lot like him, especially your eyes, your green eyes."

"What are you talking about?" he asked, every muscle in his body tightening. "Who do I look like?" When she didn't answer right away, he wanted to shake her, because this woman knew something he didn't. This woman knew who Ellie was to him.

"Janet," Chloe said, as the older woman continued to stare at him in shock. "Who does Decker remind you of?"

"Hank," Janet finally said. "You must be Decker. Little Decker has finally come back after all these years. Confusion filled her gaze. "Did you get to see Eleanor before she passed?"

He shook his head. "No. I just arrived last week. And I don't know why I'd look like Hank. That was Eleanor's husband, right?"

"I can't believe you missed Eleanor. She would have been so happy to see you again, and in her house, too." Tears filled Janet's eyes. "So many years passed. She gave up hope."

Her rambling words intensified his confusion. "Who was Ellie to me?" he asked. "Why did she care if I came back or not?"

Janet's eyes widened. "You don't know? Your father never told you? Then how are you here?"

"I came to visit a friend of mine. He said Chloe needed help to fix up a house, and I'm a contractor."

"I didn't know there was any connection between Eleanor and Decker," Chloe said.

"Your father should have told you," Janet said.

"Told me what?" he asked tightly, his heart thudding against his chest.

"Hank was your grandfather, Decker."

Her words were shocking and wrong. "That's not possible. I know who my grandparents are."

"Well, it's a little complicated. I shouldn't be the one to tell you."

"You're the only one who can."

"I don't know all the details, but this is what Ellie told me. Hank and your grandmother had an affair. Hank realized it was a mistake and went back to Ellie, but then he found out your grandmother was pregnant. She was also married, and neither one wanted to break up their marriages, so Hank paid your grandmother to take care of your dad and to keep their secret. Two years later, her husband found out and left her alone with her son, your father, Ryan."

It felt like Janet was telling him a story about people he didn't know. But she was talking about his father being the product of an affair between Ellie's husband, Hank, and his father's mother, Catherine. Still, he needed to clarify. "You're telling me that my father, Ryan, was Hank's son?"

"Yes."

He thought about what he'd learned so far. "At some point, Ellie had to know, too. When was that?"

"I think it was when your dad was about twelve. Ellie said she was shocked and felt betrayed by Hank's secret. She left him for a few months to think about everything. But he begged her to forgive him. He hadn't seen that woman in years, not since she got pregnant, and he had no relationship with his son; he was just financially supporting him."

"Was that something to brag about?" he asked angrily.

"No. I'm just telling you what Hank told Ellie. She went back and forth for a while, but in the end, she took Hank back. She told me she should have encouraged Hank to have a relationship with Ryan, but she couldn't stand the thought of him seeing Catherine again. Hank didn't want to shake things up, so he just left things the way they were with Catherine and Ryan."

"My father said he didn't have money growing up. Hank couldn't have paid her much," he said.

"I don't know."

"Did Ellie tell you when my dad found out about Hank?" he asked.

"When he was seventeen," Janet replied.

"Seventeen? That's how old my dad was when my mom got pregnant with me."

"Yes. Apparently, Ryan went to the man he thought was his father to ask for help and that man told him the truth, that he wasn't Ryan's biological dad—that was Hank. Ryan and his girlfriend came to Whisper Lake next."

"My dad wanted Hank to help him."

Janet nodded. "Yes. Ellie felt so guilty when Ryan and your mother showed up scared and pregnant. She urged Hank to help Ryan, but Hank wasn't interested. He thought Ryan needed to take responsibility for his actions, so he turned him away."

"Everyone turned my parents away," he muttered. "They were kids, and no one wanted to support them."

"Ellie did," Janet said. "She sent your father money on the side. Hank didn't know about it. And after your mom died, she tried to help even more, but she knew she couldn't do much without Hank's approval, because he managed the money. She convinced Ryan to bring you to Whisper Lake. I think you were about six. She wanted you all to be a family."

Suddenly, all the pieces were falling into place. "But that didn't work out."

"No. Eleanor said she just couldn't get Hank and your dad on the same page, and your dad left. She kept reaching out to Ryan, hoping to get him to come back. She wanted to have a relationship with him and with you, even if Hank and Ryan couldn't be father and son. She bought presents for your birthday and

Christmas, always hoping that one day she'd get to give them to you."

"All the toys in the house," he murmured. "You're saying they were for me?"

Janet nodded. "Eleanor gave up after a while, but she couldn't bear to get rid of anything. I offered to help her clean up. She always said maybe someday, but that day never came." Janet took a breath. "It's such a strange coincidence that you came here knowing nothing."

"I remember being here when I was a kid," he said. "It was a place I loved and when my friend Joel said he was here and I had time to visit, I made the trip back. I had no idea that Whisper Lake had been more than just a vacation spot for my dad and I."

"How is your father doing?" Janet asked.

He started at the question. "My father died twelve years ago."

Dismay entered Janet's eyes. "I had no idea. I'm sorry. I don't think Eleanor knew that. Even as recently as last Christmas, she talked about hoping she could reunite with you and your father."

"Well, that's never going to happen," he said tightly, feeling so many emotions he didn't know what to do with them all. He was confused, hurt, and angry. He couldn't hear anymore. "I need to go to the donation center before they close. Thanks for filling me in, Janet." He hurried to the truck, hopping behind the wheel, and pulling out before Chloe or Janet could say another word.

As he drove down the street, he didn't know what to think. His father had not felt the need to tell him anything about his grandfather. Maybe that was understandable, considering their relationship. But all of his dad's talk about moving on, living in the moment, looking to the future was really just a way to avoid everyone in the past. But what about him? Hadn't he had the right to know his grandfather? To understand where he came from?

He felt betrayed by the one person he'd always trusted. His

father had kept an enormous secret about his past, about their family. And the worst part was that there was nothing he could do about it now. He couldn't ask his dad or Hank or Eleanor about anything. He couldn't meet them or know them. Everyone was gone. The truth had come too late.

He pulled over to the side of the road, too distracted by the past to keep driving. He leaned his head back and closed his eyes. His dad's image appeared in his mind.

"We don't have a big family, Decker," his dad said. "It's just me and you. But I'm going to make it up to you. We're going to have so much fun. We won't need anyone but each other. I love you, Decker. And I won't let anyone take you away from me."

His eyes flew open at that unexpected memory. *Had his father been afraid that someone would take him away? Who would have done that?* The only person he could think of was Hank. *Was that why they'd traveled the world? Had they been having an adventure, or had they been running away?*

CHAPTER NINETEEN

"MAYBE I SHOULDN'T HAVE SAID anything," Janet said, as Chloe led her into the house. "Eleanor trusted me with her secret. I was just so shocked to see Decker. He looked like Hank."

"I don't remember Hank," Chloe said. "But I think it's good that you shared what you knew. Decker has had some memories of his trip here when he was a little boy, but none of it was making sense to him."

"It always felt like a sad story to me."

"I'll say. Hank cheated on his wife, disavowed his biological son, and when that son needed him, he turned his back. Frankly, he sounds like a jerk to me."

Janet gave her a weary smile. "Well, when you put it like that...yes. But I only heard one side. Maybe Hank would have told a different story."

"We'll never know, but I'm glad you told Decker the truth about his father, his family."

"I'm not sure he's glad. He looked angry."

"He needs to process." She blew out a breath, feeling like she needed to process, too, but first she had had to find Janet's quilts. "Shall we go inside? You can tell me about the quilts you're looking for."

As they entered the house, Janet's gaze swept the messy living room, which wasn't nearly as cluttered as it had once been, but there was still a lot to be done.

"This place is a mess," Janet commented. "I haven't been here in a long time. After a while, Eleanor just stopped opening the door."

"I don't remember seeing any quilts in the bags I've filled, but Decker may have donated them. He's been cleaning up, too."

"Well, it's not the end of the world. I just thought if they were here, I'd get them back." She paused. "I wouldn't even know where to look."

"What did they look like? I'll keep an eye out for them."

"One was a holiday red and green plaid with reindeer on it. I thought it would brighten Eleanor's days during the holiday season. And the other was one we worked on together. It had boats on a lake surrounded by mountains."

"I don't remember seeing either of those, so they might still be here. I'll look around. You might check in town at the donation center. Decker might have already taken them there."

"I'll do that. Tell Decker I'm sorry, will you?"

"I will, but you have nothing to apologize for."

"I know, but I feel like someone should apologize."

She smiled. "I'll tell him."

When Janet left, she debated what she wanted to do. She was worried about Decker. She wanted to talk to him. But he'd clearly needed some space. So, she'd just do what she came here to do—clean out more junk and wait for him to come back.

An hour later, Decker hadn't returned. She locked up the house and headed to the café. She parked in the back, frowning when there was no sign of Decker's truck. He couldn't still be at the dump or the donation center. Both had closed a while ago.

She went inside and knocked on his door just in case he'd parked elsewhere, but there was no answer. With a sigh, she went downstairs and into the restaurant. It was a little early for dinner, but there were a few families with young kids already eating. She said hello to Marian and then cleared a nearby table and took the dishes to the sink. As she moved toward the counter, Hannah came in the door and slid onto the stool in front of her.

"Here you are," Hannah said, a sharp gleam in her eyes. "Why didn't you answer my text?"

"Oh, sorry, I forgot," she said, realizing she'd gotten a text from Hannah asking about grabbing dinner right before she pulled into the house and saw Decker by his truck. And then all hell had broken loose. "You wanted to get dinner."

"Well, it looks like you're working."

"She's not," Marian interjected. "I don't know what she's doing here."

"I have an hour before I have to pick up Leo," she said.

"Then have something to eat with Hannah," Marian said. "Why don't I pour you each a glass of wine and you can sit over there and chat while I bring you the special: grilled salmon with asparagus and mashed potatoes?"

"That sounds good to me," Hannah said. "Jake is out with some old college buddies, and I didn't feel like heating up left-overs. I'd love some merlot if you have it."

"Same," Chloe said.

Marian poured two glasses of wine, and then Chloe led Hannah to a booth in the corner.

As she sat down, she said, "Is something wrong?"

"That's what I want to know," Hannah replied, giving her a pointed look. "You skated over your disappointing non-birthday celebration with Joel when we went out on Wednesday night, and we haven't spoken since then. What's going on with Joel? A friend of mine is working on his development and said he's been gone all week. I thought it was supposed to be a quick trip."

"There were more problems than he expected."

"How are you feeling about his long absence?"

She stared back at Hannah, one of her oldest friends in the world, and told her the truth. "Not great. When he gets back, we probably need to break up."

Hannah frowned. "I'm sorry to hear that. You were so excited about him."

"I was, but he's not the man I thought he was, and I'm probably not the woman he thought I was. That's why you date, so you get to know each other."

"That's true."

"I was so caught up in how good Joel looked on paper that I couldn't see who he was in real life. And he's not a bad guy. He's fine. There's nothing wrong with him."

"Well, he bailed on your birthday."

"Okay, he's very consumed with work, which reminds me of Kevin."

"That's what I was thinking."

"I didn't know that at first. He said all the right things, that he wanted to change his life, find balance, stay in one place, and just be calm, soak in the wonder of the mountains. But I think that was just a fantasy in his head. He's very ambitious. He's dedicated to his job. He wants to rise in his career. I think he was just tired when he got here." She paused. "I think he might have had his own list, and I checked all his boxes, the way he checked mine. He wanted an answer to a problem, and I did, too. Does that make sense?"

"As one of your longest friends, I was able to follow that," Hannah said with a dry smile. "You both thought you knew what you wanted, but it turns out you don't. Don't get mad, but I'm relieved."

"Really? You didn't like Joel?"

"I liked him well enough, but you didn't seem right for each other, at least not to me. He was never really that engaged with our group, with your life, with Leo." Hannah paused. "You know who does seem right?"

She saw the gleam in Hannah's eyes. "Don't say it."

"Decker," Hannah said, ignoring her order. "When you two were singing karaoke, when you were playing trivia, you were having a blast. You were your old self again, and I enjoyed seeing that girl. I think Decker has brought some fun into your life."

"I like him," she admitted. "More than I want to, but he's leaving, Hannah. He has a life somewhere else."

"He doesn't have to leave. He's a builder. There's a lot of building going on."

"It's not just about a job. Decker is an adventurer. He grew up roaming the world, and he wants to keep doing that. He enjoys being free. He travels light. He wouldn't be happy staying in one place, and I have a child. If I didn't have Leo, I'd be tempted to go wherever he was going, but I can't do that. Besides that, I haven't known Decker very long, either. I'm sure there's something I'll come to dislike."

"I'm sure you're looking for that something," Hannah said knowingly. "But let's say Decker leaves in a few months. You could still have fun now. Not every relationship has to be forever."

"If Leo gets attached to Decker, and Decker disappears like his father did, then that's going to be bad."

"Decker isn't Leo's father. And all Leo knows is that he's a fun friend who comes around. He's too little to think about anything else."

"Decker is really good with Leo. He came over a couple of nights ago to talk about house stuff," she added vaguely, not wanting to get into Decker's personal business. "And he ended up playing with Leo, getting down on the floor, making up imaginary games with him. It was so sweet. It made my heart ache."

"Decker reminded you of when Kevin used to play with Leo."

"No, he didn't remind me of Kevin, because Kevin has rarely

been around since Leo was old enough to play. And if they play when Kevin comes to town, I don't see it. But when I saw Decker and Leo together, it made me realize that's what any future relationship of mine should look like. Joel barely knows Leo. He'll just tousle his hair and say something to him like you're such a smart boy. But Leo and Decker—they have a vibe."

"You and Decker have a vibe, too."

She sighed. "Why can't I fall for someone who's going to stick around? What is wrong with me? Why do I pick men who have somewhere else more important to be, something else more important to think about?"

"Well, you fell for Kevin when you were sixteen years old. You had no idea what was going to happen when you eventually grew up. And I think Joel said all the right things. Maybe he even felt all the right things at the beginning, but as you said, he changed, or you did. As for Decker, get to know him better before you write him off. Don't push him away just because it might not be forever."

"I'm not pushing him away; that's the problem."

"Considering how hot he is, I don't think that's the problem," Hannah said with a laugh.

She couldn't help but smile back. "Let's talk about you."

"My life is definitely not as interesting as yours."

Despite her protest, Hannah had plenty to say, and Chloe sipped her wine as Hannah talked about problems at work and figuring out what to do for her anniversary. Their conversation continued over dinner, and she enjoyed catching up with Hannah on her own. They were often in a big group; it was nice to talk just the two of them.

After Hannah left, she headed out to her car, then made an abrupt turn when she saw Decker's truck in the parking lot. She ran up the back stairs and knocked on his door.

He opened it and frowned, a complete lack of welcome in his eyes. "I can't talk to you right now, Chloe."

She was surprised by his harsh tone. "Is everything all right?"

"No. And you know why."

"I'm sorry you got blindsided by Janet. She told me to apologize."

"I knew there was a blindside coming. I knew it the second you told me my dad and I stayed in the house that Eleanor owned. I should have left it alone, but I didn't. In fact, I should have left town, but I couldn't. You know why? Because of you, Chloe. I made you a promise, and I didn't want to break it. I didn't want to walk away from you." His eyes burned with a fire that heated her blood.

She swallowed hard. "I don't know what to say."

"Tell me to leave, Chloe. Tell me you don't care if I break our contract."

She sucked in a breath. "Okay. I don't want you to go. But if you want to leave, you should."

"I should go—for a lot of reasons—and I'm not just talking about what I learned today."

She licked her lips, unable to read his expression. "What else are you talking about?"

"You know, Chloe. I've been traveling two dangerous roads, one leading to questions about my father's behavior and the other leading to a woman who's dating one of my good friends. And I can't seem to get off either road. But I have to get off."

She wanted to tell him she wasn't going to see Joel anymore, but that was something she should tell Joel first.

"You need to go, Chloe. You need to go right now."

He was angry, and he was hurting, and she was tied up in all of it. She wanted to ease the pain in his heart and feed the fire in his eyes. But she couldn't do either of those things. "Decker—"

He cut her off with a shake of his head. "Go home, Chloe. I can't do this." He stepped back and shut the door in her face.

She stared at it for a long minute, her breath coming hard and fast. She wanted him to open that door again. She wanted to throw herself into his arms and tell him she didn't want Joel; she wanted him.

But then what?

There was no good answer to that question.

Forcing herself to move, she ran down the stairs feeling shaken and terribly afraid she might have just lost something incredible.

CHAPTER TWENTY

DECKER SPENT most of Sunday debating whether he wanted to put Whisper Lake in his rearview mirror, the way his father had done twenty-seven years ago. But despite getting into his truck and driving around the entire lake for two hours, he couldn't quite bring himself to take the highway leading out of town.

He'd made a commitment to Chloe, and he didn't want to leave her high and dry. It wasn't her fault that his family was a twisted mess of secrets, some of which he still didn't understand. The worst part was not having anyone to ask. He hadn't spoken to his mother's parents his entire life. And he hadn't seen his paternal grandmother more than twice in his life and that's when he was a kid. He didn't even know where she was anymore. He supposed he could track her down and ask her about her affair, but what was the point? It wouldn't change anything.

Running away wouldn't change anything, either.

But staying...well, that presented another set of problems.

He'd shut Chloe out last night, but if he stayed in town, he'd have to deal with his attraction to her and his loyalty to his friend.

As he drove back into the downtown area, he could see why his father had always wanted to keep moving. New people, new places are the best medicine, his father would tell him. And it was tempting to follow in his dad's footsteps and just move on, but he wasn't his dad. He couldn't just leave and not look back, not yet anyway.

When he finished the house, when his commitment to Chloe was over, then he could leave without guilt, but that wouldn't be today.

He drove to the rental house, happy to see that there was no sign of Chloe's car. When he got inside, the house felt different. Knowing his relationship to Eleanor made him see everything in a new light. So many things she'd kept for him. She'd wanted to preserve the family history. And he was finally here to see everything she'd gathered together.

He no longer wanted to throw it all away. He needed to look, really look, at everything. Eleanor had tried to bring his father and grandfather together. She'd tried to make his family more whole. He owed her for that, even if she hadn't been successful.

For the next six hours, he went through every drawer, every pile, and instead of seeing just junk, he saw history. In the hundreds of books in the house, he found his father's ten novels, and each one of them appeared to have been read at some point in time. He also found dozens of history books and military thriller novels, some written by a former air force pilot, who had autographed his books to Captain Hank Johnson. Hank had been in the military and loved history.

His father had never served, but he'd been a history buff his entire life, writing books in various historical periods and sometimes hard-to-reach locations. His father and grandfather had shared an interest in history, and neither one might have known that.

Once he'd sorted through the books, putting his father's novels aside, he boxed up the rest and put them in his truck. Then he started on the toys. But before he tore the train apart, he let it run around the living room, thinking about how Eleanor had set it up for him, to remind him of perhaps the one and only thing they'd done together. Or maybe it was to remind herself.

When he finally stopped the train, he took it apart and put it in a big box for Leo. He didn't want it to go to a kid he didn't know. But it would make him happy to think of Leo playing with it.

He moved on to photo albums, of which there were at least six. Thinking he might easily get lost in those, he put them in another box along with more letters and more journals, all of which would take time to read. He put that box in the cab of his truck. He'd look at it later.

Small pieces of furniture and knick-knacks to be donated filled up the rest of his truck. He made a quick trip to the donation center to unload and then headed to his apartment, taking Ellie's personal items upstairs. When that was done, he went down to the café. He wasn't sure he was ready to see Chloe or not, but it was a moot point, as she wasn't there.

"Hi, Decker," Marian said. "Can I get you something?"

"I'll take the special to go," he said, eying the board. A prime rib dinner sounded perfect.

Marian put in his order and then came back with a beer. "You look like you could use a drink."

"Thanks. I've been cleaning out Eleanor's house."

"It sounds like that's a big job. Chloe said it's a never-ending pit."

"It feels that way." He sipped his beer, then said, "Have you seen Chloe today?"

"No. She was going to come in, but I guess Joel is finally back."

He was surprised by that piece of information. "Really? I thought Joel was coming home tomorrow."

"Apparently, he got an earlier flight. I got my sister to babysit for Chloe so they could get together."

"Well, that's great." He took another long draught of beer. Joel was back, and Chloe had a babysitter. Sounded like a perfect date night. He needed to be happy about that.

When his meal was ready, he took it upstairs and ate at his kitchen table while he watched a baseball game and tried not to think about Chloe and Joel having their long-awaited reunion.

Two hours later, the game was just ending when he was surprised by a knock at his door. He was even more surprised to find Chloe standing outside.

"Don't close the door in my face," she said, putting up her hand. "I need to talk to you, Decker."

"Okay," he said warily. "Come on in."

"Well, that's a better reception than I got yesterday," she said dryly.

"I'm sorry about that," he said, as she entered the apartment. "I was having a rough day."

"I know," she said, meeting his gaze. "How are you feeling now?"

"Better."

"Good. I have to admit, I wasn't sure if you were still here or if you'd left."

"I was tempted," he admitted. "But I made a commitment to you."

"I told you that you could leave. I don't want to force you to stay. You never anticipated what you were going to learn about your family when you took the job. I won't hold you to your commitment. It wouldn't be right."

"I don't make promises I won't keep. It's something my father taught me a long time ago. I'll finish the job I started."

"I'm relieved to hear that," she said.

"I went by the house today. At first, I didn't think I could stand being in there, but as I thought about what I had learned, about my relationship to Ellie, all of her things took on new meaning. It was weird. I even turned the train on."

Chloe smiled. "That's not weird at all. You discovered that

you and Ellie had a special connection, and you wanted to feel it." She paused. "Do you believe in fate?"

"No. I think we make our fate. But I know why you're asking."

"Because it feels like the universe wanted you to find the house, wanted you to see what Eleanor had saved for you," she said.

"It feels like that," he admitted. "But it's probably just a coincidence."

"That's not as exciting of a story," she said, annoyance in her gaze.

"I know. I brought back some personal items and cleared out most of the living room. I'll keep going until I get to the end." He paused. "I want to apologize for how I treated you last night, Chloe."

"I know why you told me to leave, Decker."

"Do you?" he asked, searching her gaze for the truth.

"Yes," she said, not looking away.

He drew in a sharp breath. "I heard Joel was back, that you were out with him. So, why are you here?" he asked, thinking how spectacularly pretty she looked in a short black dress with her hair falling loosely around her shoulders.

"Joel and I aren't going to see each other anymore."

His pulse leapt. "Why not?"

"Because he's not the one I want, Decker."

"You told me Joel is everything you want. What changed?"

"You came to town," she admitted.

He immediately shook his head as blood raced through his veins. "I don't want to be the one who breaks up you and Joel."

"You didn't break us up, Decker. It hasn't been right between me and Joel for a long time. And, honestly, when I told Joel, he was relieved. We were both telling ourselves a story about what we wanted, what would make us happy. We were looking too far into the future and not seeing what was right in front of us."

"Aren't you someone who needs to look into the future?" he

challenged. "Didn't you say that you couldn't afford to make another mistake?"

"That's how I've been thinking, yes. But it's wrong, and I don't want to do it anymore. I don't want to miss what's right in front of me because I'm worried about tomorrow. Not everything has to last forever."

He could barely process what she was saying, because his brain was focused on only one thing: *Chloe and Joel weren't together anymore.*

Actually, that wasn't the only thing he was thinking about. Chloe's eyes were sparkling gold, her cheeks flushed, her lips so full, so invitingly kissable.

"Decker?" she questioned.

"I just don't want you to have regrets."

She gazed back at him, her heart in her eyes. "Then let's make it too good to regret."

Her words sent him over the edge. He wanted to make it good for her. He wanted to make it mind-bending fantastic. "Are you sure?"

"No more talking," she said, as she put her arms around his neck.

He grabbed her by the hips, pulling her soft, curvy body against his. Then he lowered his head and took the kiss he'd been craving since the last time his mouth had touched hers. His tongue swept into the moist heat of her mouth and felt like he was tasting a little bit of heaven.

There were no barriers between them, and the floodgates had opened. Desire ran through every nerve in his body. He wanted to taste her and touch her and make her as crazy with passion as he was.

Thankfully, Chloe was on the same page, her hands running through his hair, as she uttered a soft moan of pleasure. He backed her up against the wall, taking the kiss to another level, his body hardening against her soft curves. It wasn't enough. He needed to see her. He needed to feel her. He pulled away and ripped his shirt off.

Chloe's eyes widened in appreciation. "Wow," she murmured. "I've been imagining what you looked like under that shirt for a long time now." She licked her lips as he reached for the snap on his jeans. "Don't stop."

He smiled, then stepped out of his jeans and his briefs, loving the way her eyes glittered with need.

"Double wow," she said, moving toward him.

"Not yet. First, we need to get you out of that dress." He spun her around, so he could pull down the zipper of her dress, and his eyes feasted on her beautiful back and her lacy underwear as the dress fell off her body, and she stepped out of it. As she turned around, her breasts spilling over the cups of her bra, he put his hands on her, and she sucked in a quick breath as he took another kiss, his fingers slipping under the edges of her bra.

She gasped as he played with her breasts. He could feel her trembling, or maybe that was him. Lifting his gaze to hers, he smiled and then unhooked the front clasp of her bra. She helped get the bra off and then pulled down her panties.

And when she moved into his embrace, he wrapped his arms around her and then took her to bed. He wanted to go slow, but the fire was too hot, and their needs were too great. Savoring would come later. Next time, he told himself as Chloe urged him on, as they got rid of the last barriers between them. And when they finally came down from the mountain, he hugged her tight, never wanting to let her go.

An hour later, Chloe still didn't want to let Decker go. She wanted to stay just like this, her head on his shoulder, her arm around his waist, her legs entangled with his. Her body was still humming from the passion they'd shared. And she really, really wished she could stay the night. But it was getting late, and she had a babysitter who would need to go home not too long from now.

"You're not leaving," Decker murmured, his lips brushing the top of her head.

She lifted her head to look at his handsome face, his sexy mouth. She drew in a helpless breath of desire. She felt sated, but also eager for more. "I wish I didn't have to leave."

"Me, too. That was...something."

"Something. More than I thought it could be." As a shadow moved through his eyes, she frowned. "Hold on," she said. "No thinking about anything that drives the smile off your face."

"Sorry."

"Are you having regrets?"

"No. I just think... I probably should have talked to Joel before this happened."

"Our breakup was mutual, Decker. If I hadn't done it, Joel would have. He told me he won't be able to stay in Whisper Lake, that he has to move back to New York for his business."

"I believe that the breakup was mutual. But he's my friend, and I should have said something to him."

She respected his loyalty and was sorry that she hadn't given their friendship much thought when she'd come to the apartment. She'd just really wanted to see Decker. And she hadn't wanted to wait another minute. "I'm sorry. Maybe I shouldn't have come tonight. I just had to see you."

"And I wanted to see you, too, Chloe. I loved being with you. It's not a big deal. I just don't like to feel like I'm going behind someone's back."

"I know. That's why you told me to leave last night, and it's why I went. I needed to break up with Joel before this could happen. And I needed to tell him before I told you. It seemed like the right thing to do."

He wrapped his fingers around a strand of her hair. "You are amazing, Chloe."

"We are amazing together," she said.

"How soon do you have to leave?"

She looked at her watch. "Forty-five minutes."

He smiled. "A lot can happen in forty-five minutes."

She grinned. "Why don't you show me what you've got?"

He abruptly flipped her on to her back and she fell against the pillows with a delighted laugh. "I think I like where this is going."

"Oh, you're definitely going to like it."

She closed her eyes and sighed as he made good on his promise.

CHAPTER TWENTY-ONE

CHLOE WAS STILL SMILING on Monday. Not only was it a beautiful and unseasonably warm day, she felt giddy, excited about being with Decker, and she went through most of the day in a happy haze, so much so that Marian gave her more than a few questioning looks, but she didn't address any of them. She didn't want to talk about what happened. She just wanted to remember every second of her time with Decker in intimate detail.

Being with Decker had been hot, sexy, and fun. She had felt completely in sync with him, completely herself. She wasn't pretending. She wasn't trying to be someone she wasn't. And it had been mind-blowing.

Risky, too, a little voice inside her head reminded her. But she didn't want to listen to that voice. She'd been playing it safe for a long time. If she ended up getting burned down the road, she'd deal with it, but right now, she was going to enjoy it.

Decker had texted her last night after she got home, telling her some pretty sweet and hot things, which had made her dreams incredibly good. But his text this morning had been a little more tense. He'd said he was going to knock off work at noon to go on a bike ride with Joel.

She hoped there wouldn't be a problem, that Joel wouldn't

react with anger, that their friendship wouldn't be in peril because of last night, but there was nothing she could do about it, and she couldn't regret being with Decker. She'd called it off with Joel beforehand. She didn't have anything to feel guilty about.

She picked up Leo from school at two and had just given him a snack when Hannah called.

"Hi, Hannah," she said. "What's up?"

"Adam wants to take the boat out this afternoon and then we're going to barbecue on the beach."

"That sounds spontaneous and fun. Leo and I are in."

"Great. We're going to meet at the boat at four."

"That should work."

"You can invite Joel. Is he back in town?"

"He is. He got back yesterday, but I broke up with him last night."

A silence met her words, then Hannah said. "Oh, I'm sorry. Or maybe I'm not. How do you feel about things?"

"I feel relieved and free. It wasn't working. I got stuck in the idea that he was Mr. Right, but he wasn't right, at least not for me."

"How did he take it?"

"Remarkably well. He knew it wasn't working, either. And he's going to be moving back to New York."

"It sounds like it was for the best. If Joel is out of the picture, maybe you want to bring Decker."

"Maybe," she said.

"Interesting. I was expecting you to say no."

"Well, let's just say that I've decided your advice about having fun for now isn't the worst idea. I'll see if Decker can come, but he's with Joel, so I'm not sure what their plans are. If he comes, don't push us together or make a big deal. I don't want it to be awkward. And no one really needs to know anything right now."

"Got it. I won't say a word. I'll see you later, Chloe."

"Later." As she hung up the phone, she texted Decker with the invitation, hoping he would come.

Decker's watch buzzed with Chloe's text as he followed Joel along a lakeside bike path that climbed high into the hills. His legs were burning, and his breath was coming fast. He'd have to answer her text when they stopped.

A few minutes later, Joel pulled over at a vista point.

Decker hopped off his bike, breathing hard as he soaked up the amazing view.

"Was it worth it?" Joel asked, waving his hand toward the deep blue waters of Whisper Lake.

"Absolutely," he said. "Although that last incline was a killer."

Joel leaned his bike against the concrete wall and took off his helmet. Decker did the same. He needed to talk to Joel. When Joel had suggested a bike ride, he'd quickly agreed, happy to postpone the upcoming awkward conversation as long as possible, but it needed to happen, and now was probably the best time.

"I'm going to miss this place," Joel said with a sigh, then turned away from the view to look at him. "I'll wrap things up this week, hand over the reins to my project manager, and then head back to New York." He paused. "I'm sorry to bail on you. You came here to visit me, and now I'm leaving. But if I don't go back, I'll lose the company, everything I've been working so hard to get."

"I understand. You have to do what you have to do."

"I know there are other options. I could work for myself. I could break away from my family's company, but it doesn't make sense to start over when I already have a great company to run."

"You just have to run it from New York."

"Yeah. No idyllic small-town life for me."

"Are you sure that's what you really wanted?" he challenged. "You don't seem that unhappy to be leaving."

"I have mixed feelings. I realized when I got back to New York that I'd been kidding myself. As much as the city and my family make me crazy, they're also invigorating and exciting. So is Sylvie. We talked a lot and realized that we were both being stubborn and unwilling to see the other's point of view. I wanted to feel like I was living my own life, and Sylvie thought I was just running away from who I was. She wasn't completely wrong. I still want to have my own life, but I don't think Whisper Lake is the answer I thought it was."

"I don't, either. But, hey, you can always have a vacation home here."

"I will definitely look into that." He paused. "Chloe broke up with me last night."

"It sounds like you were going to do it if she didn't."

He nodded. "I was relieved she wanted to end things. Chloe is one of the best people I know, and I care about her, but we don't have much in common. And as much as I want kids, I'm not ready to be a father." Joel blew out a breath. "So, that's that."

"It sounds like you made the best decision."

"I hope so."

"There's something I need to tell you, Joel."

Joel gave him a questioning look. "Are we breaking up, too?" he joked. "Because that's exactly the way Chloe started our conversation last night."

"I'm interested in Chloe," he said shortly.

Surprise ran through Joel's eyes. "Oh. I had no idea. But you're not going to be here very long."

"I know that. But I'm here now."

"I can't imagine Chloe being interested in a short-term thing."

"What if she was? Would that bother you?"

Joel thought about that for a moment. "I'd be concerned. I

wouldn't want either of you to get hurt, and that would be a likely outcome. But Chloe and I aren't together anymore, so that's up to you and her. Just be careful, Decker. She has a kid, and I've already seen how much Leo likes you."

"I know the risks."

"Well, I think you have your work cut out for you, because Chloe is looking for a long-term relationship, a forever guy, and you've never wanted to be that. But maybe Whisper Lake will change you."

"You thought it changed you, and it didn't," he pointed out.

"I don't know about that. The six months I've been here have provided some clarity. I know I want more in my life than just work and eventually I'll get out of Manhattan. But I also realize that I like the game, the business, the networking, and the dinners." He shrugged. "Sometimes you have to step away from your life and then you either move farther away, or you go back."

Joel's words felt oddly prophetic. But he wasn't going to step away from his life. He was just going to do what he always did, have fun in the moment. Chloe knew he was leaving. He wasn't leading her on. They were both aware of the risks.

"Let's ride," he said. "I'm stiffening up."

"It's all downhill from here," Joel said. "You'll be fine."

He wondered about that. This ride might be all downhill, but he had a feeling there were still a few mountains to get over when it came to the rest of his life.

"Decker," Leo said excitedly, letting go of Chloe's hand to sprint toward the man walking down the dock Monday afternoon.

Chloe had to fight the urge to do the same thing.

As Decker picked Leo up, she said, "I'm glad you could make it."

"I'm looking forward to it. I haven't seen the lake from a boat since the last time I was here."

"You went out on a boat then?"

"It wasn't as big as this one," he said, his gaze moving past her to Adam's boat. "But I remember going in and out of some really cool coves."

"There are lots of coves around the lake. I think you'll enjoy the sail."

"I already am," he said huskily, his eyes telling her more than his words.

She wanted to tell him she'd missed him. She wanted to kiss him, but her very curious little boy was between them.

"Can we go on the boat now?" Leo asked.

"Let's do that," she said, leading the way.

Once on board, they said hello to her friends. Adam and Molly were there as well as Gianna, Zach and Hailey, and Hannah and Jake.

"Looks like we're all here," Adam said, as he put a lifejacket on Leo.

"No Lizzie or Chelsea?" she asked.

"They'll meet us for the barbecue," Adam replied. "Decker, why don't you come up front? You can help me get off the dock."

"Sure," Decker said, giving her a smile before he followed Adam.

"I want to go up front, too," Leo declared, with Hailey chiming in with the same request.

"I'll take these two," Zach offered. "Okay, Chloe?"

"Of course."

Zach, Jake, and the kids joined Adam and Decker, leaving the women in the back of the boat.

"Looks like Decker is going to get some questions," Hannah said with a sly smile.

"I thought we weren't grilling until the barbecue," she said dryly.

Hannah laughed. "Good one, Chloe. I'm sure Adam just wants to get to know Decker better."

"And let us talk about Decker behind his back," Gianna said with a gleam in her eyes. "So, what's going on? Hannah said you broke up with Joel."

"I hope that wasn't a secret," Hannah cut in.

"It's not a secret, and I did break up with him. As for Decker, he'll only be here for another month, maybe six weeks, so none of you should get too worked up about him."

"It could be an entertaining six weeks," Molly put in, a sparkle in her eyes.

She grinned. "It could be," she said, unable to hide her happiness. There was probably pain coming down the road, but for now, all was good.

"I'm happy for you," Gianna said. "You deserve to have fun."

She shook her head. "I don't think any of you should be happy for me. You should be telling me a fling is a bad idea, that I might get my heart broken again, that I should really only date someone who lives here." As her doubts came out in her words, she saw her friends' expressions change. "Sorry, I was talking to myself more than anyone else."

"All of that could be true," Gianna said slowly.

"But not every relationship has to be forever," Hannah argued.

"You have to go with your gut, Chloe," Molly said. "Follow your heart wherever it leads."

"It already led me over one cliff. I'm not sure I make the best decisions when it comes to men."

"Oh, please," Hannah said. "You were sixteen when you fell in love with Kevin. That was a long time ago."

"Thanks for reminding me how old we are."

"You know what I mean. This is totally different. You're different. You know what you want and, more importantly, what you need. I say, sit back, and enjoy the ride."

"I think I will," she said with a laugh, as the boat picked up speed. Her gaze moved to Decker, who was at the wheel and probably responsible for their speed. He was laughing with the guys and having fun. He really was an easy person to be around. Everyone liked him, and she was going to let herself like him, too, for however long she could.

CHAPTER TWENTY-TWO

"SOMEONE IS TIRED," Decker commented as he walked her and Leo to their car after the barbecue, which had ended around seven.

Leo was dragging his feet. He'd be asleep the second she got him in the car.

"I'm not tired," Leo argued, the grumpy note in his voice making that statement a lie. "Can you come over to the house and play, Decker?"

Decker hesitated. "I better go home, buddy. I have some work to do."

"What kind of work?" Leo asked, rubbing his tired eyes.

"I have some boxes to look through," he said.

"Can't you do that tomorrow?" Leo whined.

"Decker has to go," she told Leo. "Get in the car."

Leo gave her an unhappy look but climbed into his car seat. She fastened the seatbelt, then shut the door.

"Sorry to disappoint him," Decker said. "Do you want me to come over?"

She wanted to say yes, but it had been a long day and she had Leo to deal with. "I'd love to spend time with you, but Leo needs to settle down and have some quiet time before bed, so maybe another night."

"That makes sense."

"Are you really going to look through Eleanor's boxes?" she asked curiously.

"I'll see how I feel when I get back."

"How was your bike ride with Joel?"

"It was challenging. We ended up at Hawk's Point."

"That is a steep trail."

"The view was worth it."

"Did you talk to Joel about us?" she asked.

"I told him I was interested in you. I didn't go into detail beyond that."

"Was he angry?"

"No. He didn't think I had much of a chance with you."

She smiled. "You definitely have a chance."

He grinned. "Good."

She licked her lips. They were dancing a little too close to the future, and she was trying not to think too far ahead. As Leo started tapping the window, she said, "I better get him home."

"Okay." He paused, a bright light his eyes. "I can't kiss you goodnight, can I?"

"No. Leo is watching us. Although, I hug a lot of my friends. That wouldn't look odd."

"I'll take it." He gave her a tight hug, whispering into her ear. "Come by the house tomorrow, so I can kiss you again."

"Tomorrow," she echoed, as a shiver ran down her spine at the promise in his eyes.

All of Chloe's plans for Tuesday and Wednesday were derailed by Marian pulling a muscle in her back, requiring Chloe to spend long days at the restaurant. While she sneaked a few quick kisses with Decker when their paths collided at the café, she couldn't find the time to get over to the house during the day, and Decker was spending time with Joel in the evenings.

But on Thursday, Marian came back to work in the afternoon, so Chloe invited Decker over for dinner. When he showed up a little after six, cleanly shaven and smelling incredibly good, she had to restrain herself from running into his arms. Her little boy showed no such restraint, talking a mile a minute about what they were going to play as soon as Decker lifted him up.

"Slow down," she told Leo with a laugh. "Give Decker a minute."

"It's fine," Decker said. "I'm ready to play."

"How about a drink first?" she asked.

"Maybe later. I think there's a horse calling my name."

"Are you sure?"

He met her gaze. "I'm sure. By the way, something smells really good."

"It's nothing fancy, just chicken tetrazzini, which is basically pasta with chicken and vegetables."

"Perfect. I like pasta."

"Is there a food you don't like?" she asked with a laugh. "So far, you've loved everything I've seen you eat."

"I'm not picky. My dad exposed me to a lot of different foods when we traveled. I grew up eating whatever was being served, like fried caterpillars in South Africa."

"You ate caterpillars?" Leo asked in amazement.

"They were good. Crispy on the outside, like chips."

Chloe gave him a doubtful look. "I don't think they were anything like chips. But if you can handle fried caterpillars, I'm feeling good about my dinner."

"I'm feeling good about everything," he said, a gleam in his eyes. "I missed seeing you this week."

"Me, too."

"I saw Marian in the café. She said she's feeling better."

"Yes. Thank goodness. I really appreciate how much she does when I don't have her."

"Decker," Leo squealed, tugging on Decker's hand. "Let's go."

Chloe smiled as Decker followed Leo to his bedroom. She was lucky to have found a guy who was so willing to play with her kid. For the next half hour, she found herself smiling every other moment, as sounds of laughter came from Leo's bedroom.

When they sat down at the table to eat, it felt like a family dinner, the kind of night she'd envisioned when she'd first gotten pregnant. But she and Kevin had never had a family dinner when Leo was old enough to sit at the table. Kevin had been long gone by then.

Not wanting to think about Kevin, she concentrated on the man across from her. "How's the house coming along? I'm sorry I haven't been able to get over there."

"It's not a problem. I've gotten the house cleaned out. I took anything that looked personal to my apartment, but the rest is now gone, except for a few large pieces of furniture that I'll need some help to move. But I am finally able to concentrate on the renovation. Which reminds me, I need your decision on tile, flooring, and paint."

"I did that earlier today." She waved her hand toward the samples on the side table. "I wrote them down. You can take everything when you leave."

"Good. The choices I gave you were all in stock, so I should be able to pick up materials soon."

"Mommy, can I be done eating?" Leo interrupted.

"Do you want to have dessert?" she asked.

Leo nodded.

"Then eat all of your fruit and two more bites of pasta."

"What's for dessert?" Decker asked.

"Ice cream sundaes. Do you love those, too?" she teased.

"I do, but there are other desserts I also like."

She shook her head at the wicked look in his eyes.

"Mommy, I'm done," Leo declared, drawing her attention back to him.

She looked at his plate. The fruit was gone, and he'd eaten a little more pasta. "Okay, take your plate to the kitchen and then you can play for a few minutes while we finish eating."

As soon as Leo vanished down the hall, Decker leaned across the table to kiss her. It was so sweet and far too short. He gave her a smile. "I'd like to have you for dessert."

"You have to be careful," she said with a warning smile. "Leo is always listening and then he repeats things to whoever will listen."

He cocked his head to the right as he gave her a speculative look. "Are you trying to hide what's going on with us? Because your friends seem to be on board. Even Hannah, who frankly scares me a little."

"She scares a lot of people. I'm not trying to hide anything. I just need to be careful where Leo is concerned. I don't want to confuse him. Right now, he thinks you're a great friend of ours, and that seems like a good place for us to be."

She knew she was taking a risk getting involved with Decker. She could get hurt. So could Leo. But not getting involved with him would also hurt. So, she was going to stay on this ride for a while longer.

"Chloe?" Decker said, bringing her gaze back to his. "Where did you go?"

"I was just thinking. I should get the ice cream out." She got to her feet and moved to the freezer. "I have chocolate and vanilla. You can pick one or have both."

As she set the cartons on the counter, Decker was right in front of her, giving her a serious look.

"You need to tell me what you were thinking about Chloe, because a dark cloud came into your eyes."

"It was nothing. Let's just make sundaes and enjoy the evening. I really like spending time with you, and we haven't had much of that this week."

"I feel the same."

"Good. So vanilla or chocolate?"

"Both."

She handed him the ice cream scooper. "You scoop. I'll heat up the fudge."

An hour later, after sundaes, two imaginary games that Leo created for all of them to play, and a couple of bedtime stories, Chloe put Leo to bed and returned to the living room. She was surprised to find Decker sprawled on the couch, his eyes closed.

She smiled to herself as she just let herself look at him, remembering the feel of his hands on her skin, the taste of his mouth, the way his body had moved in hers. Shivers ran down her spine at the memories. It had all just flowed between them. They'd been in sync, able to sense what the other person needed. It hadn't been too serious, either. There had been a lot of light moments, a lot of laughing along with everything else.

She sat down next to him on the couch, and he stirred, his beautiful green eyes suddenly looking back at her.

He straightened. "Did I fall asleep?"

"You did. Maybe you should go home. You're clearly tired."

"I don't want to go home. But I wouldn't mind going to bed."

She licked her lips as his gaze darkened. "I wouldn't mind that, either, but you can't stay all night. You can't be here in the morning."

"We have a lot of time before the morning." He took her hand and gave it a squeeze. "I don't want you to be uncomfortable. This is your house, Leo's house, and if it doesn't feel right—"

She cut him off by putting her fingers against his lips. "It feels incredibly right," she whispered, removing her fingers to press her mouth against his.

When their kiss ended, she rose, taking his hand and leading him into her bedroom. She closed the door and drew in a breath, suddenly feeling nervous. She'd never slept with anyone else in this room but Kevin. The brief relationships she'd had since her divorce had happened elsewhere.

But since the divorce, she'd made the room her own. There was no sign of Kevin or their past life in any of the décor or the bedding. She'd even bought a new bed. But bringing Decker in here made her feel like she was really moving on.

"Chloe? You're thinking again," Decker said. "If you don't want this..."

"I do. I really do."

"Are you sure?"

Looking into his gaze, she felt more certain of what she wanted than she had in years. "So sure," she said. "I want you, Decker."

"And what do you want to do with me?" he teased, the seriousness vanishing from his eyes.

"Many things." She tugged on the bottom of his shirt. "Let's get this off for a start." She helped him pull the shirt over his head and then tossed it on the bed, taking another minute to revel in the absolute magnificence of his bare chest that was toned with fine dark hairs running across his skin. She put her hands on his chest, the warmth of his skin instantly heating her up.

As desire ran through her, she needed to get closer. She wanted nothing between them. She wanted to feel every inch of his body and for him to feel every inch of hers. Their gazes met. They smiled at the same time, then laughed together, and stripped off their clothes, because they didn't need words. They knew exactly what each other wanted.

CHAPTER TWENTY-THREE

DECKER LEFT A SLEEPING Chloe shortly before five on Friday morning, tiptoeing out of the house as quietly as he could. It felt strange to sneak out of a woman's house before daylight. It reminded him of sneaking out of his high school girlfriend's house before her dad got up. This situation was the same and yet completely different. Dating a woman with a child was an unfamiliar experience. He'd never really considered it before. He hadn't shied away from it. He just hadn't met anyone with a child that he'd wanted to date.

Chloe was different. She was special: beautiful, sweet, funny, down-to-earth, and quick-witted. She had a lot of baggage, but she was the only one carrying it, and that she rarely asked for help only made him want to help her more. But they were heading to a crossroads. She knew it, and so did he. He just didn't know what to do about it. But there was no decision to make now, so he wasn't going to make one.

When he got to his apartment, he fell back into bed, needing more sleep. It was half-past eight when he awoke; the sun streaming through his windows. He took a shower, dressed, and then headed down to the café to grab breakfast. There was no sign of Chloe, which was disappointing. He'd gotten used to seeing her in the mornings after she dropped Leo at school, but maybe he wasn't the only one who'd needed more sleep. He grabbed a breakfast sandwich and coffee to go and then headed to the job site.

He'd barely gotten out of his truck when two more trucks pulled up on either side of him, all with the same company logo. Joel hopped out of the first one.

"I have good news," Joel said.

"What's that?"

"I brought you some help." Joel tipped his head to the two guys walking toward the house. "Eddie and Lamar—this is Decker."

He nodded at the guys.

"They're here to do whatever you want for the next week," Joel continued. "It's on my dime. But I'll need them back at the development next Friday."

"Seriously?" he asked with surprise. "Why would you want to pay for their time?"

"I feel bad for abandoning you, and it's for Chloe, too. I didn't try that hard to help her with this project, and I should have." He paused. "Where do you want the guys?"

He turned to Eddie and Lamar. "There's a lot to do. What I need done first is to get the house cleared out. You can start by taking all the furniture out of the upstairs bedrooms and bringing it down here. Load up my truck and yours, and we'll take it from there."

As the guys went into the house to get started, he turned back to Joel. "This is very generous."

"You said you needed extra hands."

"And I said I was going to hire day laborers."

"These guys can do anything you need. They're both highly skilled—drywall, carpentry, electrical, plumbing—they can do it all. And they are being well compensated for their time. Oh, and I have the name of a tile guy for you," Joel added, pulling a business card out of his pocket. "I just talked to him, and he said he's actually waiting for a tile delivery, so if you can use him next week, he can do something for you."

He took the card. "This is great, Joel, but I can pay for these guys. I built labor costs into the bid."

"Not for this kind of labor," Joel said with a knowing smile. "Let me do this for Chloe. I realize now I wasn't being honest with her because I was lying to myself. I had this vision in my head that seemed so peaceful and perfect, completely different from the chaos of my life. But the truth is, I thrive on work. I love to make deals. Sometimes work can consume me, and I know I need to find a balance, a middle ground. But I also want to take my father's company and make it better than it ever was."

He nodded. "That makes sense to me. You're good at your job. And I'm sure you'll either find balance or stop looking for it."

Joel smiled. "That might be true."

"I also know you will find a way to make New York City your city. As for the help, I'm appreciative, and I'm sure Chloe will be, too."

"Hopefully, this will also allow you to get the job done more quickly and then you can get back to your life. Santa Barbara next, right?"

"Right," he said, not feeling in a hurry to leave Whisper Lake before he had to.

Joel gave him a speculative look. "What's happening with you and Chloe?"

"Just getting to know each other," he replied, not wanting to talk to Joel about Chloe. "We're both busy."

"I was a little too okay with her being busy. And she was a little too happy to go slow. I think we both probably realized our relationship wasn't what we wanted it to be but hoped we could get there eventually."

"Are you trying to tell me something?" he asked, seeing the gleam in Joel's eyes.

"I don't want you or Chloe to get hurt. And, frankly, I don't see how you end up together, Decker. You don't stay anywhere for long. You're always eager to get to the next thing, just like your dad. Chloe will never leave Whisper Lake. Her roots go deep. She has all her friends to support her and Leo. I can't see her making a move."

Nothing Joel said was wrong or something he hadn't already considered. But not seeing Chloe anymore didn't feel like an option. "We'll just have to see how things go," he said vaguely. "When are you heading back to New York?"

"Not sure. A few days. Want to have dinner tonight?"

"You're on."

"Just so you know, I'm not rooting against you and Chloe. But I think one of you will have to make a big change. If you don't see that being you, then maybe you should think about what you're doing, Decker."

"That's good advice."

Joel laughed. "Yeah, and you're not going to take it."

"I'll think about it."

Twenty-four hours without seeing Decker had made her even more excited about her date on Saturday night.

The day before Decker had been tied up with the house and then had dinner with Joel, so she hadn't seen him since he'd given her a sleepy kiss before sneaking out of her house on Friday morning. That seemed like a long time ago. Besides feeling excited, she was also nervous. It felt different to go on an actual date with Decker. To put on makeup as well as a sexy dress and heels. It felt like a different kind of evening than just inviting him over for dinner with Leo.

Since she didn't want to disappoint Leo by going out with Decker without him, she told him she was going out with friends and then headed across town to meet Decker at her favorite Indian restaurant, which was just down the street from her café.

He was waiting for her outside the restaurant, looking like he'd put a little more effort into the night as well, wearing black slacks and a charcoal gray sweater, his hair neatly styled. Of course, that only made her want to run her fingers through his hair and mess it up. He greeted her with a long, passionate kiss.

"I missed you," he said.

"You're making me want to skip dinner."

"I had the same thought."

She shook her head. "One of us needs to be rational."

"What would be the fun in that?" he said with a laugh. "But you look beautiful tonight, so we should go inside and have a real date."

"I was thinking it feels like our first date," she admitted as they entered the restaurant. "You look nice, too. Not a trace of dirt on you."

"You should have seen me earlier. I spent a lot of today under the house, working on the plumbing."

"That doesn't sound fun."

"It was successful, so that's what matters." He paused, as she gave her name to the hostess. Then they were led to a table against the wall with a good view of the open-air kitchen but far enough away to be quiet enough to talk. "It smells spicy in here," he said as they sat down.

"The food is incredible."

"I'm looking forward to it."

"Let me guess, you love Indian food," she teased as they opened their menus.

"I do. We spent a month in India one summer. We traveled by train all over the country. It was quite an experience. The people are wonderful. The food is out of this world. And the poverty can be overwhelming."

"That's sad."

"It is, but India is a country everyone should see, especially if you like yoga. My father and I took several classes with a yoga master. It was probably as much meditation as it was posing, and we had to do it in utter silence."

"Did you enjoy that?"

"It was hard to stay that focused for that long, but I think it was good for me. Even now, some principles I learned there come back to me."

"Like what?"

"Remembering to take a deep breath. To stretch the body. When you relax the body, you relax the mind, and problems are solved."

"I didn't realize it was that easy to solve problems."

He grinned. "Some problems, not all. Basically, it's just about slowing down, being in the moment, because in that moment, most things are good."

She nodded. "This moment is good."

He met her gaze. "I think so, too. Now, let's order, because I'm starving."

Over a delicious dinner of spicy chicken curry, red lentil dal, a flatbread called Roti, and a couple of glasses of wine, they talked about everything under the sun. Besides their unbelievable physical chemistry, they also got along very well.

She could talk to Decker about anything. No topic seemed off limits. Although they were both skating around any discussion of the future, but that was fine with her. Staying in the present was okay for now, and maybe the past was even better.

"You haven't said much about previous relationships," she said, as they finished their meal. "Have you ever been in love, Decker?"

"I'm not sure I'd say love, but I've had feelings for a few women."

"What happened? Why did those relationships end?"

"Most of them just ran their course. Or they ended because one of us had to move on."

"Were you the one who moved on?"

"Not always me, but sometimes," he admitted.

"You said you've been in LA for the past several years. Is there someone there you're seeing?"

"If there was, I wouldn't be seeing you," he said pointedly. "If I'm with someone, I'm with them."

"Until you're not," she said, unable to keep the disappointed note out of her voice.

"Not very many relationships last forever," he said. "You know that better than anyone."

"I do," she admitted. "What about friends? Who do you hang out with in LA?"

"I have a couple of guys from college who live near me. We bike, play softball, volleyball on the beach, that kind of thing. I work a lot. When I'm not working, I'm usually travelling. Last year, I went to Costa Rica and New Zealand."

"Did you go by yourself?"

"Yes. I'm very comfortable on my own. And I usually make friends along the way."

She had a feeling he made a lot of friends along the way. Was she just another *friend*?

She already regretted starting this conversation. She needed to get out of it. "So, have you gone through any more of the boxes you brought home from the house?"

"Still need to do that. I just haven't found the energy."

"Maybe it's not about energy but about nerve."

"Could be," he acknowledged with a nod. "I'm still wrapping my head around the fact that Eleanor's husband Hank was my biological grandfather, and he didn't want anything to do with me."

She frowned at the hard note in his voice. "That was his loss."

"Many people were willing to take that loss—like every single one of my grandparents. Was I some sort of devil spawn because my teenaged parents had sex in high school and accidentally got pregnant? Because that's the way people acted."

"They were stupid. All of them. And I understand why your

dad just took you away from all of it. He didn't want their coldness to touch you. He was protecting you."

"I want to believe that was the only reason, but since all these other secrets have come out, I've lost some of my unconditional trust in what my father told me about the past, about the family. Maybe there was a reason everyone washed their hands of him, turned their backs. Maybe he was a screwup. He definitely wanted to live life on his own terms."

She thought about that. "Well, you knew him better than anyone else. I think you have to trust your gut."

"I just wish he'd told me about Hank and Ellie. It didn't have to be when I was six, but it could have been later. I should have known. He should have given me a chance to decide if I wanted to know them."

"He must have been afraid."

"That they would take me away?"

"That and also that you might want to go with them. I don't think he could risk losing you. You were all he had. I kind of understand that feeling."

"You're not keeping Leo from anyone. You have pictures of his hero father in his bedroom, even though the guy is never there for his son. You're still trying to encourage that relationship."

"For Leo, not for Kevin. I want to be clear about that. Leo has a father, and I want him to know who he is, and I want him to love him, to have a relationship with him. I also want Leo to know Kevin's parents. They're his grandparents, and they love him. And that's important."

"How did they take the divorce?" he asked curiously.

"They were angry with Kevin. It was a little surprising because they were so proud of him. But they knew Kevin was letting me and Leo down. I've known them since I was sixteen, so I'm like a daughter to them. I run their business for them. They love me and they love their son. They didn't want to be in the middle, and Kevin and I have both tried not to put them there."

"That's good."

"It is good. Kevin isn't around the way he should be, but he's not a bad guy. I think you would actually like him. He's a man's man. And he's fiercely loyal to his team, his patriotism, and his desire to make the world a better place. That's what I want Leo to see. And I hope that down the road Kevin will be able to spend more time with his son." She paused. "But getting back to Leo's grandparents—I don't think a kid can have too much love. So I want everyone who wants to be in his life to be there."

He nodded. "My father should have seen that Ellie had some love to give. But he made sure I only had his. Was that selfish? Was he protecting me from the harsh reality that none of my family wanted to know me? Or is there more to the story I don't know."

"Maybe it's all that." She paused. "I don't know if there's anything else you'll be able to learn from Ellie's things, but isn't it time to put that question to rest? Let's get the check, go back to your apartment and look through the boxes together."

He frowned. "I had a few other things in mind for what we could do at my apartment."

She smiled. "I'm sure I would like those ideas, too, but you've been avoiding the elephant in the room too long, Decker. One thing I've learned from Leo is the only way to make sure there aren't any monsters is to look under the bed."

"What would you do if you found one?"

"Thankfully, I haven't had to find out."

"Well, let's hope we don't have to find out tonight."

CHAPTER TWENTY-FOUR

THEY HADN'T FOUND any monsters, but they had found a journal in the first box Decker had picked up. It was a journal written by Ellie during his first trip to Whisper Lake. It took only a few lines to confirm that. He didn't want to keep reading, but he also couldn't look away. Chloe peered over his shoulder, reading along with him…

Ryan and Decker arrived this morning. Ryan was eager to see Hank, but I told him it might be better to wait a few days. Hank has been battling with a cold and is even grumpier than usual. At least, that's what I told Ryan. The truth is that I want a chance to get to know Ryan and little Decker better before Ryan talks to his father, before this trip blows up in our faces. I also need time to get Hank off this crazy plan he has brewing in his head.

Ever since Kelly died, Hank has been thinking about Ryan trying to raise a kid on his own. He doesn't think Ryan can do it, and when Ryan wrote and asked him for money, Hank became even more convinced of that fact. Last week, Hank told me he wants to take custody of Decker.

I was shocked to hear him say that. Decker is six, and we're in our late sixties. How are we going to raise a six-year-old? And why would

Hank want to step in with Decker when he was perfectly content to let Ryan grow up without him?

Maybe Hank's guilt is catching up with him. He knows he didn't treat Ryan right. Now he wants to make up for it, but in the worst possible way. I need him to see that Decker is thriving with Ryan, that Ryan just needs a little help to keep his family going.

I'm also hoping that Ryan will fall in love with Whisper Lake. I think the best solution would be for Ryan and Decker to live here. Then we can all be together but also have our own lives.

I need to make that happen. I feel so guilty about Ryan and Hank not having a relationship. I know Hank didn't tell me about Ryan because we were having trouble conceiving our own child. He couldn't bear to say that he had a son with someone else. And when I found out, I didn't encourage Hank to spend time with his son. I didn't want him anywhere near Catherine, the woman who had come between us. But that wasn't fair to Ryan. It took me a long time to see that.

Decker sucked in a breath as he got to the end of the page. He met Chloe's gaze.

"Do you want to keep going?" she asked.

"I don't think I can stop now." He turned the page.

It's been six weeks since Ryan and Decker arrived, and two weeks since they left. I thought maybe things would change so I couldn't bring myself to write about any of it before now. But I've become resigned to a terrible truth that I may never see them again.

The trip was a disaster. I wanted to make things better. I wanted to heal the family, but I made everything worse.

The beginning of the visit was great. I got to spend time with Ryan and Decker. We went to the beach and played games in the cabin, but my favorite outing was when I took Decker on the train. His eyes lit up with delight. It reminded me of the time that Ryan had brought his pregnant girlfriend, Kelly, to meet us. They'd ridden the train a half-dozen times because she loved it so much.

Ryan didn't go with me and Decker on the train. I think it made him sad, reminding him of Kelly.

After that day, everything went downhill. I had to tell Hank that

Ryan was in town. Hank was livid that I'd invited Ryan and Decker to visit. I said he needed to talk to Ryan, that Ryan is his son, but there is so much anger between them. And the sad thing is that Hank is angrier with himself for being a terrible father than he is with Ryan. He just can't admit that. But he knows he let Ryan down, that his son grew up without a father, that whatever trouble Ryan got himself into was probably because he didn't have a father figure in his life. If Hank acknowledged that, he'd have to admit that Ryan's shortcomings are his fault.

I don't think Ryan is a stupid kid. He just made a mistake—a big one, yes. But he tried to do right by his girlfriend, by his child.

And now poor Ryan has suffered the loss of Kelly and another rejection from his biological father. He's in so much pain it almost hurts to look at him. I can see it roll off him in big waves. I want to help. I've sent him money before, but when he left this time, he said he didn't want anything more from me. I'm going to keep trying to reach him. I don't want Ryan and Decker to be alone in the world. I just hope someday Ryan will come back.

Hank decided against pursuing custody, which is the only good thing that came out of Ryan's visit. He said he doesn't want to talk anymore about Ryan or Decker. He's in pain, too. But his is self-inflicted. And sometimes I wonder how I can love a man and hate him at the same time.

Ryan and Decker are our family. I love them, even though I don't share their blood. I pray that one day they'll know that.

Eleanor's words were breaking his heart. He drew in a deep breath as he looked up from the journal.

"Eleanor really loved you," Chloe said.

"It seems so. I remember the night we left. We were at her house, I think. My dad was screaming at an older man. I didn't know what they were talking about, but it scared me. Ellie was playing with me in another room. She kept telling me everything was okay. They just had a disagreement. Then my dad came in, grabbed my hand, and pulled me from the house. He put me in the car and told me to look at the setting sun on the horizon. He said that's where we were going. We would have an amazing adventure and I didn't need to look back, because everything important was in front of us." He felt a knot come into his throat. "He did his best to give me that adventure."

Chloe dabbed at her eyes. "He sounds like a wonderful father, and he loved you, Decker. So did Ellie. Is there anything else in the journal?"

He turned the page. "The date from the next entry is four years later."

It's been a while since I've written. I wish I had something good to write about. The last several years have been incredibly difficult.

I've never heard from Ryan, not since he left four years ago. I can't believe that Decker is ten now. I've written them both many letters, but they always come back. I've been buying Decker toys every year on his birthday and on Christmas. I even bought an incredible train set. I can only imagine how much he would love it. I hope one day I can give him his presents, before he's too old to enjoy them. But I don't know where in the world Ryan and Decker are. I wish I did. Because I'm all alone now.

Shortly after Ryan and Decker left Whisper Lake, Hank was diagnosed with cancer. Sometimes, I wonder if the cancer wasn't the result of all that anger and stress. After a hard battle, Hank passed away last month. I've gone through so many emotions since he died. I loved him so very much, but he betrayed me, and his rigid ideas sometimes made me sick to my stomach. He was such a complicated man. I think the affair really destroyed us, even though he tried to make up for it, and I tried to forgive him. But it was never really the same after that. And instead of Hank becoming a more forgiving person, because of his own experience, he became a self-proclaimed monitor of right and wrong, creating an impossible standard against which he measured his son.

I should have stepped in earlier. I was a coward, afraid to lose what little I had left of my marriage, selfishly and secretly hating that Hank was able to have a child while I could not.

But Ryan could have filled the empty spaces in my heart if I'd let him, if I'd figured out sooner that love isn't about bloodlines; it's just about love.

Now Hank is gone, and it's just me. I'd like to reconnect with Ryan and Decker. I guess I'll see if the universe brings us back together. In the meantime, I'll keep writing letters, but I don't send them anymore, because they always come back; I just keep them in my drawer. I'll keep tucking things away that remind me of them, and pick up treats for Decker, even if it's only so I can imagine him enjoying them.

My biggest regret in life is that those two boys can't feel my love. I know they need love, because so many other people turned away from them. One day, I hope they'll be able to feel it. Ryan is a great father. I see him with Decker, and Ryan puts his whole heart into their relationship. He is not following in his father's footsteps. He is forging his own path, and he is not afraid to love his little boy unconditionally. Decker will be fine with Ryan. He'll be better than fine. He'll be happy. This is what gives me the most comfort.

Decker turned the page and the next. Everything else was blank. "She didn't write anything else."

"She said it all. She told us why she couldn't throw anything away. She wanted you to see her life, feel her love, and the universe sent you back here." A sparkling light filled Chloe's eyes. "Fate."

"The universe didn't have good timing. She was already dead."

His words killed the wonder in her eyes. "That's true."

"It's too late for her to know me," he murmured.

"But not too late for you to know her, through her journal and the train and her letters. There must be letters we haven't seen yet."

"It sounded that way." He flipped the page back to her final words, reading them once more. "My dad did love me unconditionally, and I was happy. He never let on how much pain he was in, and there had to have been pain. His mother had kept secrets from him. The father he thought was his father had walked away when he found out he wasn't. And then Hank was the cherry on top of terrible parents. It's what Ellie said. Everyone turned away from my dad when he needed them the most. He was seventeen years old when all this happened. He was just a kid."

"He had to grow up really fast," Chloe agreed. "But he made sure that his son would never experience what he went through. I know you felt anger toward him because he didn't tell you about his past, but he was trying to protect you."

Decker nodded in agreement. "He didn't want me to love any of them. He knew the kind of people his parents and in-laws were. He chose to keep me away from them. He wanted to protect me from the sting of rejection, which he felt sure would come my way." He paused. "Ellie was collateral damage, although not completely innocent, according to her own words."

"That's true. But she was also in pain. Love is complicated."

"Only because people make it that way. They hang on when every instinct they have tells them to let go."

"Fear of being alone is powerful."

"Yes." He drew in a breath and let it out. "But Ellie seemed to find some peace."

"She knew in her heart that you and your dad were okay. Should we keep looking for the letters?"

He shook his head. "Not tonight."

She gave him a compassionate smile. "I understand. There's a lot to think about. It will take time to process." She glanced at her watch. "I wish I could stay longer, but I have to relieve the babysitter in half an hour."

"That's okay."

She slid closer to him, wrapping her arms around his neck. "I also wish I had time to take the unhappy light out of your eyes."

He smiled. "You are really good at doing that. But you need to go." He gave her a kiss, then pulled her to her feet.

"That kiss was kind of quick," she complained.

"If it went any longer, I wouldn't be able to let you leave."

"I like that answer. When can I see you again? Is tomorrow too soon?"

"It wouldn't be, but I found a tile guy, and he can get started on Monday if I get the tile and one bathroom prepped before then. He only has this week to give me for work, so I have to take him when I can get him. The good news is that the bathrooms will be done in a week. But you may not see much of me for a few days."

"So good news and bad news," she murmured. "I appreciate how hard you're working. Just don't work too fast."

Her words were loaded with meaning, and she looked like she wanted to take them back as soon as she'd said them. His chest tightened. He knew that conversation was coming, but he couldn't have it now.

"I better go," she said, moving to the door.

"I'll walk you to your car." He didn't want to say goodnight, which made him worry that if saying goodnight felt this bad, how was saying goodbye going to feel? Fortunately, he didn't have to do that yet.

CHAPTER TWENTY-FIVE

DECKER TALKED to Chloe off and on by text for the next four days, his days packed with construction work that had to be done while he had the manpower. But when she invited him over to dinner on Thursday, he was thrilled to finally see her again.

When he arrived at her house, she came out the door before he could ring the bell, putting her arms around him and kissing him with a pent-up need that shook him to the core with how much he wanted her.

"Damn! You pack a punch, you know that?" he asked, when they finally came up for air.

"So do you. I've been thinking about that for four days."

"I've been thinking about doing more than that for four days," he returned.

"Me, too. But all that will have to wait until later." She grabbed his hand and pulled him into the house.

Stepping inside, he felt like he was coming home, especially when Leo ran down the hall to greet him with a big hug. These two people were fast becoming very important to him. He'd never really felt like he had a home. They'd stayed so many places that no house had ever felt more than temporary. But this was what a real home felt like. It was warm and filled with love and laughter and life. It also smelled good. He sniffed. "Are we having cake for dinner?"

"No," Chloe said with a laugh. "But you have a good nose. Leo and I are making cupcakes for his school tomorrow. The kids are putting on a talent show. It will be very cute."

"That sounds fun. Are you going to sing or dance, Leo?"

"I'm going to dance," Leo said, jumping up and down in a very unrhythmic way.

"He takes after his mother," Chloe said with a wry smile. "Anyway, we just put the cupcakes in the oven. We'll frost and decorate them after dinner."

"If you need someone to test them out, I'm in."

"Somehow I thought you would be."

"But first we have to eat our dinner," Leo proclaimed. "No cupcakes unless we eat all our food."

He laughed at the boy's seriousness. "I'm hungry, so that shouldn't be a problem."

"I'm hungry, too," Leo said. "When are we eating?"

"Dinner is almost ready," Chloe said. "I made chicken enchiladas for us, and chicken fingers for Leo. How about a margarita? I made a batch to go with my enchilada theme."

"I would love one." He followed Chloe into the kitchen as she poured him a drink. She looked so pretty in a light blue floral dress that showed off her gorgeous legs. His body hardened as he thought about those legs wrapped around him.

Chloe's eyes darkened as she put a drink in his hand. "You look like you need to cool off."

He looked around to see where Leo was, happy to see he'd moved into the living room to play with his trucks. "After that kiss you gave me, that won't be easy to do."

She sucked in a breath. "I don't know what it is about you that makes me feel so…"

"Hot?" he asked when she couldn't seem to find a word.

A smile lifted her lips. "Yes."

"Well, I know exactly what it is about you."

She shook her head, sending him a warning look. "Someone has big ears."

"Do you want me to whisper in your ear?"

"I want you to tell me about your day instead. How is the job going?"

"Coward," he teased.

"Are you on budget and on time?" she asked, ignoring his comment.

"Yes. Not just on time. I'll be done early," he said, as he sipped his margarita. "The tile guy is amazing. He's good and fast. He'll be done by tomorrow night with the bathrooms. The kitchen was painted today, and it looks good. The cabinets really just needed to be cleaned up, and the countertops are fine."

"That's amazing. The realtor was asking me today when we might be ready to do photos for the listing."

"End of next week should work."

"That soon?" she asked in surprise. "I thought we had two or three more weeks."

"The extra labor made everything go faster." He paused, seeing an odd look in her eyes. "Usually, customers are happy when I give them this news."

"I am happy. Of course, I am. My parents are eager to put the house up for sale," she said, before taking a long swig of the margarita she'd poured for herself.

"Well, good," he said. Even though he didn't feel all that good about it, either. Not that he had to leave town when the house was done. He'd planned to be here a few more weeks. He could still do that.

Chloe's doorbell rang, breaking the sudden tension between them. She put down her glass and went to open the door. He followed her into the living room, hearing someone's agitated voice. An older man was on the porch, and he was very upset.

"Slow down, Mr. Pearson," Chloe said. "What's wrong?"

"Denise is crying, and she won't talk to me. Says she needs a woman to help her. And the caregiver can't come for an hour.

She's in the bathroom with the door locked. I don't know what to do. Could you come and talk to her?"

"Of course, I'll come." She turned back to him. "The cupcakes need to come out of the oven in like seven minutes. Could you get them when the buzzer goes off?"

"Sure."

"Hopefully, I won't be too long." She hesitated. "I can take Leo with me."

"Don't be ridiculous. He's fine here. Go."

"Thanks." She grabbed her coat off a nearby hook and went out the door.

"Where's Mommy going?" Leo asked.

"To see your neighbor." He squatted down next to him. "What are you playing?"

"Trucks? Do you want to play?"

"Absolutely," he said, sitting down on the floor. As Leo explained the game to him, which in typical Leo fashion had all kinds of rules and twists and turns, he marveled at the kid's imagination. Leo could build an entire world in his head, which reminded him of his dad, who always had a story going on.

They'd barely started playing when the buzzer went off. He jumped up to check on the cupcakes. They looked okay to him, but he wasn't sure how to tell if they were done. He looked at Leo, who was peering into the lower oven along with him.

"What do you think?" he asked.

"Mommy puts a stick in them."

"A stick, huh?" He opened a few cupboards and found a box of toothpicks. That should work. He opened the oven and stuck one in the middle of the cake, and it came out clean.

"That means it's good," Leo said.

"I'm glad you're here." He pulled the cupcakes out of the oven and set them on top of the stove.

"They have to get cold before we can put frosting on them," Leo said, dispensing more valuable information.

"Got it. Your mom should be back by then." He paused as his

phone buzzed with a text from Chloe. She was probably going to be another half-hour. She needed to wait with Denise until the caregiver arrived. She wanted to know if he could feed Leo. She had half his plate made up, and he just needed to grab the chicken nuggets from the top oven for Leo. He could pull out the enchiladas, too, and eat without her. He could see the stress in her words, so he immediately texted back that he would take care of everything and not to worry. Then he got to work on dinner.

Within minutes, he had Leo's food ready to go. He took the enchiladas out of the oven as well and covered them with foil. The toppings were in bowls on the counter, so he put them back in the refrigerator to stay cold. Then he sat down with Leo while he ate his dinner.

Leo kept the conversation going with little help from him, talking about anything and everything, moving from one topic to the next without much of a segue, but he was mostly able to keep up with him.

"Are you Mommy's boyfriend?" Leo asked suddenly.

"Uh," he was surprised by the question. "Why would you ask that?"

"Joey told me that his mommy said you were my mommy's boyfriend."

He had no idea who Joey or his mom was. He also wasn't sure how to answer the question.

"So, are you?" Leo asked.

"You should finish eating."

"If you're my mom's boyfriend, then can you live with us?"

"You know what? I think it's time to frost the cupcakes. Why don't you eat those last few bites, and we can do that?"

"We have to decorate them with sprinkles, too," Leo said, as he popped another chicken nugget into his mouth. "Mommy got pink, orange, and blue."

"Got it. I should probably look for the sprinkles." He got to his feet, if for no other reason than to shut down the interrogation. He hadn't been grilled by a four-year-old before, and Leo's questions had been unsettling. They made him realize that gossip was going around town and was getting to Leo. Chloe wouldn't like that, and he wasn't sure how he felt about it, either.

Thankfully, Leo was distracted by the frosting, however, when Leo smashed icing all over the first cupcake, Decker realized that his four-year-old assistant wasn't going to get the job done. "Hang on," he said. "Let's make that cupcake your cupcake. You can eat it while I frost the others, and then you can do the sprinkles."

"Okay," Leo said happily.

He moved the remaining cupcakes out of Leo's reach and then picked one up to frost. He couldn't remember ever frosting cupcakes. One problem with growing up with his dad and living on the road for so much of the time was that they ate out a lot. While his dad cooked enough to keep them alive, they had never ever baked together. Hopefully, he wouldn't do worse than Leo.

A half-hour later, he wasn't sure that was true. His icing was messy, and with Leo's heavy-handed dash of sprinkles, the frosting was lopsided and appeared very sugary. He might need to run to a bakery in the morning and buy some cupcakes for Chloe to take to school.

With the cupcakes done, he played a few more games with Leo. Chloe sent him another text that she was very sorry, but she would be a while longer. He hoped everything was okay with her neighbor.

As bedtime neared, he got Leo into his pajamas and awkwardly helped him brush his teeth, figuring that one bad night of brushing probably wasn't the end of the world. He'd be losing those baby teeth, anyway. Then they read books in Leo's bed and after the third story, Leo was getting very drowsy.

"Time to sleep," he said.

"Will you tuck me in?" Leo asked.

He got up, set the book aside, and tucked the Spiderman comforter closely around Leo's small body.

"Can you come to my show tomorrow?" Leo asked. "I want you to see me dance."

He had an incredibly packed day tomorrow, but it was hard to dash the hope in Leo's eyes. "I'll try, but I might have to work."

"My dad always has to work," Leo said, looking suddenly sad. "But it's okay, because he's a hero. Are you a hero, Decker?"

"Nope, but I still have to work. I'll try to come, but I can't promise."

"Decker?"

"Yes?" he asked warily, not liking the look in Leo's eyes.

"I think you should be my mom's boyfriend. Then you could live here with us. We could play all the time."

"That would be fun." His heart twisted at the hope and love in Leo's eyes. "Goodnight, Leo."

He turned on the nightlight, then flipped off the overhead light. As he reached the door, he took one last look at Leo. The kid was already asleep, his arms wrapped around a stuffed horse. He smiled to himself, then left.

As he entered the living room, the front door opened, and Chloe came in, looking stressed.

"I'm so sorry," she said. "The caregiver was tied up with another patient, and I couldn't leave Denise. She had some female issues, and she's very private, and she didn't want her husband to help her."

He held up a hand. "You don't need to apologize. Someone needed help, and you were there." He suddenly realized how often Chloe probably did that. Whisper Lake was a tight community. She knew her neighbors. She cared about them, and they cared about her.

"How's Leo?" she asked.

"He's asleep."

"Seriously?" Surprise ran through her eyes. "He let you put him to bed?"

"Yep. I did a lousy job on the teeth brushing, and I'm not sure he's wearing his pajamas as they looked more like clothes to me, but he swore that's what he wore to bed."

"Let me guess, it was a shirt with a horse on it and some shorts," she said with a smile.

"Yes. I didn't think it was worth an argument."

"Definitely not." She paused, her gaze widening as it moved to the dining room table. "You frosted the cupcakes, too. I can't believe you did everything for me."

"You do everything for everyone else. Why shouldn't I do what I can to help you? But I'm not sure about the cupcakes. Leo helped decorate, and I'm not completely innocent in how they came out."

She walked to the table to take a closer look. "They're not bad."

"You're being nice. I could pick some up from the bakery tomorrow and give them to you to take to the school."

"Decker, these cupcakes will be eaten by children under the age of six at a show that will look more like recess. Please don't worry about it. They're fine. And you did them with Leo, which is very sweet."

"It was fun. I did break the rule and have one before dinner."

"But you ate dinner, right?"

"No. I was waiting for you. I put everything in the fridge a while ago, so we'll have to heat it all up."

"I'll do that. You should sit down and relax."

"You should sit down and relax," he countered. "I'll put them in the oven. Or maybe the microwave would be faster."

She nodded. "Let's do the microwave because I'm starving."

Working together, they got dinner on the table in a matter of minutes.

"I hope Leo wasn't too much trouble," Chloe said as they sat down.

"He definitely talks a lot," he replied, as he dug into his enchiladas. "He's a very entertaining child. Goes from one topic to the next. It's an amazing stream of thought."

"He has a lot going on in his head and no filter. I try to encourage him to think before he speaks, but that idea is too complex for his little brain."

"He told me that his dad works a lot. But it's okay because he's a hero."

She frowned. "Maybe I'm wrong to put it that way. I don't want Leo to think his dad doesn't love him. Because Kevin does love him. He just feels like he has a higher calling."

"It's not wrong for you to make sure Leo has a good relationship with his father. I didn't have a relationship with my mother, and I missed that. Leo's dad sounds like a good guy and maybe one day he will have more time for his son."

"I hope so."

"But doesn't it ever bother you that you were left to shoulder everything?"

"Of course it does." She set down her fork. "I've felt every emotion about my failed marriage—everything. I think of all the things I might have done differently. I hate to fail."

"It takes two to fail a marriage."

"I've come to realize that. My friends all blame Kevin for choosing himself and his needs over everything else. And I have felt the same way. But I don't want anyone to feel sorry for me. I don't feel sorry for myself, not anymore. I may get tired and grumpy and irritated, like every other mom, and sometimes I would love for someone to share that. But if I had to do anything over, I wouldn't change a thing. I love my kid. I love my life."

Her words moved him; they were so utterly honest. And she was so sure of herself. He used to feel like that, like he was doing exactly what he wanted to do, living exactly the way he wanted to live, but it didn't feel like that anymore.

Going back to his single life in LA—with a few months there, a few months somewhere else—didn't appeal to him nearly as much as it had. Whisper Lake had changed him. Maybe that's why his father had left all those years ago. He'd felt the pull to a place that might have trapped him in a life he didn't want, so he'd run away.

Maybe he should run, too. He was getting caught up in the web of Chloe and Leo, and it would be difficult to get out.

"Let's talk about something else," Chloe said, obviously sensing his tension.

He gave her a brief smile. "Sure, tell me about your week."

As she launched into a funny story about her recent book club dinner, he felt less stressed. This was what he wanted, to just enjoy being with her. He liked talking to her. He also liked it when they didn't talk.

But when they finished dinner, and she mentioned wanting him to go to Hannah's anniversary party in a few weeks, he tensed again. They were making plans for a few weeks out. People at Leo's school were talking about them. Leo wanted him to come to his show. Suddenly, there were a lot of people expecting a lot of things, and he was starting to feel like he couldn't breathe.

"You don't have to tell me now if you can go or not," Chloe said, giving him a funny look. "Are you okay, Decker?"

"The long day just caught up to me," he said, hoping that's all it was.

She frowned. "I'm sorry I turned you into a babysitter tonight. Let me make it up to you. We could go into the bedroom, and I could give you a massage. We could see where things go."

His body tightened at her words. He wanted to see where things would go in the bedroom, but he was afraid of where they were going everywhere else. He had a feeling their fun fling was heading for a disaster, and every second they spent together would make it worse.

"Decker?" Chloe asked, a quizzical look in her eyes.

"Can I get a raincheck? I have an early morning. What I really need is sleep."

Disappointment ran through her gaze. "Sure, of course you can have a raincheck. Any time."

He got to his feet. "Leo asked me to come to his show tomorrow. What time does it start?"

"Noon."

"I don't know if I can break away. I told him I'd try, but I don't know."

"Okay. That's fine. I just wish you hadn't told him you'd try to make it. His father tells him that a lot."

"Well, I'm not his father," he snapped.

"I know. I just meant—"

"I know what you meant. I'm sorry. He took me by surprise. And by the way, apparently, some kid named Joey has a mom who thinks I'm your boyfriend, and Leo seems to have thoughts about that."

"What kind of thoughts?" she asked in surprise.

"He thought that meant I was going to live here."

"Oh." She licked her lips. "I guess people are already talking about us. I'll speak to Leo. I'll let him know."

"Let him know what?" he challenged.

She hesitated. "I'll tell him we're friends."

"We're more than that."

"What do you want me to tell him?"

He ran a hand through his hair, wishing he hadn't started this conversation. "I don't know. Let's discuss it later." He grabbed his coat and headed to the door.

Chloe followed him onto the porch. "I'm not sure what just happened," she said. "But thanks again for helping me tonight."

"You're welcome." He paused. "Everything is fine. I'm just tired. I'll talk to you tomorrow." He gave her a quick kiss and then left.

As he stepped onto the porch, the chilly air hit his heated face, and he drew in a deep breath, knowing he wasn't feeling anything close to fine.

CHAPTER TWENTY-SIX

CHLOE DIDN'T SLEEP all night, thinking about how her night with Decker had taken an odd turn. Clearly, Leo's questions about him being her boyfriend had bothered him. He probably also hadn't enjoyed the comparison to Kevin. Plus, instead of making him a great dinner, she'd abandoned him and left him to take care of her son.

This wasn't the life Decker wanted. He was a single man, a wanderer. He loved to travel. He didn't stay in one place. He liked to move on to the next thing. He'd told her all of that. He'd been completely up front about it. And she had barreled past all that because she liked him so much.

She'd been hiding from the truth since she first kissed him, because she'd wanted him so much. Now things were getting complicated. She couldn't keep pushing the future off, because it was coming fast. The house was almost done. The only thing keeping Decker in town would be her. But he wasn't going to stay for her and for Leo. She'd seen it in his eyes when he'd brought up the boyfriend comment. He didn't want to be her boyfriend. He didn't want to stay in Whisper Lake. He didn't want to be a family man.

She really had only one decision to make. *Did she break up with him or wait for him to break up with her?*

That painful, heartbreaking question ran around in her head as she got Leo up and dressed for school on Friday morning. It followed her to work and then to the recital, where even Leo's silly, happy dancing couldn't quite bring out her smile.

Decker didn't show up at the performance, which was fine because she didn't know what she wanted to say to him. *What she needed to say to him.*

But when Leo got in the car and started asking about Decker, it became very clear that avoidance wasn't going to be a solution any longer.

"How come Decker wasn't there?" Leo whined as she put him in his car seat.

"He had to work, honey. He said he told you he might not make it."

"But it wasn't very long. I wanted to show him how good I can dance."

"He saw that last night." Her words did nothing to brighten the storm clouds gathering in his eyes.

"Can we go see him?" Leo pressed. "Maybe I can show him my dance now."

"He's at work. We can't disturb him."

"I want to see him. Why won't you let me see him?"

She frowned at how agitated Leo was getting. "Let's talk about this when we get home." As she slid behind the wheel, she heard Leo start crying, and a glance in her rearview mirror confirmed that. She turned back to him. "Leo, what's wrong?"

He cried louder at her question.

She blew out a breath and started the car, her heart breaking apart with each little sob that came from the backseat. When they got home, she tried to offer him lunch, but he said he wasn't hungry and then ran into his room and flung himself on the bed.

She followed him into his bedroom, a little concerned with the level of emotion she was seeing. Normally, Leo didn't get this upset, and she didn't understand it. Or maybe she did. Her little boy was falling in love with Decker. And so was she. Now she felt like crying, too. Because it was going to end so badly.

"Leo," she said gently, rubbing his back. "Tell me what's wrong."

"I told you." Angry tears dripped from his eyes. "No one ever wants to come and see me."

"That's not true. People always come to see you. I came to see you."

"Daddy doesn't. He has to work. And so does Decker." Leo burst into tears again.

"Adults have to work sometimes," she told him. "It's not that they don't want to see you; it's just that they have a job to do."

"I don't like work."

She let out a sigh. "I know. Sometimes I don't like it, either."

"I thought Decker would come because he's your boyfriend."

"Oh, honey. Decker and I are friends, and he likes you very much, but he's not my boyfriend, and he couldn't come today because he had to work. That's all. Everyone loves you, especially me. You know that, right?"

He didn't answer, but his crying eased. The doorbell rang. It was her babysitter. "That's Jessie. Let's dry your eyes and see what games she wants to play today."

Leo didn't follow her to the door, but he did roll over and pick up his horse, which seemed like a good sign.

She let Jessie in, giving her a relieved smile. Jessie was a recent college graduate who was working remotely part time for a company in Denver and babysitting several hours a week.

"Leo is not very happy," she said.

"What's wrong?" Jessie asked. "He's usually in a good mood."

"I think he's overtired, and maybe over-sugared. He had a show at school today and quite a few cupcakes. I have to go to work for a couple of hours, but I'll be home by four. He should be out of his mood soon, but if he isn't, text me, and I'll come back."

"I'm sure we'll be fine," Jessie said. "Don't worry about us."

"Okay." She grabbed her bag and headed out the door. She needed to go to the café, but instead found herself driving to the rental house. When she arrived, Decker was standing by his truck. He was on the phone, but as soon as she got out of her car, he ended the call.

"Hey," he said. "How did the show go? Sorry I couldn't make it."

"I understand. Leo was unhappy about it, though. He cried all the way home."

Decker's lips tightened at her words. "I'm sorry about that. I had an inspection. I couldn't get away. I'll make it up to him."

She shook her head. "No. You aren't going to do that. I don't blame you for not coming, Decker. But last night, I know you freaked out when Leo asked if you were my boyfriend. He said the same thing to me today, in between sobs about missing you. I was selfish to get involved with you. I knew it was going to affect Leo, and I did it anyway. This isn't the best time or place to do this, but we have to end things today. It's time. It's past time. You knew it last night. That's why you left so abruptly."

"Chloe—"

She put up a hand. "Let me finish. I don't blame you for anything. You were always honest with me. I'm not mad. It was fun while it lasted, but it has to be over." The words came out like a rush of water behind a broken dam. She felt an instantaneous release, but also a terrible pain. "I told myself we could have a fun fling, but it became more than that to me and also to Leo. And I knew better. He loves you, and you're leaving, and I just put another man in his life who is going to break his heart." She felt a knot in her throat. She wasn't just talking about Leo; she was talking about herself.

"Chloe," Decker said again. "I don't want to hurt Leo. Or you."

She nodded tightly. Now that she'd said what she had to say, she needed to leave. "I know we'll have to deal with each other because of this house, but let's just keep it professional from here on out. And I don't want you to disappear on Leo, so maybe at some point, you could say goodbye. I think he'll need to have some closure with you."

Decker stared back at her with a grim look in his eyes. She wanted him to say that she was wrong, that he wanted to be with her, to be with Leo, but he wasn't saying anything, and with the silence she felt anger mix with her sadness.

"Okay, then," she said shortly. "I'll see you."

With every step to her car, she thought he'd call her back, but he didn't. And when she pulled out of the drive, she turned her head, wondering if he was watching her go. But he was headed into the house. That hurt even more.

His father had told Decker to never look back, and that's exactly what he was doing. He was done with her. On to the next.

She drove about a mile before she pulled over by a park and let the tears come. She cried for herself, for Leo, and even a little for Decker. She thought they could have had something incredible together. But he was still following in his father's footsteps, searching the world for something that he probably couldn't even define.

Or maybe this was on her. Maybe she was the one who was too stuck in her ways, needing every guy she met to line up in exactly the right way for her. Life wasn't that simple. Love wasn't neat or organized. She couldn't check off boxes and find the perfect guy. Joel was a great example of that, and it wasn't just that Joel had left; she'd known even before he'd decided to return to New York that they weren't great together. Everything had been too forced. With Decker, it had been easy and fun. Laughter, conversation, passion, and honesty had flowed between them, which was why she'd fallen in love with him.

The buzzing of her phone snapped her out of her reverie. Her first hope that it was Decker calling was dashed when she saw Hannah's name on the screen. She felt another swell of emotion.

"Hello?" she said with a tearful sniff.

"Chloe?" Hannah asked sharply. "Are you okay?"

"No. Decker and I broke up." She bit down on her lip to stop the emotion from flowing out. "Not that we really had anything to break up, but what we had is over."

"Oh, Chloe, I'm sorry. What happened? I thought you were having fun."

"We were having an amazing time, but time was the problem. Leo fell apart today when Decker missed his show at school. I've never seen Leo cry so hard, and I realized that I'd let the worst happen; I'd let my kid fall in love with another man who wasn't going to stick around. I had to cut it off."

"What did Decker say?"

"Not much of anything. He certainly didn't say he'd stick around." She paused. "To be honest, I think he was relieved. He said that Leo asked him last night if he was my boyfriend and if that meant he could live with us. That freaked him out."

"I'm a little surprised he didn't say something. Seeing you together, you seemed like you had a really strong connection."

"We do, but we've both always known we were on different paths. I shouldn't have gotten involved with him. And, by the way, your *just have fun* advice was not that good."

"But you had some fun, right?" Hannah asked.

"Too much," she said with a sigh. "I'm sorry to dump this on you. Why did you call me?"

"Oh, right. It doesn't matter now. Just some anniversary party stuff. Don't worry about it. Anyway, I'm on my way to work. I'll call you tomorrow."

"All right."

"And, Chloe, I'm sorry it didn't work out with Decker. I know I encouraged you to take a risk on him. I thought he was a good guy."

"He is a good guy, but he's not for me."

"Well, someday everything will line up."

She had a hard time believing that, but she said goodbye and set the phone on the console. She wiped her eyes, blew her nose, and started the car. She didn't have time to sit and cry. She needed to get on with her life like Decker was getting on with his.

When she got home a little before five, Leo was lying on the couch with his headphones on, watching a cartoon on his tablet. He wasn't crying, for which she was extremely grateful. Jessie was on her computer at the dining room table. She closed it and stood up.

"I just let him have a show a few minutes ago," Jessie said. "We played in the backyard for a while, but he was pretty grumpy about everything."

"Thanks for trying."

"No problem." Jessie gathered her things and left.

As the door closed behind her, Chloe went over to Leo and gave him a smile.

He smiled back, but then returned to watching his show. Usually, she got a more excited greeting or a demand to play, but since he was relatively happy at the moment, she went into the kitchen to pull dinner together. She couldn't drum up much energy for the meal. Like Leo, she was feeling deflated. Maybe some food would help.

A half hour later, she had macaroni and cheese ready, as well as fruit and carrots for Leo to eat. She'd heated up some of the leftover enchiladas for herself, although the thought of eating them only reminded her of Decker, which didn't help her flagging appetite.

She called Leo to the table, but he didn't respond, so she went over and took the headphones off. "Your food is ready," she said.

"I'm not hungry," he said grumpily.

She frowned. His cheeks were flushed, and his eyes looked too bright. She put her hand on his forehead and was astonished by how hot he was. Her little boy wasn't just out-of-sorts; he had a fever.

"You're warm. I'm going to take your temperature." She moved down the hall to the bathroom to get the thermometers. When she got back to the living room, Leo's eyes were closed. She used the forehead thermometer to get a quick reading. It said one hundred and four, and her heart jumped into her throat. She gently woke Leo up and used the regular thermometer under his tongue. It came out the same.

"I don't feel good," Leo murmured. "Can I go to sleep?"

Her energetic son never wanted to go to bed. "I'm going to call the doctor. We might need to get you some medicine," she said, as she grabbed her cell phone. The doctor's office was closed, since it was after five, but she got the night nurse. After describing Leo's temperature, the nurse told her to take him to the emergency room, which only scared her more. The nurse reassured her it was just a precaution, but Leo had a high enough fever to warrant an examination.

She threw the plates of food into the refrigerator, picked up Leo, and carried him to the car. He started crying as she put him in his car seat.

"It's okay, baby," she said. "We're going to make you feel better soon."

Her hands were shaking as she started the car, but she ordered herself to pull it together. Everything would be fine. She was five minutes from the hospital. They'd see a doctor soon, and it was probably nothing bad.

Her mental pep talk went around and around in her head on the brief journey to the emergency room. After parking, she carried Leo into the ER where a nurse asked her to fill out some paperwork. With Leo crying and his arms wrapped around her neck, the nurse decided to put them in a room. As they entered, she asked the nurse if Hannah was on duty yet and if she could tell her they were here. The nurse informed her Hannah was on another case, but she would let her know as soon as she was free.

She sat down in the chair in the exam room since Leo refused to let go of her. His feverish body only increased her panic, and a dozen thoughts ran through her mind, all of them making her feel guilty mom thoughts. Maybe Leo hadn't just been upset about Decker. Maybe Leo had been sick all day and she hadn't seen it.

Another nurse came in and extricated Leo from her arms so she could examine him.

As he continued to cry, Chloe put a reassuring hand on his shoulder. "It's going to be okay," she told him, praying that was true.

A doctor entered a moment later and continued the examination. They wanted to take some blood, which scared her even more and also made Leo scream louder.

Finally, that was over, and the doctor said he'd be back to talk over the results.

As Leo continued to cry, she picked him up and sat back down in the chair with him, his little head resting on her shoulder as his sobs tore apart her heart.

Hannah came into the room a few minutes later, concern in her eyes. "Hey, what's going on?" she asked, squatting down in front of them. She put one hand on Leo's back and the other on Chloe's knee. "Our boy isn't feeling good, is he?"

"He has a really high fever. The doctor said something about infection or virus. I don't know. They took some blood."

"It's going to be okay, Chloe."

She'd been saying the same thing to Leo, but he didn't seem to believe her, and she was having trouble believing Hannah. "It has to be," she said desperately. "I can't believe I didn't realize he was sick. I thought he was just mad that Decker didn't come to his show, but he didn't eat much breakfast, and he's been crying off and on all day. I didn't even think to take his temperature. What is wrong with me?"

"Stop it, Chloe. This is not your fault, and it has not been that long. He danced in his show, right? That was only a few hours ago. You haven't been ignoring him. You're not a terrible mother. Your kid is ill, but we'll figure out what it is, and he'll get better. You know I never lie, right?"

"I know you don't lie, but you are my friend, and you're trying to make me feel better."

"I'm also telling the truth. Kids get fevers. His body is fighting something off, and we're going to help him do that."

Hannah's calm words finally got through to her. "Okay, thanks."

"I have another case I'm working. I'll send out a group text, get someone to come here to sit with you."

"I don't need anyone to sit with me. Please don't contact anyone. I don't want to have to fake being strong. All I need is for the doctor to come back and give me good news."

"It won't be long," Hannah said, as she got to her feet. "I'll be back as soon as I can. Positive thoughts only."

"I'll try."

CHAPTER TWENTY-SEVEN

CHLOE TOOK several long breaths as Hannah left the room, holding Leo close to her, muttering words of love and encouragement to him. He finally stopped crying, and she thought he was asleep, but that also scared her. *Was he sleeping or unconscious?*

Fortunately, her next bout of panic was stopped by the appearance of the doctor. As he spoke, she tried to make sense of his words, but all that got through was a bacterial infection and wanting to admit Leo for the night so they could start him on antibiotics and get his fever down.

After the doctor left, the nurse took them upstairs to another room in the pediatric ward where Leo was put into bed and given medication to reduce his fever and fight the infection.

It broke her heart to see his tiny body in the big bed, surrounded by scary-looking machines, but she told herself he'd be better soon. He was exactly where he needed to be.

The doctor had told her that sleep was good for Leo, but she still stood by the side of his bed, watching Leo's breath lift his chest. She'd never been so scared in her life. The love she had for her son was overwhelming. If she could switch places with him, she would do it in a second.

The door opened, and she turned her head, her heart skipping a beat as Decker walked into the room. Tears filled her eyes.

"Is Leo all right?" Decker asked, concern in his gaze.

"He has some kind of infection and has to stay here overnight. They want to get his fever down before I take him home."

"Poor guy," Decker muttered. "How are you doing?"

The question undid her. She bit down on her lip, her emotions threatening to break.

"Oh, Chloe," he breathed, as he opened his arms.

She moved into his embrace as the storm burst, burying her head against his chest as the sobs racked through her. He held her tightly, surrounding her with warmth and strength, until she was finally spent.

"I'm sorry," she said, lifting her head.

He tucked her hair behind her ears. "Don't be."

"How did you know? Why are you here?" she asked, searching his gaze.

"Hannah texted me." He paused. "I wasn't sure if you'd want me to be here, but I couldn't stand the thought of you dealing with all this on your own. And I was really worried about Leo."

"I told her not to call anyone."

"I don't know Hannah very well, but in my experience, she does what she wants," he said dryly. "What can I do for you?"

"Nothing. I feel a little better now that I cried all over you. But I'm still scared. I should have realized sooner that Leo was sick. I thought he was just upset, and now I realize he wasn't feeling well; he just didn't know how to put it into words."

"You thought he was upset about me," Decker said.

"I didn't read that right."

"Both things can be true. He could have been upset I wasn't at his show, and he could have also been sick. You did nothing wrong, Chloe. You're a very attentive mother."

"Thanks." She grabbed a tissue from the table by the bed and wiped her eyes. "Anyway, Leo will sleep most of the night. I'm going to stay here with him."

"Then I'll stay here, too."

His words shocked her. "You can't stay here."

"Is there some rule that says I can't?" he challenged.

"Well, I don't know, but you don't need to do that."

"You need to be here in case Leo needs you, and I need to be here in case you need someone, which you will."

"I won't."

"Yes, you will. You'll need a break at some point, and you won't want to leave him alone, so I'll stay until someone kicks me out."

She looked into his eyes, bemused by his words, his fierce, caring tone. "We broke up a couple of hours ago, Decker."

"This isn't about that. I care about you and Leo. The rest of it is another thing," he said with a wave of his hand. "Let me be here for you now."

Now wasn't as good as forever, but she was still touched by his generosity. "All right. I wouldn't mind using the restroom and washing my face, maybe getting some coffee."

"Go. I will text you if anything changes."

"Get the nurse if anything changes and then text me."

"Done."

Chloe had only been gone about five minutes when Hannah came into the room wearing nursing scrubs.

"How's our boy?" she asked.

"Asleep," Decker replied. He'd been standing at the bed watching over Leo from the minute Chloe had walked out of the room. He seemed to be breathing normally, although there was a flush to his cheeks.

"That's good. He needs rest. Where's Chloe? Was she upset that I reached out to you?"

"No. She just went to the restroom and to find some coffee."

Relief entered her eyes. "Oh, good. I was going to give her a break myself, but I just have a few minutes. I'm on duty downstairs."

"Chloe is staying the night, and so am I."

"I'm glad. She shouldn't be alone right now." Hannah paused. "I wasn't sure you'd come, Decker. Chloe told me you broke up earlier. But she didn't want me to call any of our friends, and I didn't want her to be alone."

"I'm happy you got in touch. I wouldn't want her to go through this alone."

"Me, either. Chloe has had to go through so many things alone."

"Leo is going to be all right, isn't he?"

Hannah nodded. "I checked with the nurse, and his temperature has already come down since he was admitted. The infection should respond well to the antibiotics. He should be able to go home in the morning."

"That's a huge relief."

"These things can come on suddenly, or they're brewing in the background, and aren't visible until the fever spikes. Chloe is beating herself up about not noticing Leo was sick earlier, but it hasn't been long. She got him here right away. Leo will be fine."

He felt better hearing the words come from Hannah, who, in his short experience with her, always seemed to tell the truth, no matter how difficult it might be to hear.

"Tell Chloe I'll check in before I go home for the night." Hannah hesitated, giving him a thoughtful look.

He sighed, sensing there was a tough question coming. "Just say what you want to say."

"When are you going to realize you're in love with Chloe?"

His gut clenched at her question, a question that hung in the air for a long minute.

"I hope you figure it out before it's too late," Hannah added.

After delivering that parting shot, she left the room.

His heart thudded against his chest, her question making him look at feelings he'd been trying to ignore. He'd never been in love, but the way he felt about Chloe was different from anything he'd ever felt before. And Leo…

He looked down at the sleeping boy and felt another overwhelming rush of emotion. It felt like love. But he couldn't give Chloe the life she wanted, and she couldn't give him the life he wanted. *Where did that leave them?*

The question was still running around his head when Chloe returned with two cups of coffee and an assortment of chips, cookies, and candy that had apparently come out of a vending machine.

"Looks like you scored." He liked that she didn't look as pale or stressed as she had before.

"I didn't eat dinner, and I wasn't sure you had, either. There is a cafeteria with healthier options, but I didn't want to take the time."

"I can check it out for you later."

"It's fine. I'm not really hungry, anyway." She handed him a coffee and put the rest of the snacks down on the side table. "Did he wake up at all?"

"No. He seems to be sleeping peacefully."

She blew out a breath. "Thank God. He's never been this sick before. I didn't know what to do."

"You did everything right. Hannah stopped in. She said Leo was doing good. She checked with the nurses, so she had first-hand information. She's going to come by when her shift is up."

"That's good to hear. Hannah is great in a crisis. She calmed me down when we got here. She doesn't always come across as the most nurturing person, but she has a huge heart and fights for anyone she loves."

He smiled. "I think you just described yourself, minus the not coming across as a nurturing person, because you are definitely that, Chloe."

"Thanks. You don't have to stay, Decker."

"You're not getting rid of me, so save your breath."

"You're really going to sit here all night with us?" she asked in wonder.

He met her gaze. "Yes."

"Why?"

"Because I want to. Because I need to."

She stared back at him, a mix of emotions in her eyes. "All right. But I can't have any more emotional conversations."

"I wasn't going to go there," he assured her. "We don't have to talk at all. It's up to you."

She thought for a moment, then took out her phone. "Maybe we should play Words with Friends online."

"I could do that," he said. "But I have to warn you, I'm really good.

A smile parted her lips. "I wouldn't expect anything else."

Chloe woke up Saturday morning with a start, not sure exactly where she was. Then she realized she was in the hospital. She got up and walked over to the bed. Leo was still asleep. She put her hand on his forehead, and it was much cooler. His hair was also a little sweaty, another sign that his fever had broken.

Turning her head, she looked at Decker, who was sprawled awkwardly and uncomfortably in the other chair, but he was fast asleep. Her heart filled with love as she studied his handsome face, the thick, wavy hair falling over his brow, the fresh growth of beard across his cheeks.

She couldn't quite believe he'd stayed all night, playing games with her online, watching over her boy when she needed a break, telling her about his travels to distract her from worrying about Leo, and then sleeping in a hard, narrow chair just so she wouldn't be alone.

Decker was an amazing man and maybe they couldn't be together forever, but she needed to stop regretting getting involved with him. He had made a mark on her life. He had shown her that there was a man out there she could count on, a man who could make her laugh, listen to her complain, and love her like no one else.

How could she regret falling for such a great person? Maybe her heart would be a little less broken if they'd never gotten involved, but she would have missed out on a couple of great weeks. And while Leo would be sad when Decker left, he'd recover, and hopefully, he'd have fond memories of him as well.

Decker suddenly shifted in the chair, blinking his eyes open as he came awake. He stiffened when he saw her watching him. "Leo?" he asked quickly, jumping to his feet.

"Still sleeping," she said quietly.

She'd no sooner finished her statement when she heard Leo's sweet voice.

"Mommy?" he said.

Whirling around, she gave him a comforting and loving smile. "Good morning, sleepyhead."

"How come I'm not in my room?"

"Because we came to the hospital to get you some medicine. Remember?"

"Can I go home now?"

"Soon," she said, kissing his cheek.

"Hey, buddy," Decker said, coming up behind her.

Leo's face lit up. "You're here, too?"

"Yes. I'm sorry I didn't make it to your show yesterday, but I want to see that dance when you're feeling better."

"I could do it now," Leo said.

"Not now," she said quickly as Leo sat up. "You're going to rest."

The door opened, and a nurse came in. "Well, it looks like everyone is up," she said with a cheerful smile. "How are you feeling, Leo?"

"I'm hungry," Leo said.

The nurse laughed. "That's good news. Let's take your temperature."

As the nurse conducted a brief exam, Chloe waited with bated breath, wanting to hear nothing but good news.

"His temperature is normal," the nurse said. "Heart and lungs sound good. The doctor will be in shortly to examine Leo, but you should be able to go home soon."

"Thank you." She blew out a breath of relief as the nurse left. "Did you hear that, Leo? We're going home soon."

"Can I have a donut for breakfast?"

"I think we can swing that." She felt like a weight had just slipped off her shoulders. Her little boy was going to be fine. That's all that she cared about.

The doctor came in a moment later and performed his own exam, confirming that Leo could go home. He would need to rest and finish his medication, but he should make a full recovery.

As the doctor left, she grabbed Leo's clothes and got him dressed. After signing the discharge papers, Leo was wheeled out to the parking lot, which he was truly delighted about.

Decker walked them to her car, and she buckled Leo into his car seat.

"Why don't I get the donuts?" Decker suggested. "I'll bring them over."

"Are you sure? You've already done so much."

"I'm hungry. I'll meet you at home."

As he walked away, she slid into the car, the word *home* ringing through her ears. She wished her home was his home. Well, for this morning, that's what it would be. At the moment, that's all she could care about.

CHAPTER TWENTY-EIGHT

CHLOE STAYED home for the next five days, happy to devote all her time to taking care of Leo, who got more restless and energized with each passing day. She hadn't seen Decker since he'd shared donuts with them on Saturday, but he'd texted her a few times to make sure Leo was okay.

On Wednesday, Leo's grandparents arrived, and they had a very happy reunion. She'd told them about Leo's illness, although she had downplayed the terror of Friday night's rush to the hospital. Since Leo was back to normal, she was okay to send him off with his grandparents. He was tired of being in the house, and she needed to get back into the world, too.

She'd had a lot of time to think the past few days, and as she got into her car and drove into town, she felt like she was seeing everything in a new light. She checked in at the restaurant first. Marian and the rest of her staff were busy but not overwhelmed. After filling everyone in on Leo's condition, she went into the back and up the stairs to see if Decker was home. There was no answer at his door, and his truck was not in the lot, so she headed to the rental house.

She parked behind his truck, then got out and went into the house, thinking about how much had changed in the last few weeks since she'd first met Decker here. The living and dining rooms were empty, the floors were done, the ceiling repaired and painted, showing no sign of the previous damage, and the walls also boasted a new coat of paint.

Hearing someone moving around upstairs, she went up the steps and down the hall. As she entered the master bedroom, she saw Decker come out of the closet with a small box in his hands.

He looked at her in surprise. "Chloe. I didn't hear you come in."

"The house looks amazing."

"It's getting there."

"What's in the box?" she asked curiously.

"The letters Eleanor wrote me."

"Did you read them?"

"Yes. They're very sweet. She told me some things about my dad I didn't know. Nothing bad, just a few personal stories. She didn't know him that well. She also told me a little more about Hank, how he'd been a military man, how he had his own demons to fight, his own shame to carry. I didn't take a lot of time to go through them, but I'll take them home and read them again, I'm sure."

She was happy that he seemed more at peace with his past. "For a man who doesn't like baggage, you're not going to be traveling as light as you once did," she couldn't help pointing out.

"That's true," he conceded. "How's Leo?"

"He's good now. His grandparents arrived today, and they're going to keep him overnight at their rental home. He's excited about having a sleepover. He's tired of being in our house."

"I'm sure you're ready for a break, too, and you probably want an update on everything that has been done here and still needs to be done. I know you wanted to stage the house for photos. And I think we're there. The house is ready for a new start."

"That's good, and I want to hear everything, but not right

now." She licked her lips, stalling as she searched for the right words.

"What do you want to say Chloe?" he asked.

"I'm ready for a new start, too," she replied. "I've been home the last five days with a lot of time to think about my life and about you. I'm wondering how you would feel if Leo and I came out to Los Angeles for a while. See if we like the city. See if we might want to stay there—with you." Her heart thudded against her chest. She was taking a huge risk in assuming that Decker would want her to follow him home. Maybe all he'd wanted was a fling. When he didn't say anything right away, she jumped back in. "But we don't have to do that if it's too much. This was fun, and maybe it's just over. If that's the case, it's okay. I just wanted you to know that I'm not stuck here. I can leave. Leo is little. He'll adjust wherever he is." She stopped and blew out a breath. "You really need to talk now."

Decker set the box on the floor and then stepped forward, putting his hands on her shoulders. "You're willing to leave Whisper Lake for me?" he asked, his gaze searching hers. "Your whole life is here. Everyone you love is here."

"Not everyone. Not you. I love you, Decker. I don't want you to leave without knowing that." She drew in another breath. "And I don't want to lose you. Maybe I'm presuming too much, and you're ready to leave, ready to be done with whatever this was, but—"

He cut her off with a sharp shake of his head. "I am not ready to be done with you, Chloe. I love you, too."

"You do?" she asked in wonder. "You really don't have to say it."

"I'm not just saying it because you said it first. I've been thinking about it for a while. I've just never been in love before, and it took me a while to realize what I was feeling, why I was so wrecked when you called a halt to everything. I couldn't imagine never seeing you again."

She felt immensely relieved and very happy. "Then can we try to make it work?"

"What would you do in LA?"

"I could work in a restaurant; I have a lot of experience. I've always wanted to live by the beach. It's warm there all-year-round, right? It would be nice not to shovel snow in the winter. But all I care about is the fact that you're there. I have some money saved up. I can pay my own way." She paused, knowing that it wasn't as simple as she was making it sound. "But I'll be upending Leo's life, setting expectations, so I have to know that you're serious about trying to make things work. It's a lot to ask when we haven't dated that long. But while I'm okay with risking my heart, I'm risking Leo's, too. And you know how much he loves you, Decker."

"I love him, too." His gaze grew more serious. "I don't want you to come to LA, Chloe."

"You don't?" Her heart turned over. "But I thought you just said..."

"That I love you? I do. I want to stay here in Whisper Lake with you and Leo."

His words shocked her. "But your life—your jobs—are in LA and other places near there."

"I found someone to take over the next job. He met with the owner yesterday, and they're happy to move on without me."

"You did that yesterday? You thought about this before now?" she asked in surprise.

"I haven't been able to think about anything else. I've been moving around my entire life, always looking for what's next, never looking back, my gaze fixed on the horizon. I've seen a lot. I've lived in many places. What I want now is to be with you, to build a life with you and with Leo. Whisper Lake feels like the perfect place for that to happen."

"What about your business?"

"There are plenty of people looking for contractors around here, including Joel's company. Zach also mentioned that if I wanted to make a move here, he could use me. I can build anywhere. And while it means a lot to me that you would move your life to LA, Chloe, I'd rather we both stay here."

"I can't imagine anything better. But I meant what I said about being able to go somewhere else. I've been here most of my life. I want to see more of the world, and I want Leo to see it, too. I don't want you to feel stuck, and I don't want to feel that way, either."

"Then we'll take some amazing vacations. It's going to be good, Chloe," he said, gazing into her eyes. "I hope you can believe that. I hope you can trust me. I know that might take some time."

"I trust you already. I know who you are, Decker. You're the man who stayed with me all night in the hospital. You're the man who sets my blood racing, who makes me laugh, who makes me want to see the world. I'd like our roots to be here. But your dad showed you the world, and one day you can show it to me and Leo."

"My father would have loved you, Chloe."

"I would have loved him. Because he raised an incredible man. And I think Eleanor, somewhere up there, is smiling down at us. Because you finally came back to the place where she thought you could be happy."

"I'm going to be happy, and so are you." He slid his arms around her, and she was overwhelmed by feelings of love. "Let's start being happy right now," he said.

"I'm in. I'm kid free for twenty-four hours. What are you going to do with me?"

He leaned in and whispered, "Love you like you've never been loved before."

Her eyes filled with teary emotion. "That's what I want to do with you, too."

"I want to say something else. No one and nothing will ever be more important than you, Chloe. I know what else is out there. And what you and I have, it's extraordinary. I'll fight forever to protect it. I'll fight forever for the opportunity to be with you."

The fierce love and desire in his eyes matched what she felt in her heart. Decker might have started out as Mr. Wrong, but he was definitely the right man for her.

"I'm going to fight for you, too. But right now, I just want to kiss you."

She closed her eyes as their mouths came together. It was the beginning of a new adventure for both of them.

EPILOGUE

A year later...

Chloe looked at herself in the dressing room mirror at the Woodside Chapel in Whisper Lake and marveled at her image. She'd never thought she'd put on another wedding dress, but this beautiful, simple white gown was exactly right.

She'd never believed she'd find a love that was so absolutely perfect it still scared her a little. But in Decker she had truly found her match, a man who was strong and independent, highly intelligent, and good at just about everything. He was also kind, loving, and romantic.

The past year had flown by. Decker had gone back and forth to LA a few times to move his life and his business to Whisper Lake. They'd had some ups and downs, some growing pains in their relationship, but she had never ever doubted that they'd end up here, because they'd each found what they needed in the other person.

Hannah came up behind her, smiling at her in the mirror. "You're a beautiful bride, Chloe."

"And you're a beautiful bridesmaid."

"Thank you for not making us wear matching dresses," Hannah said as she pressed her hands down the side of her champagne-colored cocktail dress.

She smiled. "I'm just glad you all wanted to participate. It feels a little weird since it's my second wedding."

"Oh, stop." Hannah cut her off with a wave of her hand. "It's love, and that's all that matters. I'm thrilled to see you happy again. I love Decker, and I know he's always going to be there for you. So we are all going to celebrate today."

As she finished talking, the other women, her best friends in the world, crowded in behind her, and she could see all their beautiful, smiling faces in the large mirror. Keira had come back from Miami, and she stood next to Hannah and Gianna, who she had known since she was five. Lizzie, Chelsea, and Molly were in the back. Their significant others were with Decker, and the kids were with various grandparents, waiting in the chapel. Both her parents and Kevin's parents were also in the church.

She'd thought it might be awkward for Kevin's parents to come, but they had wanted to be there for her. At first, they'd been a little hesitant around Decker, but he'd charmed them the way he'd charmed everyone else. And they'd offered to stay in her house with Leo while Decker took her on what would be an amazing trip to Africa. He wanted to show her one of his favorite places in the world, and she was more than ready to see the world with him because they'd always come home to Whisper Lake.

"Are you ready?" Gianna asked. "I know what this moment feels like."

She laughed at the dry smile on Gianna's face. Her friend had had three almost trips down the aisle before marrying Zach. "Don't worry, I'm not going to run away. If anything, I'm going to sprint down the aisle."

"You should," Keira said. "Decker is amazing. I know I wasn't here for the beginning of this relationship, but I like what I see."

"Me, too," she said, turning around. "The last several years, you have all been there for me in so many ways." Emotion choked her throat at all the memories.

"Don't make us cry yet," Gianna complained, as she dabbed at her eyes.

"I just want you to know how much you all mean to me. I couldn't have survived without your support. Leo and I needed each and every one of you."

"We all need each other," Hannah said. "And we'll always be there whenever there's sadness or joy or boredom. That's the way we roll."

She laughed. "It is. We're all really lucky."

"Let's get you married," Keira said.

She took one last look in the mirror and then moved into the chapel. It was a short aisle, and the small church was filled with close friends and family. Her bridesmaids and Decker's groomsmen lined up on either side of the church, and then she walked down the aisle to the love of her life.

Decker's gaze clung to hers with every step she took. And when she reached the front, he grabbed both of her hands and squeezed them tight.

"I love you," he whispered.

"I love you, too."

Marian cleared her throat.

Chloe smiled at her manager, who was also their officiant. "Sorry, we couldn't wait," she said.

"Then we better get started," Marian returned with a smile.

As Marian talked about their relationship, how they'd first met, Chloe gazed into Decker's eyes, thinking about how he hadn't checked any of her boxes. But Mr. Wrong had definitely turned into Mr. Right. She'd been looking for the wrong things.

When Marian finished, they each said their vows, which were honest, simple, and funny. Because that's the way their relationship was.

After they exchanged rings, Decker gave her a tender kiss and whispered, "I love that all these people are here. But I can't wait to get you alone in a tent in Africa. Our adventure will truly begin."

"Our adventure has already begun," she said, smiling into his eyes. "And I not only get to go on that adventure with my lover but also my best friend."

"I'll never stop being either," Decker promised.

They kissed again and then broke apart as Leo ran down the aisle to join them. Decker swung her little boy up in his arms as they walked out of the church as a family.

# # #

I hope you enjoyed your trip to Whisper Lake with Chloe and Decker. Have you missed any books in the series? Grab them now!

Whisper Lake Series

Always With Me (#1)
My Wildest Dream (#2)
Can't Fight The Moonlight (#3)
Just One Kiss (#4)
If We Never Met (#5)
Tangled Up In You (#6)
Next Time I Fall (#7)

WHAT TO READ NEXT...

Did you love Whisper Lake? For more contemporary romance, check out ON A NIGHT LIKE THIS the first book in the Callaways Series, about a family born to serve and protect!

Sara had always been untouchable, his sister's best friend, and the girl next door...

Smokejumper Aiden Callaway never questioned his job until a fire took the life of his friend, Kyle, and left Aiden with injuries and fractured memories. The truth may clear Aiden of blame but destroy Kyle's reputation and hurt the people he left behind.

Sara has never forgiven or forgotten the way Aiden brought their teenage relationship crashing down. But the sparks between Aiden and Sara have been smoldering for a very long time. Sara is afraid to take another chance on the man who broke her heart, and Aiden knows better than anyone how dangerous an intense fire can be.

As teenagers they weren't ready for each other. Are they ready now? Or will secrets derail their second chance at love?

Don't miss this breathtaking and emotional second-chance romance and the first book in the NYT Bestselling Series: The Callaways!

ABOUT THE AUTHOR

Barbara Freethy is a #1 New York Times Bestselling Author of 80 novels ranging from contemporary romance to romantic suspense and women's fiction. With over 13 million copies sold, thirty-three of Barbara's books have appeared on the New York Times and USA Today Bestseller Lists, including SUMMER SECRETS which hit #1 on the New York Times!

Known for her emotional and compelling stories of love, family, mystery and romance, Barbara enjoys writing about ordinary people caught up in extraordinary adventures. Library Journal says, "Freethy has a gift for creating unforgettable characters."

For additional information, please visit Barbara's website at www.barbarafreethy.com.

Made in United States
North Haven, CT
15 August 2023

40337755R00157